Praise for **where night stops**

"Douglas Light's fast-paced *Where Night Stops* is a well-executed thriller that combines genre staples with literary style."

—*Foreword*

"This sinuous narrative works neatly, both as a gripping novel and a solid meditation on identity."

—*Kirkus Reviews*

Praise for **girls in trouble**

"Wonderful collection about some rough-ass lives—this dude is the real deal."

—**Junot Diaz**, Pulitzer-Prize winning author of
The Brief Wondrous Life of Oscar Wao

"Light enters the minds, hearts, and hurts of these characters with prose that is often lyrical, and always hypnotic."

—**Heidi Durrow**, author of *The Girl Who Fell from the Sky*

"These are gems of stories, slyly, skillfully interrelated and captivating in their economy, truth, and acid wisdom."

—**Frederic Tuten**, author of *Self Portraits: Fictions, The Green Hour,*
and *Tintin in the New World*

"Light deftly explores the rocky terrain of human emotion....In the most subtle of manners, Light portrays the essential paradigm of adolescence....[He] probes beneath complex layers of what it means to be alive, revealing the occasionally magnificent terrain of selfhood."

—*Foreword*

"With this collection you will enjoy engrossing fiction tightly executed, but you will also get back in touch with your own humanity, further plumbing your own capacity for compassion and reflection."

—*The Collagist*

Light's stories go down easy....The stories are fun to read and...fun to see being put together one word and sentence at a time. Light makes it look easy."

—*Short Story Reader*

"*Girls in Trouble* is a fine and thoughtful collection of fiction, very much recommended."

—*Midwest Book Review*

Praise for **east fifth bliss**

"Set on New York's Lower East Side, this first novel by Light (founding editor, Epiphany) introduces Morris Bliss, thirty-five years old and living with his widowed father. Morris has big dreams of traveling all over the world. Unfortunately, he doesn't have a job or the means to take his aspirations beyond a collection of travel brochures and pushpins in a map on his bedroom wall. This fun read boasts a likable protagonist, other quirky and interesting characters, and vivid and humorous descriptions of New York while also providing some significant social commentary. The scene in which Morris and a former high school classmate (and father of the eighteen-year-old girl with whom Morris is sleeping) storm a vacant building in the middle of the night to roust out a group of homeless squatters is both funny and disturbing. Recommended for large public libraries with an interest in new and unknown authors."

—*Library Journal*

where night stops

where night stops

douglas light

a genuine rare bird book
los angeles, calif.

THIS IS A GENUINE VIREO BOOK

A Vireo Book | Rare Bird Books
453 South Spring Street, Suite 302
Los Angeles, CA 90013
rarebirdbooks.com

FIRST TRADE PAPERBACK ORIGINAL EDITION

Set in Dante
Printed in the United States

10 9 8 7 6 5 4 3 2 1

Publisher's Cataloging-in-Publication data
Names: Light, Douglas, author.
Title: Where night stops / Douglas Light.
Description: First Trade Paperback Original Edition | A Genuine Vireo Book |
New York, NY; Los Angeles, CA: Rare Bird Books, 2018.
Identifiers: ISBN 9781945572661
Subjects: LCSH Crime—Fiction. | Bildungsroman. | Espionage—Fiction. |
Mystery fiction. | Suspense fiction. | BISAC FICTION / Thrillers / Espionage |
FICTION / Thrillers / Crime
Classification: LCC PS3612.I3445 W54 2018 | DDC 813.6—dc23

For Micah

This frail engine, we think, and yet what murder is needed to take it down.

—James Salter, *Light Years*

CHAPTER 1

Haven, Florida

S HE SMELLS OF LEMONS and warm cinnamon and isn't very pretty. Sliding onto the barstool next to me, she says, "Can I sit here?" The bartender, the woman, and I—we're the only people in the bar. She can sit anywhere. It's not just a seat she wants.

I study her a moment then catch the bartender's eye; the order is placed without a word. Whatever the woman wants. Alcohol, like long marriages, has a language of its own, one not composed of speech.

Tuesday. The hard light of the Florida morning pours into Charm's Tavern, bleaching everything to its true ugliness. Open daily from 8:00 a.m. to 2:00 a.m., Charm's is anything but charming. *Providing hangovers and alibis since 1968,* the sign above the cash till reads. The oak bar cutting the length of the space looks whittled from a tree felled on the spot. The barstools wobble, their seats swaddled in duct tape, while stalactites of grime dangle from the exposed wires crisscrossing the ceiling. Everything in the place is warped from decades of spilt drinks.

Covering the wall opposite the bar are photographs. Hundreds, if not thousands. Floor to ceiling, people smile, shout, and hold drinks up in moments they'll never remember.

The bartender pours a gin on ice and walks it down to where we sit. The key ring looped on his belt jangles with each step.

She nods thanks.

He turns on the TV and mutes it.

She lifts the glass to her lips, downs a solid swallow. The weight of the drink seems to strain her narrow wrists. "Gin," she says, catching me with a direct stare. Her eyes are a broken blue, muted light through scratched stained glass. "A beautiful, brutal creation," she says, then touches my arm. "Was a time I could tell you everything about gin, its history, the different types, medicinal uses, even its effect on the British fertility in the mid-seventeen hundreds. Now," she says, "all I can tell you about it is how I like to drink it—cold." She tilts her head to one side then the other, like a gold finch at the feeder. "You don't like to talk?"

"I like to talk," I say. "I like to listen, too." *And I like to be left alone*, I think. It was a mistake buying this woman a drink.

She leans to me, her breath charged with loneliness. "I'm not pretty," she says. "I know I'm not pretty. I've come to accept that, and it isn't an easy thing to accept." She sways back, takes in the rest of her drink. "Now you know my problem. What's yours?"

I gauge her face, sidelong. She has me by a solid two decades, midforties. "What makes you think I've got a problem?"

She taps her wrist where a watch should be. "It's just past eight a.m. You're drinking at Charm's," she says.

Touché. "I'm working," I say, leaving it there. I'm not positive I could say what it is I do exactly, but even if I could, I wouldn't. People's perceptions change the moment you're defined. The weight of your words changes. The phrase *I can help* means something different coming from a lunch lady and a doctor.

The woman smiles. "Work." She considers me, then nods slightly, a small dip of confirmation. "You're not a hard one to figure out," she says. "I know your problem—or at least one of them." She touches her lips as though to reassure herself, ready to serve. "Gin and people. The two things I know. And what I know is that this gin"—she holds her glass up—"is French, ninety-eight proof, and the cause of many car wrecks and failed marriages. I also know," she says, "that you don't have friends."

"How's that a problem?"

She lifts her chin. "Maybe it's not," she says, clattering the ice in her glass. "Other people need them to feel they have a purpose." She folds her arms across the bar, lays her head on them. "Maybe you don't need that." Her voice is distant, longing. She closes her eyes. "You know what the problem with problems is? It's *not* solving them. You'd think that'd be the hard part but it's not. The hard part is living with the solution. It's like you spend the first part of your life trying to figure it all out. Then you spend the second part just trying to forget all the stupid things you did to figure it all out."

"You're a mess," I tell her. "Keep talking."

She sits up, looks at me without looking at me, and forces a smile. "Alcoholosophy," she says. "The act of being profoundly unprofound."

The idea of grappling naked with her seeps into my mind. There's something about her smell. I motion to the bartender—another drink for the lady. "I wasn't kidding," I say. "Keep talking. You have a nice voice. I like the sound of your voice."

"A nice voice that has nothing to say." She points to the TV bolted to the corner wall. An old black-and-white movie flashes on the screen. *The Third Man.* "See that?"

Orson Welles fills the screen. Young, still handsome, a mop of thick hair. He and Joseph Cotton are at the top of a Ferris wheel, war-torn Vienna spread out beneath them. A ruined Austria.

"That right there," she says, nodding at the TV. "That's my heart."

On the screen, Welles stares down from the top of the ride at the ravaged city. "Your heart is Orson Welles?" I ask.

"Orson Welles?" She makes a noise that's the approximation of a laugh. Her eyes brim with tears. "God no," she says. "My heart is a divided Vienna."

◉ ◉ ◉

WE'RE BORN WITH A finite number of opportunities. Attrition, bad choices, misspent goodwill, and fucked-up luck. The opportunities dwindle through a process called living. Our portfolio of prospects turns into a tattered novel of outcomes.

I am twenty-two.

CHAPTER 2

WINDSTOP, IOWA. MY HOMETOWN. When I think of it I think of summers, the heat rising in thick waves from the long, flat roads. Never-ending bike rides, tires clinging to the pavement. The rainbow, metallic spray of the garden hose, the calming sway of the cornfields, a sweet, stewing smell. Soil, sunlight, photosynthesis.

When I was a kid, there seemed nothing my folks couldn't do. My father was not only strong and good at sports, he was also an expert with tools; he could build and repair furniture, birdhouses, and nearly anything made of wood. People skills and the power of persuasion were my mother's gifts: gathering signatures for a new speed bump in front of the school, getting volunteers for a bake sale to support my Cub Scout troop, or organizing a drive to collect Green Stamps for the church. Once an idea got lodged in my mother's head, she could corral the whole community into the effort. She could talk anyone into doing anything. What she couldn't do was convince my father to care for her. And unlike one of his projects, my father couldn't hammer the relationship back into shape. They endured each other for me and acted out the role of parents as best they could. Voices rarely got raised when I was around. Arguments were fought in flat, conversational tones, the anger a strong undercurrent.

Still, I had a good childhood, filled with friends, fairly good grades, and teachers and coaches who liked me well enough. Everyone in the tiny town knew everyone else and their business. I never got away with anything. News of the occasional fight or the shoplifted candy made it home before I did. My punishment was rarely severe.

Instead of a sibling, my folks got me a dog, Mackerel, whom I loved like nothing else. Why my folks named her Mackerel, I can't say. The dog hated fish.

Since leaving Windstop, I've traveled the world and killed a few people, though always in self-defense. Always in the interest of self-preservation.

The first time was terrifying. I used to have bad dreams about it. But that passed. It's the second that really haunts me.

The Greek shouldn't have tried blackmailing me. A marble figurine of Artemis was close at hand. It seems so easy on TV. He made a savage mess as he lurched about the tiny Athens apartment.

By the time he finally dropped, blood splayed every wall.

People search everywhere for the taproot of their mistakes. They want to blame strict parents, an unsupportive school, a drunk scoutmaster, bullying siblings, or mean friends. They blame anyone but themselves.

I can't blame anyone for where I find myself now. I was taught the difference between right and wrong.

CHAPTER 3

Windstop, Iowa
Four years prior

MY RIBS CRACKLED WITH pain when I coughed. Bruises peppered my body. Still, I'd healed enough to be able to walk out. The nurse insisted I exit by wheelchair. Hospital rules. "We wheel you in, we wheel you out," she said, gliding me down Windstop Memorial General's off-white corridors. The odor of urine and pine needles, of desperation masked by cleaning supplies, filled the entire place.

I'd been born in that building and had ventured back numerous times. These were the people who had stitched my head together after the diving board interrupted my backflip, cut out my tonsils, freed my Krazy Glued fingers, and diagnosed the rash speckling my skin as a case of flea bites—courtesy of Mackerel. These were my neighbors, fellow church members, the parents and relatives of my classmates, the people my family and I depended on in times of emergency.

In the lobby, the summer light pounded through the windows, sharp and blinding. Outside, a world I wasn't ready for waited.

I had the nurse stop at the gift shop where I bought a cheap pair of sunglasses and a pack of cigarettes. "Really?" she asked. "I didn't take you as a smoker."

I slid on the sunglasses and gripped the cigarette pack. "I'm not."

A battered ambulette the color of creamed corn waited out front. As she helped hoist me into the passenger's seat, the nurse said,

"Don't forget to…" She trailed off, realizing her words—whatever they might be—were useless. I buckled up.

Nodding to the driver, I told him my address. There was no need. He knew me, knew my family. Knew what had happened. He was the father of my old church youth group leader. He used to provide apples and shelled peanuts as snacks for the group. Clamping the steering wheel like it was the last life buoy on a stricken ship, he shuttled me home in silence. Nothing new could be learned through talk.

My father, mother, and best friend Clement. Everyone in Windstop knew what had happened. Just as everyone in Windstop knew of the brutal knocks of life and bad luck my ambulette driver had endured. Within a matter of months, he'd been diagnosed with cirrhosis, lost his wife to skin cancer, and lost his son—my youth group leader—to a meth lab explosion. He'd been stripped of his reasons to live. Still, the magical mechanism propelling life continued to churn deep inside him, pushing him forward.

During one youth group meeting, his son made everyone kiss the blade of a hatchet while he explained that our own birth and death were the only two things we could truly call our own.

But he was wrong. His father was proof. I was proof. Your death is owned by family, friends, and creditors, the people left with the burden created by your absence.

The van pulled to a stop in front of my house. Loneliness cauterized my blood, burning it dry in my veins. I didn't want to be here, but then again I didn't want to be anywhere. I slid out, then turned and offered my hand in thanks. Disdain flashed over his face like the sharp, fleeting shadow of a passing plane. His misery didn't need the company of mine. My tragedy had upstaged his, stolen the town's sympathy, and left him even more hollow.

That first night home, I lay in my parents' bed and listened to soft noises work their way through the empty rooms: the drip of the tub's faucet, the rattle of a loose window screen, the scrape of some small animal making its way through the walls. All sounds my father had said he'd get around to taking care of. Now they were mine. Everything that was once my folks was mine.

It'd been my plan to start college in the fall at the University of Iowa. I had my dorm room, my class schedule, and an oversized black-and-gold Hawkeyes hoodie. Forty-five hundred freshman would swarm the campus. New friends and interests, experimentation and exploration, learning and change awaited me. Or that was the hope.

I'd applied to five schools total, each for reasons other than their programs. My love of the whole grunge era drove my desire to go to the University of Washington in Seattle. I'd applied to Columbia University after reading that Kerouac had studied there. The University of Cincinnati? Because the Bengals were my favorite football team. And Tulane because, well, it was in New Orleans. I was accepted to all of them, but cost and proximity won out. University of Iowa it was.

But plans change. College, it now seemed, was the avoidance of the inevitable. Life was looming, waiting to take hold. *Better to face it head on,* I thought. *Better to start it now.*

Word got around that I was out of the hospital. Heavy casseroles made with Campbell's soups and topped with fried onions arrived on my doorstep. Food to satiate my grief. I threw them out.

Small, somber cards from my uncles and aunts, from the Hendersons, Joneses, Dices, Wagners, Nees, Reeves, Critlens, Peters, Franks, Lynchs, and Smiths arrived in the mail. I threw them out.

People who had never taken an interest in my parents when they were alive called to offer their condolences, their advice. Everyone knew what I should do. Close out accounts, sign documents, decide on the font for my parent's tombstones. They called to instruct me on decisions I wasn't prepared to make.

Life went on, at least for everyone else.

At first, the money my parents had in the bank seemed like a lot. Then it didn't seem like enough. Mortgage, utilities, taxes, insurance, and the cost of simple upkeep. Why did anyone want to own a house? What kind of dream was that? My dream was to be free of it all, out from under all the things my folks had gathered over time, the debris that defined them. I wanted to shed the load that had been heaped on me and walk away.

I rang a real estate broker. My mind tangled with all the tasks of selling the house: the prepping, the showings, the strangers wandering from room to room, examining my life on display. If an offer actually came in, there'd be haggling, the back-and-forth, and the struggle of closing the deal.

I hung up the phone. There had to be a quicker, simpler way to cash out.

The answer was in the pile of bills—homeowner's insurance.

It seemed an easy way out. But the moment the flames took the kitchen, a crushing sadness gripped me. I'd made a mistake. I was destroying the last bit of my parents, the remnants of what I once was.

By the time the fire department rolled up their hoses, there was little left of the house. A flooded, charred frame surrounded by a dark halo of burnt grass. Filled with regret, I held to my story: the lawn mower had somehow set off the blaze.

Insurance investigators don't so much sniff out lies as not believe anything. Cops, though, know a lie. They're fed them daily. They cultivate a palate for what's true and what's not.

Windstop's sheriff visited me at my motel room, my temporary residency. "Shit, really?" he said. "The lawnmower?" It was the ninth time in two days I'd told my story, each time exactly as before. I'd learned that the words inflammable and flammable meant the same thing. It was astounding how many household products were just that.

The sheriff sat next to me on the bed. "Listen, I never much liked your father. Me and him never got along. So seeing his house— your house—get burnt down doesn't get me misty in the least. But that doesn't mean you can—" He broke off, stared at me hard.

I couldn't hold his gaze; I had to look away. The only thing worse than fucking up is getting caught fucking up. Needing something to do, I pulled out the pack of cigarettes I'd bought at the hospital. They were still unopened. "Mind if I smoke?"

"Yeah. I do." He stood, hovered over me. "Get up."

Out at his cruiser, I asked, "Want me in the back?"

"I want you to shut up."

He drove me to the next town over. Parking at the bus stop, he said, "You know anything about quantum mechanics?"

I didn't.

"Well, me neither. But I saw this thing on TV about it. Don't know why, but they talked about putting a cat in a bunker with a grenade or bomb or something that had a fifty-fifty chance of blowing up in the next minute. Then they closed the lid tight and waited for the minute to pass." He bit at a hangnail. "Thing is, no one knows if the cat is dead or alive until the lid is opened. So the cat is both *dead* and *alive*, as long as no one opens the lid."

I didn't understand.

"Right now," he said, "you both *did* and *didn't* burn your house down." He pulled out his wallet, tossed seventy dollars on my lap.

I picked up the bills. "What's this?"

"Opportunity." He opened his door and climbed out. "I'm getting a coffee. When I get back, I'm going to have to crack open that lid." He drilled me with a hard stare. "You understand what I'm saying?"

I did.

I bought a bus ticket.

Wedged tight into a window seat, I watched the sheriff slowly make his way back to his cruiser, coffee in hand. He kept his back turned as the bus started up and then lurched westward, kicking off a gray cloud of diesel exhaust.

As the day slipped to night and Iowa disappeared behind me, I tried to sleep, but the woman beside me kept elbowing me awake with her knitting. It was only when dawn found us nearing Sioux Falls, South Dakota, that the worrying thought took hold of me: *Why sell cigarettes at a hospital?*

CHAPTER 4

OFTEN, I THINK OF Clement and how he and I ended up best friends by chance in first grade. Assigned seats next to each other, we'd stuck together ever since. If I wanted to try out for the basketball team, Clement did too. If Clement wanted to ride dirt bikes, so did I. We both wore blue Chuck Taylors, both had a crush on Trish Rineholt, and both wanted to get fire-red convertible Corvettes and drive down to Mexico. It was our mutual dream to escape Windstop once we were old enough.

At age eight, we were into collecting baseball cards. At eleven, starting fires. When we were twelve, we took to blowing things up. With money stolen from our folks, we'd head to Larry Cockran's house, a classmate of ours. It wasn't Larry we wanted to see; it was his older brother, Chris.

Chris had a footlocker filled with wonders: Rambo knifes, Chinese throwing stars, and fireworks. We passed on blades and the kung fu stuff and instead bought some Black Cats, Thunder Bombs, and all the sparklers he had. First, we started small, blowing up soup cans, milk cartons, and bottles of Clement's mother's perfumes. Then we stepped it up and made sparkler bombs—duct-taped two to three hundred sticks together and stuffed a fuse in the core. No mailbox was safe.

Mr. Preston's mailbox was our downfall. He'd driven up just as we lit the fuse. The sheriff was called, then our folks. But we got off easy, only had to pay restitution for the mailboxes and serve ten community service hours, which meant a lot of riding around in the back of a pickup truck and picking up trash.

Bows and arrows became our passion the summer before high school. We were out to live off the land, survive in the wild. Pricking our thumbs then pressing them together, Clement and I swore a blood oath to protect each other from the dangers of the two acres of woods behind my house. If one of us was killed by a wild boar or a cougar while we were out hunting, the other was to create a funeral pyre, burn the body, and avenge the death by tracking down and killing the guilty beast, then eating it's heart. The warm days lazed by while we traipsed about the woods with our shirts off and headbands on, firing at squirrels and birds, always missing.

Clement came up with the idea of creating a twelve-foot-long headband crafted from torn T-shirts. We'd each tie an end around our foreheads, the length connecting us. Soon, we found ourselves bolting through the trees, firing off arrows while we screamed war cries. When a tree came between us, the headband tethering us together stopped us dead in our tracks. Our necks snapped back. Our feet flew from under us.

The more hurt we were, the harder we laughed. We were blood brothers, joined together forever.

On quiet nights, even now, I find myself wondering: *If Clement had never sat next me in first grade, would he have been my best friend?*

Would he be alive now?

CHAPTER 5

THE MOMENT THE BUS crossed into South Dakota, the trip turned into a tiny taste of hell. The toilet overflowed, a fight broke out, and someone set into a meal that reeked of fried baloney. The woman next to me came alive with questions. She wanted to know everything about me: my family, my dreams, my faith. "I love talking to anyone. Muslims, Jews, Christians, even Buddhists. Everyone but Mormons." She forced a laugh.

I told her I was a Mormon, which shut her down. She knitted furiously, elbowing harder until she finally got off in Billings, Montana.

Seattle was my goal. My money had a different idea. Nearly broke, I landed just outside of Spokane, Washington, where I signed on as a day laborer picking pole beans. My wages covered my daily existence and little else. When the harvesting season ended, I hitched a ride with a group of Phish phans on their way to a Vancouver show. They dropped me off in Seattle. It'd been five months since I'd graduated from high school, since I'd left Iowa altogether. I was in a chilled, strange town with no money, no friends, and no prospects. After a couple days wandering aimlessly and sleeping on the street, I ended up at the homeless shelter.

My education was just beginning.

CHAPTER 6

THE SALVATION ARMY'S LIGHTHOUSE Shelter for Men. Two stories, in Pioneer Square. No drugs, no alcohol, and prayers before every meal. No one was allowed to remain in the shelter during the day; we had to be working or looking for work, though the truth was that most of the men spent the hours in an aimless limbo, wandering the sidewalks, camped out in the park, or napping in the library when it was too cold out. Because we had to blow on a Breathalyzer to prove we hadn't been drinking before being allowed in for the night, the smart guys smuggled in pints of vodka and drank it in the privacy of the showers.

Dinner was served at 6:00 p.m. The front door locked at 7:00 p.m. If you weren't in by then, you weren't coming in. Eight thirty, lights out.

The shame of being homeless was nothing next to the humiliation of being processed into the shelter.

Under the watchful eye of a shelter employee, I squeezed out a urine sample for drug testing. My fingers were inked for prints. Multiple photos were snapped for my file. The rules and regulations were repeated three times to me, in case I was slow.

After being inspected, prodded, and recorded like livestock at a 4-H fair, I was finally handed a wool blanket that stank of night sweats and mildewed wet dreams, and was assigned a cot positioned just in front of the restrooms. At night, a bright beam crossed me each time the restroom door opened, like a searchlight cutting across a prison yard.

We slept on the second floor in an open space that held ninety-eight men at varying degrees of destitute. Half were tapping the system, exploiting it for all it was worth just to avoid the responsibilities of being an adult—of working, paying bills, feeding and taking care of themselves or a family. No point working for something when you could get it for free. The other half were broken men, crippled by the full press of life. Being able to work, to get back on their feet, was their dream.

Ray-Ray had the cot next to mine. My first night there, he eased himself onto the edge of my cot. His hair looked like something straight out of a men's magazine, perfectly styled in salt-and-pepper waves. "Raymond's my name, but friends call me Ray-Ray." He asked if I wanted to be his friend.

"What's that entail?"

He smiled and said my birth name aloud: first, middle, and last.

I hadn't told him, hadn't even spoken to him.

Ray-Ray held up a wallet—my wallet. "Nice driver's license photo. Very handsome. Do you have a photo I could keep?"

I grabbed the wallet from him. "How'd you get this?"

"I reached into your back pocket and took it," he said. "Listen, if you're going to be my friend, you have to be more cautious. I'll watch out for you as much as I can, but I can't protect you every minute of the day." Ray-Ray's thin fingers found my chest, touched me gently. "I hope you'll keep an eye out for me in return."

"What am I watching for?"

Ray-Ray studied the room, the men lulling about, talking, listening to music. He scooted even closer to me on the cot. "I want you to know something about me. I hate disloyalty. So if you're going to be my friend, don't fuck me over." He stood, motioned to my soap dish. "Hide your soap."

My soap, a bar of Dove I'd poached from the Korean store, sat in a plastic container in my footlocker, still damp from that evening's shower. "Why?"

"Someone will steal it."

"Who, you?"

His face flashed with hurt. "Why would I steal a friend's bar of soap?"

I ignored Ray-Ray's advice. When I woke the next morning, I found the soap box where I'd left it.

The soap, however, was gone.

CHAPTER 7

Ray-Ray and I became friends. Of sorts. Proximity drew us together, not fondness. We shared meals and idle talk, games of dominos. We only discussed the immediate and near future. Our pasts, our histories, had stopped at the shelter doors. Whoever we were before, those men weren't here now.

The only payout for being poor is an abundance of time. No work to fill the hours, no money to help make time pass. My days were long. I spent most of them at the Seattle Central Public Library, reading magazines and newspapers and halfheartedly looking for jobs online in that broken birdhouse of a building.

One day I found Ray-Ray there, studying world atlases.

"Planning a vacation?" I asked.

He didn't acknowledge me. In unison, he turned the pages of each atlas, studying one, then the other, in silence.

Just as I was turning to leave, he spoke, "Who do you think decides the colors and names of the countries?" He motioned to the two different atlases resting side by side before him. Rhodesia, filled in light green on one page; Zimbabwe, a muted blue on the other. Congo, a muddy ocher on one, transformed to Zaire and a cold gray on the other. Names and history. "Do you think it signifies anything, the different colors, the different names?"

"Doubt it."

"I was a different person before now," he said, flipping the page. He pointed out an area in Iran near the border with Russia. "This is where I'm from."

He told me he'd been a child soldier in the Iraq-Iran War; after the war, when he was seventeen years old, he flew to Canada on a fake passport. Eventually, he entered America illegally. He spent a year traveling about, then ended up in a small town in Florida and married a woman there. "Not much of a marriage," he said. "She expected certain things I wasn't able to provide, things like sex." He smiled. "But I got my green card." Though husband and wife, they had separate rooms, separate lives. The union was all for show. Eventually, she dumped him. "I was crushed when she left."

"But you just said it wasn't even a real marriage."

"I'm Iranian," he said, "but people here in America say I'm Persian. Did I change? No. But people's perception of me did. Same with my marriage. It wasn't much of a marriage but it was still my marriage. It was who I was," he said.

After the divorce, he packed up and moved to the Northwest, got his beautician's license, and went to work at a hair salon. Eventually, he saved up enough money to open his own shop. "Beauty by Ray-Ray," he said. "I had five girls working for me. We were booked two months out. I was a success."

He closed the atlases and shelved them. "You want to know what happened, right? You want to know how I ended up in a homeless shelter."

I said I did.

He reached out, tugged on a lock of my hair. He offered me a haircut. He offered me a blowjob.

I took the haircut.

Back at the shelter, he broke out his scissors, draped a towel over my shoulders, and meticulously trimmed my hair. He did a great job. "You're really good. Why don't you cut hair again? You could make lots of money."

He brushed the hair trimmings into the trash, snapped out the towel. "Living in a homeless shelter doesn't mean I don't have money."

"A prince among paupers," I said. "So you just enjoy living with all the misfortunate?"

"Unfortunate, not misfortunate," he said. "Most everyone here is unfortunate."

"There's a difference?"

He packed away his scissors. "There's a difference."

CHAPTER 8

Haven, Florida

THE BARTENDER SETS A new drink before her. She hits the fresh drink hard, taking most of it down in a single swallow. Then she gets up, ambles off to the bathroom.

I check the time. The meeting's set for noon, three-plus hours off.

The Germans have a chess term. *Zugzwang*. It's when neither player can move without landing in grave danger. It's when both players find themselves in a fucked situation.

Is it possible that an event becomes inevitable only after the fact, only after the disaster has struck and the damage is done? It's obvious to me now that something awful had been building for the last four years. The road behind me is littered with signs I couldn't see as I passed them. *Stop before it ends badly*, they warned. *Stop before you get killed.*

Now, in the middle of the mess I made, I have to find a way out.

The woman straddles the stool. Her hands are dripping wet. "They're out of paper towels," she says, then, "ask me a question."

"What's your name?"

"No, I mean a real question. Ask me something real." She grasps her glass with both hands.

I think. "Have you ever been in love?"

"Yes," she says. "What about you?"

Sarah comes to mind. I remember all the things that started out good, which I turned bad. "No."

"You've never been in love?"

"Well, it seemed like love at the time, but then, after…" I let it drop.

She smiles, showing teeth uneven but lovely. "Have you noticed that people in love always describe love like it's—" Breaking off, she looks lost for a moment. "I don't know. They describe it like it were a *thing*, something you can hold or touch or put on the shelf for display. And yet they never can give a clear description of this *thing*." Her voice lifts then drops like lapping waves. "I probably sound like an idiot for saying it, but love isn't an object, it's an action. A verb, not a noun," she says, digging her nail into the scarred wood of the bar. "You know, I've been married three times." She corrects herself quickly. "No, only twice. I've been married only twice. And all my men I met here."

"In Charm's?"

She nods, touches the bar. "I was married to him." She points out another spot. "And him."

It takes me a moment to realize she's pointing to names carved into the bar in block letters. MASON the first one reads. MASON reads the second.

"You were married to the same guy twice?"

"Two different guys," she says. "Same name."

"Uncommon name."

"Uncommon men." She swivels around on the stool to search the photos on the wall, then points. "That's Mason One," she says, getting up to touch a photo showing the back of a man's head. Black hair, slightly wavy. "And that's Mason Two." She moves to set her fingertips on another. This one smiles at the camera. Young, large eyes, dark skin, and wavy black hair, like the other Mason.

The photos could be a front and back shot of the same person.

Names. A person is bound tight by a name from the moment of birth. It breaks down the bones of a man's being, forces him into its own form. Manners, sensibilities, even a person's face is shaped by the sound of the name he's given. They form the person. Ashleys are always Ashleys, while Andrews are Andrews.

And Masons are Masons.

I am my name.

"Are you still married?" I ask.

She sits back on the stool and tilts her head slightly, giving me a look. "I lost Mason One," she says, making it sound like she gambled him away. "Lost him in the Persian Gulf. I used to say the Iraq War but it confused people. They'd ask, 'The first or the last?' And I'd have to explain it was the middle one. Operation Desert Fox. Nineteen ninety-eight," she says. "Most don't remember it even happening. The people who do usually try to correct me. 'Just six days of bombing,' they say." She drinks. "It was an action, they say, not a war. They tell me I lost Mason One to an action." She runs her hand over her forehead like she's trying to rub away a memory. "I lost Mason Two, too."

I wait for more. There is no more. I sip my drink. "How?"

"I'd like to say it was to another woman," she says. "At least with another woman, I could have fought for him, made my case. But it wasn't a woman. It was bear claws." She pauses. "The pastries. Mason's Hoosier bear claws! 'Don't let the breakfast growl getcha!'" A strange giggle bubbles up from her throat.

I've had Mason's Hoosier bear claws. A bibbed, smiling bruin is on the wrapper. We sold them in the gas station where I used to work a few years ago. They are good in a bad way. They make you feel sick but you can't stop eating them. "That's your Mason?"

"That *was* my Mason," she says, finishing her drink. "My Mason Two. The king of the bear claws. And for a while," she says, "I was queen."

A silence settles. Then a jangle of keys sounds. The bartender heads down to our end and sets a new drink before her without a word—her third. She swizzles the fresh drink with her straw. "I'm being unfair. It wasn't bear claws I lost him to," she says. "It was Indiana that took him. And it was all my fault." A sip of gin. "I talked him into moving there after we married so he could open up a pastry factory. Cheap land. Middle of America. Great for shipping." She lifts her hand, lets it drop. "We had a nice house, nice friends. Really, we had a nice life. But after two years—" She breaks off, takes another swallow. "Have you ever been to Indiana?"

"I've been." It's the one place I've been arrested.

"Miserable place, right? It's like being caught at the edge of a sneeze. A constant, awful feeling of wanting to do something you can't seem to make yourself do," she says, her brow wrinkling. "Indiana is waiting for something you know can't happen."

"What did you expect to happen?"

She lifts her hands, empty. "Life. Or something. Anything. Shit, I don't know. I was just circling stuff I wanted in catalogues with no money in the bank. It was just a bunch of expecting, hoping, wishing. I honestly believed," she says, "that just being with Mason Two would be enough. That was happiness. Having Mason Two would make everything all right. I'd change. I could make myself into something."

She leans to me. "Know what sucks?" She doesn't wait for me to answer. "We are born complete. Can't change. You realize that, don't you? We're stuck with who we are."

"People can change." I've seen them change, right before my eyes. It isn't pretty. "Situations shape a person."

"We can't change," she says again. "Situations only show different bits of a person. Like turning a statue around so the light hits it another way. The statue doesn't change. Nothing changes. You're just seeing it differently." Her gaze flickers to the far end of the bar, her attention caught.

I turn, expecting to see someone I don't want to see. But there's no one there. It's just us.

"You've never done anything of importance." Her voice is like paper catching fire.

"I'm twenty-two."

"And soon you'll be thirty. And then forty. And then so on," she says, then swiftly leans in to press her lips to mine. Her kiss tastes like quinine and cayenne pepper. It heats and sickens me.

Breaking, she says, "I don't want to be alone right now. I don't think I can live with being alone right now."

I know this for what it is. A request. A proposition.

"Okay," I say, flagging the bartender to have him call a car. "Let's go."

CHAPTER 9

SUNDAY NIGHT AT THE homeless shelter. I'd been out all day, walking about Seattle. Pondering. Wishing. Wanting.

Money and time are inversely related. Lots of one means very little of the other. The heavier a person's pocket is with cash, the quicker the minutes pass. Days, weeks, even years are consumed by the act of spending or trying not to spend. Being broke liberates a person. Time halts in its tracks when there's no money to do anything. The day, free, aches by slowly.

That morning, as every morning, I showered, shaved, dressed as best as I could, and got as far from the shelter as possible. Save Ray-Ray, I didn't socialize with any of the other men. I didn't want to be recognized for what I was—homeless.

I've read studies and reports that claim society ignores the homeless. They are invisible to most people. Irrelevant. A silent blight. But I felt anything but invisible. I felt like I was on fire in a pitch-dark theater, the crowd quietly watching as I ran through the aisles screaming. Nothing in my actions, I felt, went unnoticed, no matter how innocuous.

I skipped dinner, returning just before 7:00 p.m. Checking in, I was stopped by one of the men. "Bad news," he said excitedly. A big fight. Ray-Ray had been jumped by Big Bass. "He killed him."

My heart seized. "Killed him?"

He nodded. It had happened at dinner. Big Bass, a white, ex-Boeing worker, attacked Ray-Ray with a soup ladle. "He caught Ray-Ray pissing into his toothpaste tube. Gave him a customized ass-beating, Bruce Lee–style," he said. "Bashed him on the head two, three times, then chopped him to the floor." He made a chopping motion with his hand. "*Whack, whack.* Blood everywhere. The faggot has been crying like a pussy ever since."

I was confused. "Who's crying—Big Bass?"

"No, Ray-Ray."

"He's not dead?"

"Ray-Ray dead?" he said. "Why would you think he's dead?"

"You said Big Bass killed him."

"Yeah, well, he *did* kill him," he said. "Just not, you know, kill him dead."

I found Ray-Ray sitting on his cot, reading a lesbian street-gang novel called *Razor Clit.* His left eye was the hue of an overripe banana.

"Hey," I said.

He looked up, gave a slight nod.

I sat across from him, motioned to his eye. "I heard about the fight."

He barked out an angry laugh, put the book down. "Fight is too grand a term for it. It was a tussle at best. The real fight is still to come." He shifted over next to me and leaned in. "Everyone starts out in clover with me. It takes a lot to get on my bad side," he said, conspiratorially, "but once you do, it's a miserable ride. Big Bass is now on my bad side."

He rested his hand on my knee, his fingers caressing my leg.

I stood.

"Sit," he said.

I sat.

Ray-Ray put his arm around me. "I know who I am. I can understand why someone might hate me. But there's a freedom in being hated, in being despised," he said. "There's no burden of responsibility. I can act any way I want and the results are the same—hatred." He gingerly touched his bruised eye, asked if there was anything he could do for me. "Anything at all."

Thanks, but no.

I showered, went to bed.

The next week seeped by, then the following. A month.

Near dinnertime one Tuesday, I returned to find an ambulance idling out front of the shelter, its lights flashing. The men had gathered outside, watching as the medics carried someone out on a wheeled stretcher.

Big Bass, his face Jackson Pollocked with blood. A brace clamped his neck and his body was held to the gurney with straps. "He's fine but fucked up," the EMT said. Someone said that a rat bit him, another that he'd fallen off the building's roof. It looked more like he'd been hit by a truck full of pitbulls.

I found Ray-Ray lounging in the TV room, reading an article in *Cosmopolitan* magazine. "How to Get Your Man—No Matter His Age."

I pulled up a chair next to him. His shirt and pants were wet, like he'd walked through an open fire hydrant. He didn't look up, didn't acknowledge me. We sat silent until I finally said, "You heard, right?"

Ray-Ray turned the page slowly. "Heard?"

"About Big Bass."

He nodded. "I actually saw the man naked on the shower floor." He gave a slight shiver. "A pretty nasty sight."

"Were you the one to call the ambulance?"

He shook his head. "Though you could say I brought it," he said, his eyes on the magazine. "Big Bass. Such a fitting name. The fucker flopped about like a fish each time I punched him."

◎ ◎ ◎

THERE WAS BIG BASS, Bed Bug Bill, Two-Tone Hank, Johnny B., Johnny R., Little Johnny, Johnny Socks, Rathead Ron, Five Bucks Frank, Deadfoot, Old Steve, Crazy Steve, Big Steve, Small Dick Steve, Terry the Plumber, Doctor P., Viet Tom, Tommy Deaf, David the Jew, Sal the Jew, Cigar Jude, Pat Pizza, Buckshot Bill, Dollar Bill, Broke Bill, Billy Bill, Tiny Boy Bill, Skid Row Randy, Red Eye Wally, Stink, Dan the Man, Tacoma Tim, Utah Earl, Sam Francisco, London Larry, Hoosier Harry,

Jelly Ben, Ben the Boy, Ben Nasty, Boots, Socks, Toothless Chris, Jesus Chris, Chris Cross, Gramps, Big Mac, Scabby Doo, 401Karl, Toothless Teddy, Chomper, Dentures Donny, Donny Lemongrass, Donny Keys, Four Fingers Alan, Double L Allan, Alen with an E, Lawrence the Lifer, Bob Noxious, Horseface, Paki Paul, Mick Jagged, Heath Bar, Jailbait James, Jimmy Come Nightly, Jimmy Skis, Jimmy Goat, Johan Not John, and Ray-Ray, to name just a few.

In the shelter, no one had a last name.

CHAPTER 10

"YOU NEED PURPOSE." RAY-RAY ran his fingers gently through my wet hair, caressing my scalp.

Haircuts had become a regular ritual between us. Every few weeks, we'd spread out newspaper on the bathroom floor and drape a towel around my neck. I'd sit on a plastic stool while Ray-Ray hovered over me, snipping and trimming and combing my thick hair.

"I have purpose," I said.

"And what is that?"

"Get some money together. Get my own place," I said. "Get out of here."

He paused his hands. "That's action, reaction. Cause and effect," he said. "You eat, you shit. You sleep, you wake. Purpose," he said, "is knowing the why of what you're doing."

I'd overheard a couple guys at dinner talking about Big Bass. He was in a coma. Or had moved to Arizona. They didn't know. The truth probably was that he was sleeping on the streets, ashamed and too frightened to come back to the shelter.

Ray-Ray had feigned ignorance of the whole thing, slipping out of suspicion like it was a soiled shirt.

Tipping my head under his palm, I asked him what had sparked the fight in the first place.

Ray-Ray studied the length of my sideburns, then snipped at them. "Things happened."

"I heard he caught you pissing in his toothpaste."

He set his hand on my shoulder and laughed. "Are you saying I somehow pissed *into* a tube of toothpaste? How is that possible?"

I laughed, too.

He smoothed a comb over my scalp, the teeth biting slightly. Bits of my hair peppered the floor. Ray-Ray raised his scissors and paused. "We're not done talking about your why," he said.

That night, as I faded to sleep, Ray-Ray said something.

"What?" I propped myself up, looked across the dappled darkness.

"It was his toothbrush," he said. "He caught me pissing on his toothbrush."

CHAPTER 11

THE WINTER DAYS BEGAN late and collapsed early, the sun visiting briefly before shunting off. All I wanted to do was sleep.

The shelter expected everyone to work and required a small monthly fee from each resident. I got an off-the-books job at a gas station. The pay was awful, but I was allowed any snack I wanted, within a limit. Slim Jims were my favorite.

Winter crept into spring. My birthday came and went. I plotted out a simple goal: get out of the shelter and into my own place.

I managed to build some savings from my meager pay, which was handed to me each Friday in the form of worn bills. My cash was always with me, even when I showered, kept neatly folded in a plastic sandwich bag. But it seemed something was always calling on me to tap it. The sole of my left boot tore through or my one pair of work pants were stolen. Fate pissed in the boat while I was trying to bail out the water. Still, nine months, I figured, of saving and scrimping, and I'd have enough money for my own apartment. Come Thanksgiving, I could move out.

With spring coming on strong, the shelter population turned over. The men celebrated the nice weather by hitting the street, cleansing themselves of the months of Christian charity by rebaptizing in drink or drugs.

"You should look to get out of here," Ray-Ray said one morning. "You should be focusing on your future."

"I'm working on it."

He eyed me. "Not fast enough."

A hot skewer of anger and embarrassment drove up my spine. "Yeah? Well, I don't see you fighting to get out," I fired back. Failure glared at me no matter where I looked. Ray-Ray's reminder didn't help. "I don't see you out there taking on the world. Why is that? Why don't you get out of here?"

Ray-Ray glanced at the walls. He didn't speak for a moment. "I'm probably jinxing myself by saying so, but I'm inconspicuous here."

"That's a good thing?"

"It is when you don't want to be recognized."

Ray-Ray was recognized the next week by a new man at the shelter. He was gangly, with a pockmarked face, and had been assigned a cot the row over. He couldn't keep his eyes off Ray-Ray.

"Not good," Ray-Ray said, stealing glances at Pockmark. He was rattled.

While ugly, Pockmark seemed normal to me, or normal enough. No one in the shelter was normal. That's why we were all there. "Who is he?"

"I don't know," Ray-Ray said. "But just look at that mouth. That's a mouth I'd never kiss. It's a mouth of a harbinger." He took my hand in his as a woman would and looked me in the eye. "Promise me," he said, holding my fingers tight, "that you'll shower tonight."

I pulled my hand free. "I already showered today."

"Tonight," he repeated, his gaze steady. "When you get back from work. Promise me you'll shower."

"Okay."

"Say you promise."

"Okay, I promise."

"Good," Ray-Ray said. Fear blanched his face. "Good," he said again, sounding anything but good.

When I got back that evening, smelling of oil and gas and Slim Jims, Ray-Ray was gone, his cot stripped of its bedding and his footlocker empty.

Resting on my cot was a bar of Dove soap. My bar. The one that had been stolen my first night at the shelter months earlier.

I grabbed a towel.

The soap bar came apart in the shower. It'd been sliced lengthwise, sandwiched back together. Between the halves was a narrow strip of paper with three lines written in pencil.

Line one: *YMCA.*

I ended my shower. As I toweled dry, the mildewy white plastic shower curtain was yanked back and I stood face-to-face with Pockmark. His skin was a warzone: pitted, torn, and scarred. Our eyes locked. A rumbling sounded from deep in his chest. "You done?" he asked.

I nodded, grabbed my things, and left.

CHAPTER 12

H E FLAGGED DOWN THE cocktail waitress. "This isn't my lipstick," he said, holding up his scotch glass. A red lower-lip print kissed the rim of the glass.

"That..." Her face wrinkled with worry. Flirting was in her skill set. Processing a situation—not so much. "I'm sorry for that," she said. He'd already drank most of the scotch, which was forty-three dollars a shot. "If you'd like—"

"Yes, I would," he said. "And don't just pour the drink into clean glass. Get me a fresh scotch." Gratis was stated by the firmness of his tone.

Glass in hand, the waitress made her way back to the bar like a tightrope walker with a head cold.

He glanced around the place. A handful of people. Candles on the tables, a sound of hushed conversations, a spark of laughter. No one looked at him twice. That's what he liked about hotel lounges. They weren't destinations but pauses on the path from Point A to Point B. No one would remember him, save the waitress, and even that was doubtful.

He touched the knot of his tie and turned his attention to back out the window to the building across the street. *How did ties ever become a thing?* he thought. Probably something to do with protecting your neck, not exposing your jugular to the enemy. And a business suit is a form of armor. Handshakes, he knew, evolved from the act of foes proving to each other they weren't holding weapons. I come in peace, an extended, open palm said.

Battles and fighting in high-polished shoes. That's the definition of business: war without blood.

Well, the man thought. *Mostly without blood.*

He keyed out a text on his phone, signed off with name. His nickname. What everyone called him.

He deleted it, signed off with his surname: *HIGGLES*.

Business. Formal. Professional. No bullshit. That's what this is. Work. Respect was required.

The waitress set a fresh drink down and tried to salvage her chance for a big tip by lightly touching his shoulder. "Again," she said, "I'm sorry for the dirty glass."

But the man didn't hear her.

His focus was out the window.

On the young man.

Entering the YMCA.

The man downed the scotch.

He hit send on his phone.

He stood up. "Charge the drink to room three twenty," he said to the waitress. "Add a twenty dollar tip."

The man wasn't staying at the hotel.

CHAPTER 13

A T THE YMCA, I asked for a day pass. The desk clerk tried hard to upsell me into a full membership. "You should really think of your health," he said.

"I constantly do," I told him.

Line two: *Locker 129.*

Dank and foul, the basement locker room was a moldy hole of wet towels and slick tile.

Line three: *33-24-11.*

I spun the tumbler right, left, right, popped the lock, and pulled open the door.

It's only much later, long after the event has passed, that we realize the gravity of certain moments, the weight that one choice places on our lives. It etches its mark deep in the tablet of our days. We endure the trauma of our decisions. We gain knowledge. We grow sure that we could wisely navigate such an experience should it ever arise again.

But it never does. Situations never repeat themselves in the exact same way.

In hindsight, I shouldn't have taken the fanny pack full of money that was in the locker. I shouldn't have powered up the cell phone that was with it.

CHAPTER 14

MY FATHER LOVED VODKA. He amped-up every drink with it: orange juice, coffee, Gatorade, even beer.

His problem wasn't alcohol, which he held astonishingly well, never showing the slightest tipsiness. My father's problem was sobriety. It made him hard, complicated, and contradictory.

He couldn't handle a clear head. Life was too distressing for him. The world's edges were too sharp, the situations too vivid, and people too real. He couldn't hold on, so he comforted himself with drink, from morning to bedtime. It fastened him down, smoothed the corners, rounded off the roughness of the day.

Drinking made him a better person.

It made him a better driver, too.

◎ ◎ ◎

IT SOUNDS LIKE FORTUNE cookie bullshit, but it's true. With choice comes morality.

CHAPTER 15

Haven, Florida

OUTSIDE, THE LIVERY CAB honks.

I pay up, tipping the bartender generously, then lead the woman out. Her skin is cool in my hand.

Stepping from the comfort of Charm's, I'm staggered by the Florida light, the sun making my head piston violently. Even in February, it's strong.

The woman laughs, lifting her hand to shade her eyes. "My mother used to hate going out in the daytime. Said it made her look her age."

She slides into the car first, her pale legs flashing sharply from inside her skirt. I follow closely.

My battered, white Schwinn cruiser stands chained to the signpost. I should have the driver toss it in the trunk, then tell him to drive us to a motel. Instead, I ditch the bike and I hear myself break my own rule.

I give the driver my address.

In all the years of Kam Manning, I've never revealed where I live. In all the cities I've been, I've never taken anyone home.

The lemon and cinnamon scent of her skin reminds me of Sunday breakfasts with my family, of lazy summer days filled with heat and sweat. It makes me think of the first girl I kissed.

The woman takes my hand and laces her fingers with mine. She's strong.

The car flows smoothly through the thin morning traffic. Rush hour lasts ten minutes here, from five to nine to five after nine. She says, "I dreamt about bananas last night."

I laugh.

"I wish it was funny." Her face is somber. "I found it terrifying."

"Why?"

She leans on me, laying her head to my shoulder. "I don't know why," she says, turning her face up to me. "It just was." She takes my mouth with hers.

A taste of juniper and lost opportunity floods my system, sparking a crippling erection.

We kiss for a minute, for an hour, for a lifetime. The car grazes along, pausing at red lights and accelerating through greens.

Breaking the kiss, she says, "I'm sorry for this. For what's happened, for what now has to happen."

"What has to happen?"

Her lipstick is smeared, a slash of kidney red. She turns and stares out the window at the buildings clicking past. "The people who read about us—"

"Read about us?" Now she's frightening me. "What are you talking about?"

"In our story, if it ever gets written." She taps the window with her fingertip. "Of course, no one would believe it because it's all true. People don't like the truth. At least not normal people's truth."

"You're normal?" I say, wishing I could retract the words the moment they're out of my mouth.

"Just as normal as you," she says. "That's why our story won't fly. It makes too much sense. People reject what they can relate to."

"People can relate to drinking at the crack of dawn?"

"There's nothing odd about that. Anyone can do it. What people want are stories about things that they long to do, things that they could never bring themselves to do. Take my Mason One. He wanted to be an oceanographer but was scared of water," she says, the words bubbling out of her. "Terrified of all the things below the surface he couldn't see, all the things hidden under there. That's what scared him most. But he always confronts his fears, so guess what he did?"

"Became an oceanographer."

She shakes her head. "Wasn't smart enough," she says. "No, he got a job on a fishing trawler for a season, confronted his fears that way. Joined the army out of fear, too. Fighting, shooting, killing, Mason feared it more than he feared water."

I say nothing, thinking of my situation. Of Ray-Ray, of Higgles, of how afraid I am of them both. By day's end, this whole life will be over.

Blocks from my place, the car slows to a stop at a red light. The old highway tears before us, trucks rumbling past at top speed.

The woman holds my hand. Charm's is already forgotten. I ask her name again.

She says, "How many girlfriends have you had?"

"Does it matter?"

"Of course not, but I still want to know."

I think. "How do you define girlfriend?"

"Anyone you've slept with."

I mentally count. "Three." It's the right answer for the moment.

"Is that three to the third or fourth power?"

I laugh.

Out the left side window, there's a large, sun-bleached poster in a storefront, the corners curling. It's red, white, and blue, with cartoons of George Washington and Abraham Lincoln advertising a Presidents' Day special: buy one box of Mason's Hoosier bear claws, get one free. With coupon.

Presidents' Day was yesterday. Banks and government agencies were closed. I pushed both Higgles and Ray-Ray off with that excuse. I didn't have what they wanted; it was in a safe-deposit box. They're both expecting I'll have it today.

I don't have it.

I've never had it. Don't even know exactly what "it" is.

The light turns. The car accelerates. She takes her hand from mine, her eyes mournful. "Often, I do things not because I want to do them, but because I know that if I don't do them I'll hurt someone else." She stares out the front window. "Does that make any sense?"

I think of my parents enduring each other for all those years for my sake. I say, "It does."

She touches my face gently. "I feared that," she says, then swings open the car door while we're still in motion. She bolts like a cat sprung from a box, gracelessly stumbling out. But she doesn't fall.

The driver slams on the brakes, halting the car. I step out, call after her. "Hey!" But she's gone, already down the street, heading back the way we came, back toward Charm's. Back toward where we began.

CHAPTER 16

M Y MOTHER WAS A handsome woman, much to her disappointment. She'd rather have been plain, even homely. Handsomeness, she said, was for deer hunters and heads of state, not for women. Handsome women were burdened with responsibilities they never asked for. They were relied on even if they were unreliable, and leaned on in times of trouble.

My father, on the other hand, was anything but handsome. The strange geometry of his face should have repelled people, but instead it drew them in. He had an inexplicable allure, a tempting animal charge that canceled hesitancy. Babies regularly waddled up to him, their arms outspread. Women turned flustered and flirtatious when he entered a room. Men longed to be his friend.

Together they were an arresting pair, a study in contrasts, on the surface and beneath. My mother had to have everything planned. My father left most everything up to fate. My mother was a morning person, my father a night owl. They couldn't agree on anything. Even their shared memories didn't match, fractured along some invisible fault line like separate histories of the same thing. Their stories became stories of stories, muffled echoes of the incident, distorted by time. Their tales shifted and changed with each telling, moving further and further from what really happened. In the end, I'm not even sure there was much truth left in either story.

They couldn't even agree on when they first met. Each version had the smooth, well-handled edges of the believable, though neither, I'm positive, was true. They'd made their own vivid fairy tales and presented them as fact so often that they came to believe their own lies. My mother claimed they first met in the fall, at a friend's barbecue. "Your father spilled a drink on my dress," she said.

"It was the only way she'd take notice," he replied, but then said that they'd met before that, over the summer. "Bowling," he said. "You and that one guy you dated, the one with the weird ears—"

"Richard Southwright. And I never dated him." Her voice was even, hiding her agitation.

"Right, him. Your boyfriend with goofy ears. You and him were bowling partners against me and another girl. We beat you, as I recall."

"Which girl?"

My father lifted his chin, shrugged a half shrug. "Just some girl," he said, topping off his drink.

My mother said no. Impossible.

"Why's it impossible?"

"For three reasons," my mother said. "First off, I'd remember."

"Apparently not."

"Secondly," she said, "Richard—who was never my boyfriend, mind you—got killed the spring before you and I met. Dead men can't bowl."

"He was killed the spring *after* we met," my father said.

My mother thought on this. "Well, even if that's true," she said, "the third reason makes it impossible."

"Which is?"

"I've never bowled in my life."

◎ ◎ ◎

MY PARENTS' DEATH WAS my fault.

CHAPTER 17

Seattle, Washington

WITH RAY-RAY'S CASH, I checked in to Water's Edge Motel on Alaskan Way, threw down a fistful of dollars for a room. The thought of going back to the shelter to claim my few ratty things turned my tongue thick with worry. Pockmark was there, waiting.

Inside, I turned on the light, dead-bolted then chained the room's door. The space smelled of air long trapped, of failed liaisons. It smelled like nothing good had happened there in months. A trail from the bathroom to the bed was worn in the room's carpet. The bed was troughed in the middle. I stripped, took a long, hot bath, and scrubbed myself with the plastic-scented motel soap. Lying in the tub with no worry of others barging in, I listened to the calming drip of the faucet. There is a luxury to quiet, to being alone, something I'd forgotten since leaving Iowa.

Wrapped in a tiny, rough towel, I counted the money. Two hundred dollars, a little more. Mostly soiled twenties and tens with a few ones. No fives.

I powered up the cell phone. The screen lit.

There was a chime.

One text.

Instructions. A simple task with a nice payout. The last line read, *Are we clover?*

The contact's name: HIGGLES.

I turned the cell phone off, clicked on the ancient TV. The image buzzed to life. Flipping through the channels, I searched for anything other than reruns or news. The phone stayed off. Finally, after ten minutes of finding nothing on TV, I went down the street for food and a six-pack of beer. Walking the empty night street, my kidneys rattled with anxiety. The quiet, the being alone, ate at me.

I got a couple slices of pizza, some beer, and hurried back to the seeming safety of my room. I powered the phone back up, read the text again. The errand seemed stupidly easy. It seemed safe. Which meant it was neither simple nor safe.

Higgles—whoever he was—instructed me to go to the Number Won Sun Chinese restaurant in the International District, where I was to ask for Kam Man, and tell him I wanted a large order of chicken feet. And a Diet Apple Slice.

Kam Man then would hand over some documents with instructions on what to do with them.

For my efforts, I'd make $300 cash.

Simple.

I slept soundly that night, no loud snores from others shaking me awake.

In the morning, I strapped on the fanny pack and checked out.

Heading south, toward the International District, I stopped at a trash can, took the phone out. I had a couple hundred dollars, no real obligations. I saw it as seed money Ray-Ray had supplied me to launch my career. A career in what, I didn't know. I didn't have a clue who this Higgles was, or what Ray-Ray was tangled up in. I could take the money and buy a bus ticket to somewhere, anywhere, and try to start fresh. Or I could tie on a really good drunk, sober up in a handful of days no better off than I was.

One thing my father loved to say was that small actions can vastly change your life. He had plenty of personal examples. Tons of "if onlys." If only he'd had a firmer handshake when he interviewed for the manager's position. If only he'd loaned Sam Milestone, now Windstop, Iowa's richest resident, the five hundred bucks he needed to launch his landscaping business. He believed that taking a right turn instead of a left alters your life's trajectory. At first, it may be unnoticeable. But, over time, the distance between where you were headed and where you ended up becomes substantial.

I turned on the phone and reread the text.

Stay clear, I thought. *Keep the cash, toss the phone. Keep clean.* Don't get caught up with this Higgles character and whatever Ray-Ray was messing with, whatever it was that had made him run.

We're clover, I thumbed, then hit send.

CHAPTER 18

I WISH SOMETHING HAD gone wrong on that first job, that my nerves had cracked or that I'd fucked up, then maybe things might have turned out different. But aside from my gut flaring with fear, the job went off flawlessly. It seemed like a joke, how simple everything was.

After pacing past the Number Won Sun three times, I finally gathered enough grit to head in. The clatter of pans, the violent sizzle of flaming woks, and the shouting of orders banged off the gritty walls of the tiny rat hole of a restaurant. The place reeked of pork grease and soy sauce, the stench coating my lungs with each breath. An old woman sat in the corner booth, her eyes jaundiced, a full-moon yellow. She looked like she hadn't moved in months.

"Yes? Yes?" the counterman said, not looking up from the pile of pennies he was counting.

I asked for Kam Man, my voice breaking.

"Who?"

"Kam Man. I want a large order of chicken feet and a Diet Apple Slice."

The counterman picked up a meat cleaver. His dark, tired eyes met mine, taking me in for what felt an eternity. My heart sheered the bolts holding it to the chassis of my chest, rattled wildly about my ribcage.

The counterman turned his head, shouted toward the back, then raised the cleaver. He deftly started cutting chunks of chicken. "Three ninety-five," he said.

I paid.

A moment later, a tiny man with a face like an old orange hobbled out from the back. He handed me my order and an envelope. "Are you Kam Man?" I asked.

"Enjoy!" He bowed slightly, then shuffled back toward the rear of the restaurant.

Outside, I tossed the order of food and peaked inside the envelope. An endorsed check, a document written in what looked like Russian, and a Post-it with instructions. *Seattle Public Library. 613.04244 Ou71. Page 527.*

Wandering the library aisles, I searched out the call number. *Our Bodies, Ourselves.* Page 527 was the chapter "Midlife and Menopause." There, in the pages, was another Post-it. *Leave envelope*, it read. *Money in 914.97 W521B. Page 444.*

I slipped the envelope in the book, shelved it, then went looking for 914.97 W521B. Rebecca West's *Black Lamb and Grey Falcon*, a travelogue of the Balkans in the 1930s. "Chronicling the history of violence, the pride, the beliefs, and the schism that divided a weary people."

Between pages 444 and 445 were three hundred-dollar bills, crisp and smooth and waiting.

I pocketed the cash, shelved the book, and headed toward the exit, planning a big lunch at TGI Fridays. But curiosity gripped me. I went back to *Our Bodies, Ourselves,* flipped open the book to page 527.

The envelope was gone.

CHAPTER 19

WITH OVER FIVE HUNDRED dollars in my pocket and the prospect of earning even more, I didn't go back to the shelter. I didn't go back to the gas station, either. Ray-Ray had connected me with Higgles, set me up with a paying job. It was like a paper route, only better paying.

Two, three times a week, Higgles texted instructions. The pick-up points were always different, the coded phrases awkward.

At the car wash in the Central District, I asked that Javier give me a full undercarriage treatment and lavender interior scenting; I had no car. At the gynecologist office on Queen Anne, I requested an appointment with Dr. Mendelbaum on Thursday at 8:00 a.m. and said I'd bring the donuts. And at the pet grooming shop in Bell Town, I asked for Teri and inquired about cat leashes and ordering twenty pounds of chinchilla dust.

Each time I was handed an envelope with a check already endorsed and some documents or a flash drive. Each time I was instructed to leave the envelope in a book in the library.

I called it "Kam Manning."

One summer in high school I had worked in a factory buffing the metal burrs off of small pieces of die-stamped metal. The piece would then go on to be dipped in anti-rust coating, painted a flat, matte black, and shipped off. A toy, a truck, or weapon's technology. I had no idea what the piece fit into, what the importance of it was, or even how the final product was used.

My Kam Manning was the same. I had no idea how I fit in the grand scheme of things—or even what the grand scheme was. I simply followed the instructions.

The names on the Kam Man checks would be different each time. Some were for individuals: Jasper Hogan, Molly Simmestere, Bradley D. Arsenault. Some were for businesses: Production Plastics LLC, Unipower Inc., Madson & Hopewell. Always, they were written for $42.17, memo line scrawled *For the orphans*. Each and every one.

The books I left drop-offs in differed. *I'm Okay, You're Okay*. *The Pregnancy Bible*. *Iron John*. But the three hundred-dollar bills were always between pages 444 and 445 of *Black Lamb and Grey Falcon*. Each and every time.

Two months passed, then six. Winter came again. Ray-Ray was long gone, probably in another city, in another state, maybe even back in Iran. I kept Kam Manning, kept convincing myself I was clear of any worry. I wasn't doing anything illegal—that I knew of. I could walk away scot-free.

Or so I kept telling myself.

It's disturbing how swiftly we deceive ourselves.

But then Higgles went radio silent. A week passed with nothing. I texted Higgles. No response. Two, then three more weeks passed with no word, no Kam Manning gigs. For over a month I sat around worrying. My messages to Higgles went unanswered. No reply. I bided my time, did crossword puzzles, worried, and waited.

Then came the text. *Tacoma. Tomorrow morning. Wear pink oxford buttoned to the neck.*

I wore a pink oxford buttoned to the neck, rented a car, and drove to Tacoma. Once there, I parked downtown and waited for instructions.

At two o'clock my phone buzzed. I was to meet my contact on the back deck of the Mandolin Café at three. She'd be wearing a green John Deere T-shirt, her hair done in pigtails.

I found her instantly. She sat at a table littered with empty coffee cups, plates, and a bowl. No surface was exposed. It was like she'd finished a party.

As I sat, she rose. "Pink isn't your color," she said, tossing a package into my lap. "It makes you look like an idiot."

"Hey," I called to her, holding up the package. "What am I supposed to do with this?"

She strode back to the table, cupped her hand to my ear. "Perhaps you could call a bit more attention to us," she whispered. She touched my cheek. "This is all about skullduggery, possibly a little killing, too."

I swallowed hard. "Killing?"

She let out an angry laugh, loud in my ear, and poked the check into my shirt's breast pocket. "God, you're such a fuckhead. How should I know what's in the package?" Her hip bumped the table as she walked away.

After I settled the bill, I returned to my rental to open the envelope.

Inside was a wad of pesos, an airplane ticket to Cancún for that night, and a South African passport with the name Tomas Cartright.

The photo on the passport was of me.

CHAPTER 20

CRUSHING HEAT, SWELTERING SAND, blazing sun, and tequila that tasted like toilet cleaner. The contact, a strikingly beautiful woman who didn't speak English, left me with a virulent case of crabs.

Cancún sucked.

CHAPTER 21

A LOUD, SINGULAR KNOCK on the door.

Higgles stood from bed, his bare feet on the cold tile floor. The Kite Factory Condos, #2D. Capital Hill, Seattle. No one knew he was here, not even the owner, who, according to her online postings, was in Hawaii for another three days.

Another knock, this one sounding twice. Then a man's voice. "Are you decent?"

The tension of the unknown was replaced by the worry of the possible. Higgles knew the voice, knew the man. A former colleague of sort. Someone he definitely didn't trust, not after the man's betrayal.

"You'll have to call the office to make an appointment," Higgles said. Their working relationship had ended in gunshots a little over a year ago. Now the man had tracked Higgles down.

Laughter rang through the metal door. "This isn't about business. It's an apology."

Higgles sidled up to the door and put his eye to the peephole. The man held a bottle of wine and flowers. An apology? Looked more like a date. He noted the wine. Beaujolais Nouveau, a cheap bottle made even cheaper by the fact that the vintage was three years ago. *Typical,* Higgles thought. The man gets the only wine that worsens with age.

Both stand on their side of the door, not speaking for nearly three minutes. Then the man said, "I'm out of it all. For good."

This time Higgles laughed.

A look of hurt skimmed the man's face. He set the wine and the flowers down in front of the door. "Just wanted to clear the air between us." The man backed away from the door, pulled out a small envelope from his back pocket, and held it up. "I even got tickets to the Seahawks game tonight," he said. "You and me, I thought. Beers and hotdogs and bury the hatchet. Make everything clover."

Clover, Higgles thought, remaining silent. *The fucker failed to steal my business so he steals my phrases instead.*

"The seats are on the fifty yard line." He spoke loudly and slowly, like he was giving directions to a foreigner. Putting his own eye to the peephole, the man said, "I'm here to atone for being a dick."

Higgles shifted back. The sight of the man's eye fishbowled through the door and left him queasy. "The window to your soul needs cleaning," he said, adding, "watching grown men in tight pants stand around is your way of atoning?"

"It'll be a start." He dropped the ticket next to the wine and flowers and turned. "Let me make this right with you."

Higgles watched the man exit via the stairwell. Envisioning him lumbering down the stairs, Higgles counted silently to twenty. Then moved to the window overlooking the street. A minute. Two minutes. The man didn't exit.

No way he made it out that quickly, he thought.

He checked the peephole again. Save the peace offering, the hall was empty.

Higgles watched out the window for a solid five minutes. Nothing.

Maybe I missed him, he thought, heading back to the front door. *Maybe he went out the side door.*

But another thought—a thought that came too late—sliced across his mind as he turned the door's knob.

Football season had yet to begin.

CHAPTER 22

"YOU'RE A SHIT HOST," the man said. Scouring the apartment, he'd found a laptop but no phone. *There had to be a phone*, he thought, pulling cushions off the sofa. "Quite rude, in fact. No courtesy."

"I'm a visitor here, too," Higgles said, his hands zip tied to the radiator leg. "So perhaps you can show me some courtesy and fuck off."

"Gladly." He tapped the laptop. "Tell me the password. Tell me where you hid your phone. Tell me about the kid you got working for you. Then I'll be out of your hair."

Shit. He knows about the kid, Higgles thought. He had only himself to blame. Not just for the emerald-blue knot the size of an avocado seed on his forehead. But for the situation in general. "I can't tell you the password," he said.

The kick caught Higgles in the kidneys. Bright amebas fireworked across his vision.

"Seriously," the man said. "Make this clover and I'm gone."

Again with the clover. Higgles spit, expecting to see blood. *The blood will happen later*, he thought, *when I piss*. "Imitation is flattery and all that bullshit," he said. "But really, you need to stop stealing from me."

The man's head dipped back like he was dodging a punch. "Stealing? What have I ever stolen from you?"

"My business, my words, even my ex. You're like an autistic cousin mirroring my every action."

This time, the kick caught Higgles in the face. His head bounced off the radiator. He slumped, unconscious.

"You're the retarded one, cousin," the man said to the limp body. He stood silent a moment, confused as to what to do next. "Fuck." He needed Higgles conscious, needed information from him. That's all the business was, information. The money happened when it was passed along.

The man lightly slapped Higgles on the cheek. No response. He looked at the laptop. *Okay,* he thought, picking it up. *This is good enough. I can work with this.*

He stopped at the front door. *Autistic cousin,* he thought, and headed back to the kitchen, where he found a pair of scissors. When the man was done, Higgles looked like a chemo patient, tufts of hair hacked from his head. *That'll piss him off,* he thought, smiling.

Back at his hotel room, it took the man more than five hours to hack into the laptop. It took him less than five seconds to realize Higgles hadn't been lying. He didn't know the password.

The laptop wasn't Higgles'. It was the condo owner's, the woman who was on vacation in Hawaii.

He winged the laptop across the room. It frisbeed into the wall, divoting the drywall. *Fuck technology.* He stood. *I'll do this the old-fashion way. Find Higgles again, torture him a little.*

But then he had another thought. The kid. The one Higgles had working for him.

"That's the way," he said, thinking through the plan.

CHAPTER 23

O N MY WAY BACK from Cancún, I changed planes at LAX. That's when I saw him. Pockmark. I'm positive—nearly positive—it was him standing by the Wok & Roll in the terminal's food court, his glare hard on me. He disappeared in a flash, swallowed by a passing crowd, but seeing him jammed a pike of dread into my liver. I was being watched, followed.

Back in Seattle, I hit the pharmacy for Lindane shampoo to address the crab issue and then texted Higgles that Cancún was complete. I had the package.

He texted me a call number. 613.69 Sw35N. *National Geographic Complete Survival Manual.*

That afternoon, I slid the package between pages forty-three and forty-four of the book. My money was in the standard place, *Black Lamb and Grey Falcon.* Pocketing the cash, I grabbed a magazine and sat at a table in the far corner of the floor, staking out the shelf where I'd left the drop. I texted Higgles, then didn't move from my spot all afternoon, hoping for a glance of my mystery employer, or at least whoever made the pick-up.

Night edged in. Only a handful of people had wandered down the aisle the entire time I was there. No one had stopped, pulled the book from the shelf.

At closing time, a security guard came by, gave me the nod. "Learning time's over," he said. I was the last person on the floor.

On my way out, I quickly checked for the package. It was gone, the book's pages empty. Higgles had been there, and somehow scooped up the documents.

I took the cash, headed back to my room at the Marco Polo Motel. I wasn't making mint, but the jobs paid enough to support me—covering a place, shopping trips to Old Navy, dinners at the Olive Garden. It was high living—if you were low rent. I was glad for it, though. I didn't question the set up. Luck's lips occasionally brush a man's cheek.

But now that I'd spotted Pockmark, I knew the kiss wouldn't linger long.

After the LAX sighting and Higgles' magic trick at the library, my paranoia built. I became overly cautious. Before, I'd show up clean shaven, a smile on my face. Now when I went on a Kam Manning, I buried my head in a ball cap or hoodie, hid my face behind sunglasses and a week's worth of stubble. I had a new disguise for every job in every town and made roundabout journeys to my pick-up point. I'd cut through department stores, ride the bus a few stops one way then take another bus in the opposite direction, grab a cab to race me five blocks past my destination. No one was following me. Ever.

Weeks passed swiftly. I grew tired of moving from hotel to hotel, decided to lease a gutted loft in a raw part of town and hunkered down.

I took an entire floor and made the mistake of paying six months upfront, all cash.

The landlord eyed the stack of bills, then eyed me. So much for trying to be inconspicuous. Overhead, pipes and wires ran their routes, exposed—the nerves and veins of the building. "What do you plan on doing here?" he asked.

"When?"

He gazed at me stiffly. "This is a commercial loft. It's not zoned for residential living." He asked me my business.

"Twist ties," I said. It's what came to mind.

"Twist ties?"

"Yeah, you know, the green-and-white wire thingies that seal bread bags." I made a turning motion with my fingers. "I supply thirty-four percent of Indonesia," I said, adding, "one in three Indonesians use my ties."

It took him a moment to process. "Didn't know they ate much bread."

"More than you'd imagine."

He nodded slowly, handed me the keys. "Best of luck with that."

Home. For now.

The back windows looked out on an alley while the front gazed up on the Puget Sound. I set up a couch and a hot plate. A shower entailed standing in a plastic bin and rinsing with a hose hooked up to the bathroom faucet. The used water I dumped in the toilet.

The industrial neighborhood huffed out noise and exhaust fumes during the day, but went silent at night. I shopped exclusively at the dusty-shelved deli across the street. I didn't flash about, which wasn't difficult. There was no place to flash about. The warehouses were mostly dormant, there were few real businesses. No shops, restaurants, cafés, or offices; the neighborhood was a pass-through, not a destination.

After 7:00 p.m., activity collapsed completely. The street emptied. I'd sit on the fire escape and watch the lights of the Puget Sound ferries as they made their cheerless journey across the water. I had no plans, no agenda, no dreams or goals.

Friendless, I invented friends, spinning elaborate stories about the one or two people who got on the express bus that stopped a block away. I made up histories for them, created names, imagined successes and failures.

I fell in love with a woman on the 7:42 p.m. Or at least, my version of her.

From my perch, I studied her as she waited, weaving new threads into her backstory. I came to anticipate her comings, watching her appear from behind a building and walk the half block to the bus stop, the sound of her heels clacking on the pavement. She was always professionally dressed—a secretary or warehouse manager, maybe?

At first, I made her a thirty-one-year-old from South America. Argentina. Then I rewrote her into something else, something more exotic. She was part Inuit, part Creole.

For weeks I watched her, imagining her returning home from a long day of work to a condo with a view of the mountains and water. I knew her kitchen cabinets were nearly bare: a few cans of tuna, some strawberry Crystal Light packets, and nothing else. She rarely drank, but when she drank, it was prosecco.

And I knew her name. Marya.

In Marya, I saw my new life. I saw myself setting up house, getting a job that I'd have to shower and dress for every morning, filing taxes, mowing the lawn. I saw us having a couple of kids, spending Friday nights lazily sharing take-out or watching a movie or playing cards. I saw us as an old couple, the kind who've lived together so long that they no longer speak in full sentences. We were predestined to be together. She was waiting for me. And for that I was thrilled. All I had to do was start the process, put the inevitable in motion.

All I had to do was introduce myself. The rest would play out.

Friday night.

I broke out a new shirt, headed down to the stop. We could jump a plane someplace south, Marya and I. Run away to Napa Valley or Costa Rica or Charlotte, North Carolina. Anywhere. We would be together.

A swarm of jitters chewed my stomach. *Calm down*, I told myself. This was Marya. My Marya. It wouldn't be hard. Just talk to her, say "Hi." Then what?

I didn't know.

It didn't matter.

She didn't show up for the bus that night.

I worried that something had happened to her, that she'd gotten fired or was in the hospital, but then I convinced myself that she must have just taken Friday off.

Saturday and Sunday ached along, dragging the weight of my fantasy behind them. Monday finally ticked around.

Again, I stood ready at the stop. I tried to appear relaxed as I watched each passenger board. Again, no Marya. The driver eyed me. "You getting on?"

I shook my head.

The bus rumbled off, leaving me on the deserted street.

I waited each night that week at the bus stop, reading old newspapers people had left behind. Tuesday, Wednesday, Thursday, Friday. No Marya. I brimmed with anxiety. Was she on vacation? Sick? I asked other passengers getting on if they knew her. All I got was confused or frightened looks.

Another weekend. Monday night finally arrived.

The bus rumbled to the stop, the brakes squeaking painfully, picked up the waiting passengers, then lumbered off.

I turned to leave, but then heard the *click-clack* of heels. Marya. Racing.

The oxygen in my lungs ignited. I stood ready to take her in my arms, hold her like she was life's last breath.

She approached, winded.

I stepped forward. "Hi," I said, then motioned down the street. "The bus took off. You just missed it."

She turned to me, her face a mix of caution and inquisitiveness.

I felt the moment start to escape and quickly fumbled to recover it. I introduced myself as Clement Martin. "Can I buy you a drink?"

Gravity failed as I waited for her reply. Everything loosed from the earth, shooting off into the darkness of space. Misery settled in my heart in the silence.

She paused a moment, thinking. "Sure," she said, and laughed.

But she wasn't my Marya. From her first word I knew she wasn't anything like I'd imagined. For one, her teeth were bad. And then there was her laugh. She sounded like a goat hitting a barbed-wire fence every time she found something funny.

Her name, Jasmina, reminded me of a cheap air freshener, and I knew it'd never work between us.

Still, I had a drink with her.

Still, I went home with her that night.

CHAPTER 24

B UT IN A WAY, Jasmina did carry my fate with her. Returning to the loft after our night together, I found a box at my door. It was large enough to hold a horse's head. No name on the outside, no address, no markings at all.

Warily, I lifted it. It had some weight to it. My mind spun through the catalogue of things that came in unmarked packages; none were good.

Inside, I found twelve dusty, hardbound books, each with a number markered on the cover. There was a postcard included: *Florida is hot in the summer. The beach is filled with dead jellyfish. Don't lose the books.* I turned the card over. A picture of Hersheypark in Pennsylvania.

Brighton Rock. Lover's Guide to Paris. Sex Kittens Take Seoul. The books were a mix of literature, trash, travelogue, and memoir. I picked up book eight, *Homage to Catalonia* by George Orwell, and began reading. The pages were ready to fall out, the binding weak.

Around me, the evening settled, shadows bleeding across the loft until it was too dark to read.

I turned on the light and the shadows shot back. The place was still, quiet, the night embracing. I looked at the book. I looked at the box. I reread the postcard.

A damp cold took hold.

Higgles. He knew where I lived.

CHAPTER 25

IT BOTHERED ME FOR weeks, like a floater skimming across your peripheral vision, never quite coming into focus.

Then one morning, long after I'd forced it from my mind, the answer came to me in the shower—a sudden rush that left me grasping for support.

My photo on the Tomas Cartright passport.

I realized where it had been taken.

The snap of the camera on my first day at the homeless shelter. The day I first met Ray-Ray.

◎ ◎ ◎

RAY-RAY. ONE OF OUR last conversations. Him telling me I needed to find my "why." The reason to exist. To continue. The thing that made me get out of bed in the morning.

My why was not wanting to die.

Which isn't the same as wanting to live.

CHAPTER 26

HIGGLES SENDING THE BOX of books spooked me. I moved places, hoping to hide.

The apartment I took in the Yesler Terrace just east of downtown Seattle could be mistaken for a closet. The view was of the back of a building. The fall was sweltering, ninety-plus degrees even in mid-October. Otter Pops and Corn Flakes were all I ate, my stomach revolting against me.

Popping out for toilet paper and milk one afternoon, I returned to find a padded envelope propped against my door.

Fuck, I thought, my skin trying to run off without me. This was no Welcome Wagon coupon book.

Inside my place, I bolted the door, threw the envelope in the trash, and then washed my hands for good measure. For over an hour, I ignored the envelope in the trash, but the allure of the mystery was too much.

I dug it out of the garbage, slowly tore it open. Inside was a SIM card.

I swapped it with the one in my cell phone. A text pinged. *Book 2,* it read. *Thursday. Meet me there.*

Higgles, I thought, even though he didn't sign off. *Don't lose the books,* he'd written on the postcard. I hadn't. I'd dragged them along. I scanned my library. Book 2. *Brighton Rock* by Graham Green. Higgles would be waiting in Brighton, England.

I was finally meeting the boss face-to-face.

Clover, I texted back.

Seattle to Newark to London. At the station, I got a meat pie, four tabloid papers that stained my hands black with ink, and took a train south. Brighton.

I waited four hours and was about to give up when Higgles texted the name of a pub. *The Uppin Arms.*

How will I know U?

You'll know me, was his response.

Stocky, oily faced, and huffing for air, he didn't look anything like I thought he would. His hair was shaved down to his scalp and spittle glossed his mouth. He reminded me of a horse after a hard race.

"That you?" he said, seeing me. I expected an English accent. He was a solid American.

I nodded and he wrapped me in a sweaty hug.

We settled in at a table in the back and ordered drinks, a whiskey and a beer each. "This is great, sitting down like civilized men to talk," he said. "So, tell me a little about yourself, your background, hobbies. Where do you see yourself in five years?"

I sat back in my chair, studied Higgles. "Is this a job interview?"

He flitted his hand about like he was clearing the air. "Of a sort," he said. "You've been a courier for—what?—a year-plus now? I just figured you're ready to start making some real money."

"What's real money?"

He threw out a number. It had a comma in it. I sipped my beer. "I'm listening."

"Good." He leaned toward me, his weight tipping the table a bit. "What do you know about Africa?"

"I know it's a continent."

"That's a start," he said. "I've got a job, a little something on the side I need done. It's not the regular nine-to-five you've been doing. To pull it off, it has to be *Hart to Hart.* It needs to be *Magnum, PI.*"

I tasted my whiskey, which burned my tongue. "You've lost me."

"It needs someone credible," he said. "Someone with a good facade, calm demeanor, and continuity of character." He smiled a mouthful of blue-white capped teeth. "I need someone who can hold their drink and be charming."

"You need a James Bond."

"But without the gadgets."

"A lo-fi James Bond."

"Try no-fi." Sniffing his whiskey, Higgles made a pained face.

"Go on. I'm listening."

He nipped at his drink, then rubbed his hands together like they were cold. "You know what hawala is?"

"A Turkish dessert?"

His look told me no. "It's a money transfer without money movement. Popular in the Middle East. And that's kinda what we're doing here. Just without the money bit. And there is a bit of movement involved."

"So it's not halva at all."

"Hawala," he said. "And it is like one because it's off the books—if you know what I mean."

I didn't. "And?" I said.

"Basically, I need you to be on the scene before the scene starts. I need you to influence the results." He tried his best for a friendly smile. "You'd be amazed at what can be accomplished with a head start."

I asked who we were getting a head start on, knowing it didn't matter. The whole set up—the new SIM card, the face-to-face, the blatant skullduggery—raised my guard. I didn't trust Higgles. But I trusted myself and my abilities to run his gauntlet, best him at his own game, and walk away richer.

"Everybody else. But don't worry. The everybodies are mostly nobodies. Underlings, creeps, hobos," he said. "We're not concerned about them."

"So then there's no risk?"

He held up a hand. "Of course there's risk. There are some people out there who don't like getting fucked."

"Does anyone *like* getting fucked?"

He tapped his nose. "You've got a point," he said. "But the big people, the bosses running everything, like it even less. That's why, once we set this in motion, we never speak a word of it again. We keep it a secret, between you and me." His eyes shot bright with a thought. "Let me see your phone."

I handed it to him.

He pulled out a safety pin and popped the SIM card, which he snapped in half. Then he dropped the phone in my pint of beer, killing it.

I fished it out, irritated. "Why'd you ruin it?"

"I'll get you another beer," he said.

"I meant the phone."

Digging in his pocket, he pulled out a new one and handed it me.

"I like my old one better."

"From now on," he said, ignoring my comment, "no calls, no texts to the old numbers. I'll get in touch when we need to get in touch," he said, working down his whiskey. "What should my handle be?"

"Your handle?"

"My name."

"What's wrong with Higgles?"

He laughed. "Higgles," he said. "Love it. Perfect. Call me Higgles! Now what about you?"

He was fucking with me now, I could tell. Working through Ray-Ray, he'd okayed my Kam Man recruitment at the homeless shelter, gotten me the Tomas Cartwright passport, and sent me around the world on jobs. He's just now getting around to asking my name? "Call me Ray-Ray," I said.

"Fantastic." He clapped his hands. "Ray-Ray," he said, pointing to me. "Higgles." He touched his chest. "Great. Now let's talk details of the deal." He pulled out a notecard, read off the points of the gambit. West Africa. I'd meet a man. He'd give me some documents and cash. I'd fly back to the States and wait for further instructions. Higgles leaned back in his chair, placed his hands on his belly. "Simple, yes?"

It sounded vague, dangerous, anything but simple.

"Of course," he said, "if the whole thing turns Confederate, heads south, then it goes without saying that—" He broke off, not saying. "You in?"

Broadly stroked and extremely rough, the plan relied on facts and factors far outside my soundings. It was like packing for an Arctic trip without ever having seen snow.

"I'm in."

Higgles sealed the deal with a clank of glass. Whiskey and beer were followed by whiskey and beer.

"Tell me something about yourself," he said.

I hesitated.

"Come on," he said.

"You tell me something first."

He tilted his head back, scratched his chest. "Well, like what?"

"What'd you do before doing this?"

"Before Brighton?"

"Before before," I said. "CliffsNotes your life for me."

"Well, I was born, did the military like everyone else in my town, got married, got divorced, worked in the shipping department for FedEx, then got on with AT&T. Now I'm here."

"What were you doing at AT&T, customer service?"

"Systems analysis," he said. "I was the best they had. Could get into anywhere, get into any system, figure out any problem, and fix it."

"Why'd you leave?"

"Ah, well...we had a disagreement over my job responsibilities. Semantics, really. What I called digital exploration and investigation, they called hacking. So did the FBI." He shrugged.

"So what's your connection to the homeless shelter? And how'd you get those packages out of the library so smoothly? I never saw you once."

A shadow of confusion crossed his face. "The shelter? The library?" He sat up in his chair, cleared his throat. "Trade secrets," he said. "Now's time you tell me something about yourself, *Ray-Ray.*"

I said my birthday was the next day. It wasn't.

"A birthday boy!" He ordered yet another round and lifted his glass to toast. "Here's to making money the old-fashioned way," he said, his voice warm. "Stealing it."

The night hazed on, shifting to black.

I woke on a sticky bathroom floor with a blazing hangover.

In the other room, Higgles snored like a derailing train amid a litter of Wimpy Burger wrappers and uncapped pens.

I vomited, showered, then vomited again. Dressed, I prodded Higgles, trying to wake him. No response, not even a shift in his chugging snores. Taking one of the markers, I scribbled a note on a hamburger wrapper: *Clover.*

It was afternoon. I had a few hours until the train clattered me north to London. From London, it was onward to home where I'd set the scheme in motion.

The Brighton day seeped gray, like a wound that wouldn't stop bleeding. I felt like shit. I must have looked even worse. People commented. The fish-and-chips counterman laughed when he saw me, saying something in a phlegm-coated accent so thick that I didn't understand a word.

Dropping down on the bench at the end of the pier, I sucked the salt off french fries, and hit a huge bottle of water. The waves sprayed over the pilings. Seagulls screeched above me, wheeling in the air.

An old woman with a face like a cable-knit sweater hobbled past smoking a pipe. It was a beautiful pipe, the bowl carved from a bone of some kind, crafted into the head of a man with a pointy beard. Maybe a sultan with many wives, even more camels. The smoke was sweet and spicy, like melting pumpkin butter, overwhelming. I coughed up a mouthful of bile into the fry bag.

She paused. "Just have a birthday?"

"No," I said. "Why?"

She pointed the stem of her pipe at me. "From the look of your face," she said, and sat down next to me. Stoking the pipe strong, she kicked out mouthfuls of smoke.

I got up, my stomach churning. She grabbed my arm, gripped it tight. "Sit."

"The smoke—it's too much."

She tapped her pipe out, the tobacco sifting away in the breeze. "Sit."

I sat, sweating out toxins, and waited for her to start in on the state of England, how it had lost its way in the world. I waited for her to say something cryptic like, "The turtles follow only the purest moonlight."

She didn't. She didn't say a thing, just took a small notepad and a pencil from her purse. She drew two lines, the top line slightly longer, then held the pad up to me. "Which one is longer?"

"The top."

She nodded, her cold pipe hinged tight in her jaw. Turning to a fresh page, she drew two new lines, one with an arrow on each end and one with an arrow only on one end, a hard stop on the other. She held out the pad. "Which one is longer?"

The top line shot off toward infinity in both directions, but the bottom line stretched only one way. Half of infinity. "The top line."

The old woman packed her pipe with fresh tobacco. "What you believe you want," she said, "isn't what you truly want." She stood, lit a match, and tendered the tobacco. The pipe bowl flamed, the smoke swirling thickly. She hobbled off in a cloud, saying, "Clean up. Go home."

The Brighton train station. The odor of industrial grease mixed with fresh-baked rolls. The PA muttered an announcement for trains soon departing. Heels clattered on the hard floor, racing from one track to another.

Seeing me, the ticket girl broke open in laughter.

My hangover flared. "What is so fucking funny?"

The girl bit off her glee, seeing I wasn't in the mood. "Sorry," she said. A zit beaconed on her forehead like a third eye. "Just having fun, it being your birthday and all."

"It's not my birthday."

She made a noise of embarrassment. "Really?"

I said nothing, gazed at her toxically.

She pulled a compact from her purse and held it up to me.

I eyed the small, oval mirror. Across my cheeks, my forehead, my nose, was written *Birthday Boy* in black marker.

CHAPTER 27

ABIDJAN IS IN CÔTE d'Ivoire, Africa. I found this out after Higgles texted me to fly there for the job.

After two days waiting for instructions, Higgles finally contacted me. Things had fouled, he texted. My contact died in route, had a heart attack on the plane as it crossed the Atlantic. He was found with three different passports and over $17,000 cash, a chunk that was to be mine. *Hold tight*, Higgles wrote. *I know a guy. Might be able to salvage the job.*

I texted him that I still expected to get paid. "And some plus-plus."

Côte d'Ivoire, a country of coup-spoiled dreams. The heat was incredible.

My hotel room looked like a large shower, the entire place tiled in glossy brown. The AC barked out foul, tepid air that tasted of bus exhaust, so I spent my days sitting in the shade out front of the Paris Amerika, a makeshift café decorated with *Beverly Hills 90210* posters. Brenda, Brandon, Kelly, and Dylan. All had a film of grit covering their faces. I stuck with Lipton tea.

Abidjan had nice areas. This wasn't one. Trash and rubbish piled up on the road out front of the café. As I sweated out my essential salts and waited for instructions, men roamed past with chained hyenas and rifles. Gang protection. The women hauled loads on their heads that would buckle me.

Foreign money is like Monopoly money, its value mysterious and shifting. My first day at the Paris Amerika, I over-tipped, kicked out twenty thousand CFA francs—around forty American dollars—for my cup of tea. I became the proprietor's new best friend.

Across the road was a line of shantytown stalls filled with items hoping for a second life. Africans may not have invented recycling, but they've mastered it. Besides a few stands of withered fruit and a kid who mended shoes using dental floss, all the other tables were stacked with items begging for another go at it. Cracked porcelain mugs, a handleless pot, skirts Frankensteined together, and totes made from the blue tents the UN provides refugees—all carcasses of items long stripped of purpose.

Wedged in the middle of the mess was an herbalist selling homebrewed cure-all remedies. Shielded from the sun by a tattered tarp, the woman sat at a table crowded with corked glass Coke bottles filled with an amber-green liquid. A crudely painted sheet of canvas advertised ABEGONE'S MIROCLE'S ELIXIR with vibrant images of a man breaking a chain tethering him to the liquor bottle and what appeared to be a woman burning a penis.

On my fourth day at the Paris Amerika café, the woman ambled heavily across the sweltering road toward me, a bottle of elixir in her hand. Her face was a fire-scorched log: charred, glossy, and crackled. She spoke in French. I replied with my Berlitz.

"You are American?"

I hedged—Canadian. No one ever said bad things about Canadians.

She held out the Coke bottles. "You are interested." It wasn't a question.

"What is it?" It looked like urine mixed with lime Jell-O.

"It is Abegone's Mirocle," she said. "It kills vices. And helps the digestion process. Your skin, too. And vision."

"What doesn't it do?"

She shrugged.

"So it kills vices?" I asked.

She nodded.

"Any particular vice it's good at killing?"

"It kills them all." She settled into the chair next to me.

The proprietor clapped his hands at her like he was scaring off a bird and upbraided her in French.

She snapped her fingers at him, gave him an evil look, and shooed him off. The man backed away, frightened. The woman had power, and not just physical.

Holding out the bottle, she said to me, "If you are a man who likes alcohol, you will no longer like alcohol. If you are a man who steals, you will not steal. If you are a man who cheats on his woman, you will not cheat." She rolled the bottle about in her hands, her dark eyes on me. "One bottle will kill the vice. It attaches to the seed that powers the bad and burns it out of your body. Destroys the"—she groped for the word—"*impetus* of the act."

The impetus of the act.

I took the bottle and uncorked it. It smelled of grass clippings and gasoline, like an overheated lawn mower. Still, I peeled off francs and laid them in her palm. It was the easiest way to get rid of her.

Encouraged, she urged me to buy more; five, ten bottles. "I give you a discount."

I didn't see myself handing out Abegone's Mirocle's as gifts. "Why would I need more than one bottle?"

"One bottle cures one vice. And I can tell," she said, laying her hand on mine, "that you're a man of many vices."

CHAPTER 28

After I spent eleven days slathered in an African sweat, Higgles texted to say the Abidjan gig was scrubbed. "The beavers have found the biscuit," he wrote.

I had no idea what he meant. All I knew was that I was pissed. I hadn't traveled half the world for a stench that wouldn't wash off and a stomach virus that had me vomiting and shitting every twenty minutes. But that's what I got.

That, and a bottle of Abegone's Mirocle's vice-killing, all-purpose elixir.

After showering for the sixth time that day, I pulled the scratchy blanket off the bed, folded it, and sat on it in my underwear. The once cream-colored linoleum was worn to a scuffed pewter gray. Fluorescent bulbs buzzed and ticked overhead, kicking out their thin blue light. I couldn't sleep, and the thought of food made my stomach wince. It wasn't yet 10:00 p.m. I had some eight hours before my flight out. Cairo, then London, then the States. Home, or at least the place I kept my clothes.

I said my real name aloud, then said it again, over and over. I hadn't heard it spoken in so long, it sounded strange to me. Foreign. I couldn't remember the last time someone had used my name.

My mother only called me by my full name when she wanted to share a secret she didn't want my father knowing, like the fact that she regretted taking his last name in marriage. "When I hear my name, it makes me think of a funeral home," she once told me. There was no lyricism in saying it, no lilt or joy. "It's a terrible last name, not one I would wish on anyone."

I pointed out that it was my last name.

Ignoring me, she said, "I should have held on to my maiden name." Her eyes gathered tears. "There are a lot of things I should have held on to."

"Like what?"

She wouldn't say. Taking my hand in hers, she said, "Whatever you do, promise me you won't make the mistakes I made."

What were her mistakes? What had she done wrong?

She shook her head. "Just promise me."

I promised. It was a blind, pointless promise. Did she really expect me keep it?

Time and distance rarely brought clarity. If anything, things grew more muddled. But with her death, I think I understood what mistakes my mother was referring to. They weren't mistakes of action, things she'd done, then come to regret. Her mistakes were mistakes of definition. Husband, wife, family, happiness, commitment. The dictionary my mother referenced was vastly different from that of my father's. She had thought she knew what he meant when he said he loved her, only to discover too late that the words they used held unique meanings for each of them. They spoke the same language but couldn't understand each other.

There in Africa, sweating and sick, my body was speaking a language I didn't understand. I sat cross-legged on the floor, shook a cigarette out of the pack, and lit it. I don't smoke, but it tamped down the taste of bile I kept choking up.

Aspirin, whiskey, tea. I'd tried everything to settle my stomach. Nothing seemed to work.

I picked up the bottle of Abegone's Mirocle's elixir. If it killed vices, maybe it killed viruses, too. Certainly smelled like it would.

I poured a Styrofoam cup full, then hit the toilet, my bowels once again revolting.

Ten minutes later, after I showered yet again, I found that the elixir had eaten through the cup, spilling over the table and onto the floor. The table's finish had turned milk-white, and the splatter on the floor had bleached the tile.

I stayed clear of the elixir, kept both my virus and my vices.

They killed less quickly.

CHAPTER 29

MY FATHER HAD A special trash can in the garage for garbage he couldn't admit was ours. Things he felt tarnished the family name, like frozen-pizza boxes, period pads, used Q-tips, empty tubes of hemorrhoid cream. He had a master list of things he didn't want the trash collectors to see. "Those garbage guys go through everything," he said. "They're urban archeologists. And what they find says a lot about us, the type of people we are."

"They're garbage men," my mother said, making a face. "They're idiots. They have a high school education at best."

Wrong, he said. "Where do you think the term 'trash talk' came from?"

So, this unworthy trash of ours had its own bag. And every Tuesday and Friday night, under the cover of darkness, my father would sneak down the street to dump the incriminating bag beside the Marksons' or Peabodys' or Sterns' trash.

As for his liquor bottles, he had an entirely different system. I never did see an empty bottle in the trash.

The night before my high school graduation, after his midnight trash run in a downpour of rain, my father woke me, his breath ragged and sour with drink like he'd just run the length of the county, stopping at every bar along the way. Soaked, he sat heavily on my bed, causing my sheets to snug me tight, trapping me like a straitjacket. Silhouetted in the darkness of the room, he loomed over me, threateningly. I lay still, my throat clamped shut with fear. Bending toward me, he said he had something important to tell me, something I had to know. "And don't tell your mother I told you," he said, the weight of his wet body heavy on me.

I worried he was going to say something terrifying, that he'd just hacked up the neighbor's dog and needed help burying it, or that he'd cheated on my mother with my gym teacher—something I didn't want to know. Something that would shift our relationship, turn it even more awkward, more stilted. Parents are parents, not friends. Not equals or companions. And definitely not confidants.

He said my name twice, then told me his secret.

Babe Ruth, he said, never pointed out where he was going to knock a homer. He was holding up two fingers, indicting the strikes against him.

The storm lasted through the night and all the next morning. By late day the rain had stopped, leaving the road glistening. Saturday collapsed into evening.

My parents were arguing over the best route to the restaurant, who would drive, the time of the reservation, whether the place took American Express.

I'd just graduated from high school and—as the card my mother gave me read—I'd "exited one stage of life and entered a new one." My aunts, uncles, and cousins were coming to the house the next day for a party. But tonight my parents wanted to take me out for a celebratory dinner.

My mother said, "I'm driving and that's final."

My father snatched the keys out of her hand and actually growled.

"Well then," she said, like she had any say in the matter, "you can drive. As long as you promise me you won't order the fried chicken for dinner. You know how you get after eating their fried chicken."

He violently jangled the keys as he unlocked the car door. "Please, tell me," he said, his voice flaring with irritation, "how do I get with chicken?"

We climbed in the car, me in the back.

"Crabby. Or crabbier." My mother turned the rearview mirror to study her makeup. "What's your problem tonight?"

"I have no problem." He readjusted the mirror, then started the car.

The problem was that he was sober. And my father was a terrible dry drunk.

I was the reason he was sober.

That morning, my best friend Clement had come by on his new bike, a used red Kawasaki Nighthawk. Five hundred ccs. His graduation gift. We'd grown up riding dirt bikes, the puttering 125ccs that kicked out a trail of black smoke and a whiney howl. Now Clement had moved into the big leagues, or a bigger league.

I was envious. We always competed, tried to one-up each other. He'd beaten me with the bike, but I'd won out on plans after high school: I was going to college while he was staying in Windstop. School wasn't Clement's thing. He'd struggled through English, cheated his way through math, and spent more time in the principal's office than science class. None of it mattered to him. He'd always claimed to want to leave Windstop, but it was always his plan—or at least his parents' plan—that after he got out of high school, he'd take over the day-to-day operations of the family business, the town's one hardware store.

In a way, Clement had it made. Everything was laid out for him, the burden of choice eliminated. His purpose defined for him. I could easily see him getting married in a year or two, probably to Marianne Clark, the girl he'd been dating since his junior year. It wouldn't surprise me if he had two or three kids by the age of twenty-two. Clement would happily live out his life in Windstop.

My own plans were more directional than defined. I was going to college, had been accepted to University of Iowa for the Fall term. Beyond that, I didn't know, though. That didn't stop people from constantly asking. When I tried to think beyond the high school graduation parties I was going to that night and the lazy summer ahead, I couldn't see much. The years ahead were vague shapes against the present, like trees at dusk, darks against the fading light of the sky.

Clement had let me take his new bike for a spin. I tore around the neighborhood, then hit a county road and opened the throttle. The wind crashed about my face. It was a terrifying, freeing feeling, the tires spinning smoothly as asphalt blurred beneath me. I felt I could ride forever.

Clement grinned when I rolled back up my driveway. "Pretty sweet, yeah?"

"Yeah, very." I slid off, my legs a little stiff.

Clement sidled up next to me. "Hey, man," he said, "my hook-up fell through. Think you can get some liquor off your dad? For tonight?"

I thought a moment. Why not? I'd snuck drinks before, watering down the bottle to cover my tracks. All the other dads drank beer or cheap whiskey, but vodka was my father's drink. He thought that no one could smell the fumes on his breath. I pilfered a liter from his stockpile in the garage, shifted the bottles around to hide the theft.

After lunch, my father asked if there was something I wanted to tell him. He'd been in the garage, had instantly noticed the missing bottle. "Maybe something you accidentally took without thinking," he said. An offer of amnesty.

I mulled it over—or acted like I was—then said, yes, I had taken something of his. A pair of his socks. "I was out of clean ones. Sorry."

He was thrown. "Anything else?"

I shook my head. "What are you missing?"

His face folded with confusion. Had he drunk that liter already? Had he become so secretive with his habit that—somehow—he'd hidden his drinking even from himself? The idea seemed to rattle him, which I guess is why he decided sobriety would be the song of the day.

We all regretted his commitment. With no fuel of drink, he lost his calmness, grew cagey, sharp, and grouchy. He snapped at me and my mother, got irritated by the tiniest things.

At the restaurant, my father didn't like the table we were seated at. He asked that we be moved. The second table was no better. We moved again. Instead of the fried chicken he wanted, he ordered steak, medium rare. He sent it back because it was too rare—then sent it back again because it overcooked.

My scalp prickled hot with embarrassment. Clement was probably getting primed for the parties while I was stuck watching my mother slowly cut, then chew each bite of her meal, resting between each forkful like she'd just climbed a flight of stairs. They ordered dessert.

Finally, the table was cleared and the check came. I stood. "Sit down," my father said. "I want to tell you something."

Speaking in a grumble, like he begrudged the fact he had to speak at all, my dad told me how proud both he and my mother were of me. Finished, he reached into his inside jacket pocket, pulled out an envelope. "Here," he said, handing it to me. It was five hundred dollars, a graduation gift.

Anxious to get home and to the parties, I offered to drive.

"Not on your life," my father said.

Again, my mother tried for the keys. No luck.

Rolling out of the parking lot, my mother lit into my father for driving right past the restaurant's hand-painted stop sign. "It's not a real stop sign," my father said. "It's an elementary school art project."

"A stop sign is a stop sign, hand-painted or not. It's a law."

And so the volley began, my mother firing one barbed remark after another, each answered with a growl or grunt of dismissal. They went at each other the entire ride home.

Or nearly the entire ride.

We never made it home.

CHAPTER 30

AFTER THE FAILED AFRICA job, I made a three-day layover in New York City. Sightseeing, relaxation, and a trip to check out Columbia University was the plan. College seemed more appealing with each passing day. Maybe I could swing a few classes, Kam Manning on the side to cover tuition.

My long weekend turned into a seven-month stay. And in all that time, I never once set foot on campus.

Sarah was the reason.

When I met Sarah at a loft party in Brooklyn, I asked if she spelled her name with an "h" or not.

"Actually, I spell it with two *h*'s, both silent," she said.

"Really?"

She smiled, bit the meat of her thumb, then laughed. "No."

We made out on the fire escape, while across the East River the buildings of lower Manhattan lit up the night sky. I walked her across the Brooklyn Bridge and back to her apartment, as dawn stabbed the city.

Morning. Then the following morning. The entire weekend we tore the sheeting from the bed, leaving each other sore.

I missed my flight, rescheduled, and missed that one too. "You don't have to leave," she said, getting ready for work Monday morning. "You can stay." She shrugged while pulling on her leg warmers. "For a while, at least."

I was staying at a crusty hotel in Chinatown and had no desire to return. I had nothing calling me back to Seattle, either. Higgles, the Kam Manning, everything was done by text. I had no home, lived in a shitty apartment, no real roots. With its rush of activity and chattering crowds, New York seemed the perfect place to be a stranger. It seemed the perfect place to explore. And the convenience of having a girlfriend with a place was appealing. But convenience always comes with a cost. Living with someone isn't something to take lightly. It was more than just sharing a sock drawer.

What I liked about Sarah, what made her *her*, was that she had grown tired of: fun but flaky friends, a sublet on Rivington Street, her job at an art gallery on the Lower East Side. She was bohemian, a pioneer, albeit one spending most of her salary on rent. "I mean, just look at this place," she'd complain. The five-flight walk-up one bedroom at the back of building never got sunlight. The linoleum flooring curled in the corners and the bathtub emptied sluggishly, taking the afternoon to drain a five-minute morning shower. The oven was barnacle-encrusted with memories of old meals boiled over. And the centerpiece of the small space, Sarah's gray-sheeted bed, rested against a soot-darkened window.

Still, I liked it. It was welcoming, cozy, a home. More of a home than I'd had, anyway.

Lying in each other's arms in the morning, she'd spin stories of her pet peeves. "Even the term 'pet peeve' is a pet peeve of mine." So were toe rings, white pantyhose, chunks of apple in white wine, men who spoke with authority on topics they didn't understand, women who carried their lunch to work in a Victoria's Secret bag ("What's that supposed to say, 'I'm wearing sexy panties while eating my sandwich'?"), and Yorkies that scooted along the dirty sidewalks, rat-brown and yapping sharply. "They're the dog of my nightmares."

I told her I hated people who left teabags in the sink. "Is it really so hard to just throw it away?"

She smiled. "You know, I came here thinking New York City was like—I don't know—a Frank O'Hara poem, I guess. I really thought it'd be the place I'd find myself, that I'd have all this opportunity for excitement and that I'd become this stunning, incredible person. But instead I've become something else." She paused, looking lost. "I think I've become my mother."

Sarah had swept into the city with a liberal arts degree from an overpriced Midwestern college and a hungry ambition. She wanted to be the opposite of everything she'd grown up with. She wanted to be famous, unique, and sought after. But she ended up crowded in a two-bedroom apartment share in Williamsburg with four other Midwesterners who had come to New York wanting the same things. These strangers were identical to her old friends back home—want-to-be artists who made forgettable music, wrote mediocre short stories, painted amateurish paintings.

The only difference was that they were in New York and they were determined to have the time of their lives. After a year, Sarah realized no one was noticing her genius. The city didn't even notice she was there. Worse, she had a disturbing feeling that her uniqueness was the same as everyone else's.

Things soured. She no longer liked her friends, especially the one who stole toilet paper from cafés to save money for three-hundred-dollar skirts at the Barney's Warehouse sale. She no longer liked the constant buzzing activity and was discovering that everything she discovered had been discovered before. Her apartment share had too many roommates moving in or out, too many one-night-stands rolling through, too many hangovers, too many STDs, and too many bedbug scares. So she moved, got a place of her own that she could barely afford. "I wanted less of the bad and more of the better." But being on her own turned out to be no better.

She was living the life I'd wanted, full of light and sound, but she'd grown tired of it. She talked of leaving the Lower East Side in a year and heading some place quieter, like New Jersey. She wanted more room, more air, more everything.

I wanted more of what we had right now—the hustle of the city, the nightlife, the staying out until dawn. Our conflicting wants made it difficult to build anything on what we had. We unsuccessfully tried to shape each other into the people we desired. It was only after months together, months of being content but not really happy, that I came to realize that we shared little more than a bed. The idea of leaving her, leaving New York, cast a shadow through my thoughts, but I didn't take action, didn't initiate my next move. Why I didn't leave sooner, I can't really say. I was like a frog in the pot of heating water, comfortable enough to be oblivious to fact that the boiling point was approaching.

My parents had been that way, forcing a fate that shouldn't have been forced. They weren't meant to be together, but they got together, stayed together, and made compromises that undermined their happiness.

I didn't want to follow that same path with Sarah. Yes, I was planning on quitting the Kam Manning, maybe to go back to school or to find a nine-to-five job and settle down to a domestic life. Just not yet.

CHAPTER 31

Haven, Florida

THE CAR SERVICE PULLS up to the curb in front of the small two-story building where I live. I pay and climb out into the heat, alone. Any fantasies about spending time with the mysterious woman have evaporated in the hot morning air. She's gone. It's probably for the best.

My apartment is upstairs, the entire second floor. On the street level is Silk Cigars, a storefront with a few battered mix-and-match chairs and a display case humidor full of cigars. A shaved-headed Cuban rolls cigars in the window from 7:00 a.m. to 7:00 p.m., crafting perfect ones each time.

I've read it takes ten thousand hours to perfect the art. I'm sure that's true of pretty much everything. It's certainly true for lying, something I've yet to master.

When I was in the shelter, Ray-Ray told me a story about a sheriff he dated. He was the best liar Ray-Ray had ever known. Consummate. Flawless. They'd been lovers, he and Ray-Ray, even though both men were married at the time. Whenever they'd meet, at a fishing cabin or a duck blind, they'd plan their future together, talk of running off to Puerto Rico, buying a shack on a deserted beach. But after they'd had their violent go at it, reality would set in. A life together would never work. Buckling his pants, the sheriff would threaten to cuff Ray-Ray, arrest him for sodomy. "That was his sense of humor," Ray-Ray said.

"Anyway, anything he said sounded true. He had a believability to him. When he spoke, you wanted to trust him, even though it was a lie."

"Whatever happened to him?"

Ray-Ray smiled. "He's a state senator now."

Heading to my building's door, I nod to the old Cuban sitting inside. He lifts his chin toward me, a cigar smoldering in the corner of this mouth.

I've been here, in Florida, in this town, this apartment, less than three weeks, yet the pungent stench seeping through my flooring has already stolen five years of my life. My walls are the color of old horse teeth from the smoke.

Until moving here, I never understood the appeal of cigars. I hated the smell, I hate it more now than I ever have. But now I see what the smoke really carries. Downstairs, it's like an old-school men's club, a respite from work, wives, and the worries of regular life. The place is a cross section of society. The town mingles. When I pass, I see men in Rolexes bullshitting and bonding with guys in janitor's scrubs.

A few days ago, feeling hollow from loneliness, I clambered down my steps and went into the shop. I bought a five-inch fifty-ring-gauge Robusto, Dominican filler, Nicaraguan wrapper. I got a V cut, lit it with wood matches, and settled down in a chair with the stuffing coming out. The place was full of men and smoke. The conversation was about diets. It was about stock tips. And about sports, colognes, vacations, cheeses, and auto insurance. It was about everything but women.

I sat for nearly an hour, offering the occasional comment on a football team or politician to the conversation while drawing down my stick of tobacco, taking in everything that was said. I envied the men who hang out there. They have a closeness with each other, friendship. Smoking isn't about a need for nicotine, it's an excuse to bond, to be part of something.

Warm with feelings, I was determined to become one of the members, to meet with the gang every day for a laugh and a smoke. I saw myself heading to their homes for weekend barbecues, going out for drinks, maybe even giving golf a try with my new brothers. I would become part of something larger than myself, a member of a group. But then a rush of lightheadedness and nausea from the smoke hit me and I barely made it outside to the gutter before vomiting. I felt sick for the rest of the day.

I open the building's door and slide into the dimness of the stairwell, my eyes fighting to adjust. A single flight of steps drives straight to my place. Thirty-three total.

Lifting my gaze toward my apartment, my heart vaporizes. Someone is there, sitting on the top stair. Waiting. My legs seize, refuse to function. *Shit*, I think. *Ray-Ray? Higgles?* It's too early for either. Twelve noon is when they're coming, but then again it'd be just like one of those fuckers to show up three hours early. Then I think, *Pockmark. He's here to kill me.*

A voice drifts down, strong but smooth. "Sorry about bolting. I needed to walk a bit." The woman. Somehow, she's beat me to my own place. "Plus, I didn't have money to help pay for the car."

"How'd you know where I lived?" I ask, knowing the answer before I've finished the question. The car service. I told the driver my address. *How did you get here so fast?* is the question I should ask.

She stands, runs her fingers through her hair. "You're expecting to see me naked, aren't you?"

Honesty isn't always a bad policy. I move up the stairs. "I am."

"You're expecting we'll have sex."

"It's crossed my mind." I reach the top, study her.

Her eyes graph a life of disappointment. She starts to speak but closes her mouth. Her face says it all.

"Let's just call it a morning," I say, oddly relieved.

I offer to call her a car service to take her back to the bar.

Her voice is soft, gentle. "Will you come, too?"

"No."

Standing pigeon-toed, she looks at her hands as if they hold all the answers, then up at me. "Then let's blunder on," she says. Her lips find mine.

We fall into a tangle of mouths and tongues, sucking what little oxygen is left out of each other's lungs.

Pulling free, she says, "Unlock the door."

Like every place I've lived since I left Iowa, my life here is stripped. Pure function and absolute basics. My place could never be mistaken for a home. It's depressing. No TV, no pictures framed, no knickknacks of my travels. A broken window AC. There's little comfort. It's a crash pad at best: scarred hardwood floors, a mattress on the floor, a Formica-topped table, a weathered red recliner, a straight-backed chair, and my library stacked in the corner. Higgles' books. My amulets. I know each by heart, the titles, the characters, the settings. They remind me of my travels, of all the schemes, of the successes and failures that have built the horror I'm now facing.

Every bit of the past two-plus years is burnt into my brainpan. All the cities, the flights, the street names, the dates, the weather on those dates, the faces and voices of each contact I met, I remember. I even remember the account numbers. I remember everything that has happened to me.

The facts, though, have somehow disassociated themselves with the truth. The details have fragmented, jumbled themselves up. Images of New Jersey come to mind when I think about the raid, but it was in Indiana that that happened. I keep thinking that I got the scar on my head in San Francisco, but it was in Seoul that I took a beatdown. Even with Sarah I've grown confused. I've thought of her so often that I'm no longer certain which conversations we actually had and which ones are only in my head.

The woman strides in, sniffs at the heavy air. The place is Florida hot, incessantly molding. She sizes up my digs. "Spartan," she says, idly fingering my copy of *The Memphis Sky Above*. "Seems like you live on very little."

I offer her a drink.

She kicks off her heels, revealing dirty feet, then collapses on the tatty red recliner.

"Just a glass of ice water," she says. "Unless you've got gin."

I do have gin, a new bottle of Randerskin Diamond. A gin made for the royal family of Nepal.

Breaking the cap's seal, I pour her a double and crack out some stale cubes from the tray. The cubes dink dully together as I hand her the glass.

She takes a swallow, makes a sound of satisfaction. "It's been a long time since I last had this," she says, holding her drink up to the light.

"You just had three at Charm's."

"I mean this brand," she says. "I haven't had it in over ten years."

"You can tell the brand?"

She holds out the half-empty glass, coy. "I'll need a bit more just to be sure."

In the kitchen I refill the glass, bring it back brimming.

She dips her nose over it, sniffs the sticky scent. Then she runs the tip of her tongue over the surface, testing it like a snake, and lifts the glass to morning light. "You must have money or connections," she says. "Or both."

The comment chills because it's true—though not in the way I would hope for. Both the money and connections are tainted. It's never bothered me before, but then it's never been something I've thought too much about. "Is that so?"

She nods, tilts her glass. "A hint of plum and pine, a good viscosity, the sharp but clean aftertaste. This gin is excellent. And expensive." She sips the drink. "It's Randerskin Diamond."

I'm impressed. "You weren't kidding. You do know your gin."

"And I know how to read." She points to the kitchen. The bottle sits in plain view. "I can see the label from here."

◎ ◎ ◎

WE'RE FIRED FROM AN unknown gun, shot at a target unseen. Life is making the best of a bad trajectory.

CHAPTER 32

"WHOTTA WHOT!" THE MAN lumbering up the driveway gave Robert Tanke a wave.

Tanke waved back and instantly wished he hadn't. He had no idea who this man was and had no interest in finding out. He hadn't been home in over a week. All Tanke wanted to do was get inside his house, kick off his shoes, spoon out some ice cream, and pour himself a tall whiskey. All he wanted was to be left alone.

"Robert—Bobby—I need a favor," the man said. "If you could—"

"Not interested," Tanke said, cutting him short. He unlocked his front door and opened it. *Who is this guy? How does he know me?*

The man grabbed Tanke firmly by the shoulder. "Invite me in, listen to what I have to say."

"I'll take a pass," Tanke said, shrugging his way free. Ducking into his house, he swung the front door closed.

The man's foot stopped it. "At least let me freshen up a bit," he said. "I'm pretty ripe from staking out your place for five days straight." He motioned to a minivan on the street. "Do you know how hard it is to shit into a Taco Bell bag? Nearly impossible not to make a mess."

"What do you want?" Tanke leaned his body hard to the door.

"Honestly? To fuck with your amigo."

"My amigo?"

Through the door's opening, the man smiled. He'd done his research, found a thread, and followed it here. "Think of it like a game of Jenga. You're a block in an already wobbly tower. It's time the whole thing falls."

"What the fuck are you talking about?"

The man shouldered his way in, knocking Tanke to the floor. "Higgles," he said, standing over Tanke. "I'm talking about your friend Higgles."

CHAPTER 33

New York City

ARAH WAS SHOWERING WHEN I received a text from Higgles that snapped me back to reality. A job in the Dominican Republic, my first since I'd settled with Sarah.

"You know, you're just like that boy," she said, toweling off.

"Which boy?" I lay in bed watching her, my mind churning over the prospect of the new job and how best to break it to Sarah. I didn't want to set any ripples in motion with our relationship. While a marriage proposal was nowhere in sight, I liked what we had going. The idea of having a place I actually *wanted* to return to sent a warm glint of contentment through my body.

"The one from the kid's book. I know you know it. A little boy who runs away from home, gets trapped in a bad place. It's a classic."

"*Where the Wild Things Are?*"

"No," she said, buttoning her blouse, "not that one."

"*Harold and the Purple Crayon?*"

"No, a different one. I *know* you know it." She explained the story as best she could. She didn't remember much. "What I remember was that he was a brat."

I smiled. "So you're saying I'm a brat?"

She picked out a skirt. "Well, yes, but that's not why you're like him. Or not the only reason." She tried to explain. "Something happened to the boy, his mother dies or she's a lesbian or she runs away—I don't remember, but something happens and he does something he shouldn't do."

"What?"

She shook her head.

"You are the worst storyteller in the world," I said. "Go on."

She poked me in the side, then leaned down and ran a finger across my lips before continuing to dress. "Well, he does something he can't change and ends up in this place that wasn't day and wasn't night. It's where night stops being night, you know?"

"I've been there," I said. "It's called the DMV."

She pouted in the mirror. "I'm being serious."

"So am I," I said. "How am I like this boy?"

Lifting her head, she studied the ceiling for the answer. Her face was still sleep-swollen. "Sometimes it seems like you're not really awake."

"Explain."

"Well, you know when you're asleep and dreaming but you're kinda conscious of everything going on around you in the room? You seem like that," she said. She paused in front of the mirror, studied her outfit. "Trapped and you can't get home." She looked at me. "How's this outfit look?"

"Great."

She grabbed her purse and keys.

"Hold up," I said. "I've got something I want to talk to you about."

The words stopped her. "You mean like *talk* talk? You're not planning on breaking up with me just as I head out for work, are you?"

"What? No."

"You have an STD?"

"God, no," I said. "I just need to leave town for a few days, that's all."

She kissed me goodbye. "Tell me tonight when you buy me dinner. I heard about a new place in Harlem I want to try."

That evening, I met her at the gallery and we took a cab up to Strivers Row.

Princess Big Thighs was a twelve-table restaurant with burlap tablecloths, a cigarette-scarred piano, tin ceilings painted orange, and sixty-watt lighting tucked away in a brownstone. No telephone number, no sign. You'd ring apartment A2 and tell whoever answered that you wished an audience with her highness. After being buzzed in, you'd walk through the parlor of the ground-floor apartment, pass an old man watching a Mexican dance show and eating marshmallows, and through a kitchen that smelled of burnt popcorn and out the back door into the yard. Crossing the small scrub of lawn, littered with broken chairs and coffee cans filled with cigarettes, you'd find yourself at the basement door of the abutting brownstone. Knock twice, pause, knock once, pause, then knock twice again.

The door would open to reveal a thick-set woman, heavily bejeweled. Princess Big Thighs. "Uh-huh?" she'd ask.

You'd tell her you'd like to have some dinner. She'd gaze over you, then, if she felt you were worthy, shoo you in.

Sarah and I were shooed in and pointed toward the last open table. We were the only whites in the place. Princess Big Thighs came around with water.

I asked for menus. "Menus?" she said. "No menus, sweetmeat. You sit. You eat. You pay. It's that simple."

Princess went to the piano and banged out a song she'd made up on the spot. "Scrawny white girls ain't nothing but lies," she sang, her voice like that of a bus engine starting.

Fried ham, squash, walnut bread, and gravy. "Red or white wine?" Princess asked. We ordered a bottle of red, which ended up being excellent. Sarah held the bottle up to the light, read the label aloud. "Remember the name. And that it's vintage," she said, then went on about the importance of wine being vintage. She wouldn't stop talking about it.

There was a red-eye to Santo Domingo. I had my Tomas Cartright passport and cash on me and planned to fly out in a handful of hours. I planned on coming back, though I hadn't figured out how to break the news of my Kam Manning to Sarah. I didn't know if it'd mix well with a steady relationship. But as the meal went on, I found myself pouring forth, telling her my life story, things I'd never told her before.

Things I'd never told anyone before. Growing up in Iowa, the death of my parents and Clement, even my time in the shelter, but not about Ray-Ray or Higgles. I stopped short of telling her about either of them or my Kam Manning.

Sarah sat back in her chair, her face expressionless but her eyes heavy with tears. Then she leaned across the table and kissed me and cried while Princess Big Thighs sang.

For the first time in a long time, I felt cared for. Safe.

Even loved.

Pulling back, Sarah shook her head. "This is all…we need to slow this down."

"Slow down?"

She nodded.

"You mean—"

"Yeah. We need to take a break."

"From each other?" A fit of laughter and crippling nausea battled their way up my stomach, fighting to be the first out. "I don't understand. What just happened?"

"It's just that, I don't know. Your unloading on me makes me realize that we're…" She didn't finish.

After five minutes of awkward silence, punctuated by even more awkward talk, I got up to leave. "I just need some time to think," she said, and ordered another bottle of wine for herself. "The red vintage," she told Princess Big Thigh.

On Malcolm X Boulevard I hailed a cab and told the driver to take me to JFK. Rattled, confused, and panicked, my brain couldn't fire a clear thought. It was the same way I felt after my parents' death.

Crossing the Triborough Bridge into Queens, my phone rang. It was Sarah, crying. "I've had time to think," she said between sobs. "Come home. I want you home."

My voice sounded before any thought formed. "I'll be back in three days," I said. "I promise I'll be back."

CHAPTER 34

O N THE FLIGHT TO the Dominican Republic, I studied the maps in the back of the in-flight magazine. I'd taken up Ray-Ray's habit of studying atlases, charting my travels, understanding where I'd been. I tried to see if there was a pattern, some logic. I tried to figure out the course I'd taken so I could see what was to come next.

I had to see my future.

But even after four cocktails and two hours of staring at the dots marking the cities of the world, I saw only a map.

I tried to sleep, but my mind refused to shut down. The Sarah situation bothered me, especially how impressed she has been that Princess Big Thighs served vintage wine. She took it to mean that the wine was good, but vintage has nothing to do with the quality of the wine. It simply means that all the grapes used in the wine were grown and harvested in that year.

In the background churned another thought, one that seemed to always be running, consuming energy. Had my father been drunk that night, the car wreck never would have happened. I'm positive they'd still be alive.

When I landed in the Dominican Republic, I found out the job was actually in Haiti. Getting over the border was easy, though the drive was slow and arduous. I found my contact, a Swiss UN aid worker in

Petionville who couldn't keep his eyes off the young boys. "It must hurt very much," the man said, handing me a packet filled with documents.

I took the packet, stuffed it in the waistband in the back of my jeans. "What hurts?"

"Your testicles," he said. "Your boss has a very tight hold on them."

I told him to fuck off and headed out.

Getting back across the border wasn't so easy. Some asshole winged a beer bottle at my rental. It smashed on the driver's side door, the glass sparking through my open window and cutting my cheek. The Dominican border guard labored over my paperwork, saying it could take hours to process me. Sixty bucks sped me through.

When I returned to New York three days later, Sarah and I picked up where we'd left off. She acted like our night at Princess Big Thighs had never happened, that she hadn't backpedaled when I'd opened up to her. All was forgotten. It was like time had been edited, the part she didn't like clipped out and discarded. As for my Kam Manning, she didn't ask where I'd been, wasn't concerned about the cut on my face. She didn't even seem to notice.

My wound healed quickly, but a heaviness hung over me like a lead wool blanket, the kind used at the dentist when you're X-rayed. The question *why?* cropped up more and more. Why Kam Man? Why Sarah? Why wake in the morning? I forced my way through the days like they were paint-by-numbers, everything plotted and prescribed. I made the motions, followed the instructions, and when night arrived, I had created something that loosely resembled living.

I texted Higgles. *Send an address. I'll FedEx.*

I set up a PO Box in Chinatown, gave him the number, and told him to send the payment—plus an extra $600 for expenses.

No reply to my request. It was like I had spooked him. I looked at the documents, which seemed innocuous: a bunch of flowcharts, a note from some guy named Fritz to Liz congratulating her on her promotion, and an old-school floppy disk. The kind that are actually floppy. In my hands, the information was worthless. I had no idea how or where it fit into the big picture. Keys with no locks.

I heard nothing from Higgles for four days. I texted him again. Another day passed with no reply. Finally, he texted an address. It was a residential area in Seattle. *Send it to Robert Tanke*, he wrote.

The name chimed a note in my memory. He was the director of the homeless shelter. The whole game shifted more into focus. Higgles, whoever he was, must have known the director.

Robert P. Tanke, JD. Those who can, do. Those who can't, teach. And those who can't teach, run homeless shelters. Attorneys have a reputation for being sharks, but Tanke had the backbone of a newborn. A stern look would topple him over. I could easily see how Higgles, possibly living or working at the homeless shelter, could use Tanke to his advantage, setting up the Kam Manning headquarters there with little-to-no fear of blowback. It was probably where he met and recruited Ray-Ray. Then Ray-Ray had recruited me. The Amway business model.

A week after I'd overnighted the package, I got my money. Or at least part of it. Higgles had gypped me expenses.

Atlanta was the next Kam Man. I texted Higgles that I wouldn't do it until he paid up full for the DR job. He swore I'd be paid in full once the new job was done.

I wasn't. Nor was I paid in full after Turks and Caicos, Vancouver, or Salt Lake City. Higgles always held back a few hundred dollars, enough to be irritating but not a deal breaker.

I kept sending the packages to Tanke's place, but I played it cautious, changing up the PO Box where my payment was sent, not wanting Higgles to know exactly where I was. Still, a tickle of worry often ran over my skin. Out for walks, I'd find myself stopping in the street and quickly turning to gaze behind me, certain I was being followed. I felt eyes on me, but I never found anyone.

Never once did Sarah question my taking off for a handful of days. She never asked where I went, what I did, how I made money. I should have been thrilled by the lack of scrutiny. I had a free pass, the ideal situation. Strangely, it depressed me. The less interested she seemed in what I did, the more urgent my desire was to tell her. Only, I didn't. Princess Big Thighs was my lesson learned. Opening up to her only made her retreat. So our conversations, our interactions, stayed surface level, never dipping very deep.

Until one hot, late spring afternoon, as we lie in bed listening to the shouts and laughs of children playing in the street, she surprised me by asking, "Do you want kids?"

The room's air swirled thick with the scent of sex and fig-scented candles. The bedsheets lay on the floor in a tangle.

"I hadn't really thought about it. But no, not now."

Sarah wiped the sweat from her face with a pillow, then picked a pubic hair off her tongue. "Not ever, you mean." She lifted a hand to stop me from interrupting.

I wasn't planning to interrupt.

"Which is fine, I guess," she said. "Hey, at least you know. At least you're honest." Sarah stood, her naked body pale, lovely. "Most people aren't even smart enough for that," she said. "They think just because they *can* have kids they should have kids."

"So you don't want kids?"

She leaned her head out the window, eyeing the street, the children, the action. She spoke over her shoulder. "I want them, kinda feel entitled to them. But then what are feelings anyway? Just a mix of chemicals, a stew of stuff."

Pulling herself back in, she turned to me, her eyes hard with a thought. I could see that she'd come to some decision. "I wasn't going to ask," she said, "but what do you think about visiting my parents for the Fourth of July?"

The words *sounds great* formed but got caught in my throat.

Sarah was moving the relationship forward by settling. I could see that. It wasn't so much that she desired to spend the rest of her life with me, but that I was available. My guess is that she'd assessed her life and determined that I, while not ideal, was good enough. First was the visit to the folks, then, when her lease ran out in the fall, a move to Queens or Jersey City. Add to that the talk of kids and it was clear that my status was being upgraded from casual boyfriend to serious boyfriend. Fiancé, then husband, wasn't far behind.

A flush of blood surged to my head. Having a wife, a family, wasn't an idea I feared, but not like this. Not as a consolation prize, something based on convenience. On giving up.

"So what do you think?" She picked up an old *Art in America*, flipped through the pages, playing the whole thing off like it was no big deal.

I swallowed hard before I spoke. "You know, Sarah, it's just that I'm broke."

She closed the magazine, looked at me confused. "What do you mean? I thought you had money?"

"I do have money. I just mean…listen, I don't think I can do this and do it right."

She didn't understand.

I got out of bed, slipped on my underwear. "Why don't we get a coffee or something?"

She laughed, but it was forced. "God, what's wrong with you? You act like I just told you I'm pregnant."

My stomach twisted like a slug being salted. "Are you?"

She shot me with a look of disgust. "You know, just forget it." She kicked my pants toward me. "Buy me a coffee."

At a café brimming with laptops and Ray-Bans' we settled at a sticky table. The waitress delivered a chocolate croissant and two lattes. "I'm sorry," I said, taking Sarah's hand.

She pulled it away. "You should be. I mean, it's not a big deal."

"It's not that I don't want to meet them, it's just that I've been thinking about us, and I think—"

"Ah, shit." She stared at me, stunned. "Really, you're doing this here? Breaking up with me?"

A thorn of ice scraped the edge of my heart. *No*, I thought. By the time I finally got it out, it was too late. Sarah was crying loudly over her croissant. "Why?" she asked again and again. "What'd I do?" The café crowd kept their heads down, focused on their phones or laptops, acted like they were ignoring us.

"Listen, I'm not breaking up with you."

"Then come with me for the Fourth."

I shook my head, feeling gutted and awful. "Let's be healthy and see how things go."

The tears came hard. "Wow. 'Let's be healthy'? What the fuck has our relationship been, unhealthy?" She took my fingers in her hand, wrenched them back hard. It hurt. "I let you move in, become part of my life. I open myself up to you and this is what I get?" she asked. "I gave you the best days of my life."

I didn't know what to say, and so I said the wrong thing. "We've only known each other seven months."

"Seven days, seven months, seven light-years. Whatever," she snapped, standing. "Betrayal is still betrayal, no matter the amount of time."

Light-years, I wanted to tell her, are a measure of distance, not time.

"I didn't expect much," she said, "but I expected more."

The crowd couldn't help but stare as she stormed out, banging against tables on the way.

I sat motionless a moment, feeling the heat of glares on me. Finally, just to do something, I picked up the croissant Sarah hadn't finished and took a bite. I couldn't get it down. *Chase after her*, I told myself. *Say you're sorry, that you'd love to meet her parents.* Instead, I called the airline, booked a flight back to Seattle. Laying down a twenty, I told the waitress to keep the change.

Only after, with my flight airborne, winging westward, did I wonder why I had done what I had done.

Twenty on a fourteen-dollar tab. A forty-three percent tip was far too much for mediocre service.

⊚ ⊚ ⊚

Rule one of breaking up: Do it in a public place.

Rule two: Do it *after* you've paid the bill.

CHAPTER 35

BACK IN SEATTLE, I couldn't settle. Jittery and depressed, everything irritated me: people, places, things. Name a noun and it bothered me.

Sarah flooded my thoughts day and night. Even if being with her wasn't right, it had ended the wrong way. I dialed her a handful of times, hoping to talk, to apologize, maybe even—I don't know—beg to come back. She wouldn't pick up.

May slipped into June. I found myself waiting anxiously for Higgles' next call. I read a lot—newspapers, essays, foreign and fashion magazines—but after a while I found myself wandering out, heading down to the Pike Place Market or to a Capitol Hill coffee shop. I struck up conversations for no reason, introduced myself to people as "Charles but call me Chuck," and found myself talking about real estate, college basketball, and the weather with anyone who'd talk to me. The challenge: be normal. I packed my time with activities, but nothing helped break that persistent foul feeling. Everything I did disgusted and angered me.

It was while I was sitting on a folding chair in the back of the elementary school cafeteria during an emergency PTA session to debate whether Kwanzaa was a real holiday and should be recognized by something special at school—say, cupcakes, or a screening of *The Lion King*—that I realized what was wrong with me.

I was frightened.

Terrified.

But not by the things most people fear. What panicked me were the things that filled the cracks of everyday, the small things that chewed up the minutes—the laundry, the television, the line at the post office, the worthless chitchat while shopping. The things that make normal people normal.

Everyday events pushed me deeper into a funk: replying to the checkout girl's "Hiya," petting an overly friendly dog, waiting in line at the bank. The tally of my existence turned into tiny hash marks. Internally, I raged at the chubby middle-aged woman who bragged about drinking a six-pump no-foam caramel macchiato on her blind date. Outwardly, though, I became taut, controlled. I appeared rigidly calm.

Listening to the people at the PTA meeting hotly debate the definition of a true holiday, I realized that this was it. Life, really, is nothing but taking a stance and fighting over things that, ultimately, mean nothing. I realized I couldn't hide or avoid that fact.

So I determined to move toward it, to embrace the mundane. Embrace what I feared.

I picked a religion and started going to church, a nice, boring Protestant one, even joined their choir and got my own shiny powder-blue satin robe.

Soon I was making a name for myself at potlucks with my Iowa cheddary potato delight.

The cancer hospice center appreciated my stopping in twice a week to read stories to the dying.

I spent time at a group home for retarded men playing board games and watching *American Idol*.

Bridge with a couple from church became a weekly activity.

My days brimmed with healthy, good-person activities.

I'd never been so miserable. Each time the guy at newspaper stand updated me on his car restoration or the woman working at the deli told me a new recipe, my soul sputtered and seized like an airplane engine choked with birds. To these strangers, "Charles but call me Chuck" was a friend, someone they knew and could trust. He provided them with something—purpose, love, meaning, I don't know.

In public, I fought to keep smiling. Alone, I fought not to cry.

CHAPTER 36

SOON AFTER MY EPIPHANY at the PTA meeting, I saw Ray-Ray. The perfect hair, the smooth, upright walk, the confidence of manner—I caught only a glimpse, but I'm positive it was him. I'd just finished participating in a charity Scrabble tournament to raise money for Afghani orphans. Four depressing hours playing a game I didn't like and definitely wasn't good at. Walking through Pioneer Square afterward, I passed by the Lighthouse Shelter for Men, the place Ray-Ray and I met. That's when I saw him. He was heading in. Thursday evening, a few minutes to seven. The sight of him sent a scorching chill through me.

I followed, determined to—what? Say "hi"? Give him a hug? I wasn't sure.

The security guard stopped me just inside the shelter doors. "Whatcha wanting?"

"The guy that just came in," I said, motioning toward the stairs leading to the second floor, the area where men slept. "That was Ray-Ray, right?"

His face creased in puzzlement. "Who?"

"Listen, the guy who just came in, he—" I broke off, thinking. "He dropped some money."

The guard held out his stubby hand. "I'll see he gets what he deserves."

"Yeah, well, I'd feel better if—"

"If you're thinking you're heading up there," he said, "then don't be thinking it. Residents only."

I started to tell him I used to live here then thought better of it. What did it matter? I took a new tact. "I'm a friend of Director Robert Tanke. I was talking to him this morning—"

The guard knocked his fist loudly on the counter as if to ward off bad luck. "What, now you're some sort of ghost whisperer?" His voice was low, worried. "Tanke got killed something like three, four months now."

My stomach wrung tight. That's about the time I sent the Haiti package to his address. "Killed?"

The guard's thick head bobbed once. "Robbers cracked into his house when he was asleep. Didn't rob much, 'cept for his life."

That night, I lay awake, worry scrapping at my heart. Had that really been Ray-Ray I'd seen? Why was he back at the shelter? Who'd killed Tanke? Who'd collected the packages? And what did this all mean to me?

The more I tried to figure it out, the angrier I became.

First thing the next morning, I went out to Tanke's place, determined to find some answers. What I found was a shuttered house, an overgrown lawn with a FOR SALE sign posted in it, and a pile of weathered fliers and junk mail littering the front stoop. The doors were padlocked tight. The place was empty, abandoned by death. No clues that I could see.

I looked for Ray-Ray, but that proved a waste of time, too. For two days straight I hung around outside the shelter, waiting for him to exit or enter. He didn't. Or at least not that I saw. But the whole time I lingered outside the place, I felt certain someone was watching me. Who, I couldn't say. But I could feel a cold stare slicing deep into my spine. The coldness stuck with me for days.

There was no specific reason for my leaving Seattle. The town was like a party after the guest of honor had left. The drinks still flowed, but the welcome was waning. What did it matter if it had been Ray-Ray I'd seen, if he was back in the shelter? Sure, he'd set me up, got me going on the Kam Manning, but our lives had separated, headed in different directions.

I packed up my books, the few articles of clothing I had, and bought a plane ticket to Cincinnati. Home of the Bengals, my favorite football team.

CHAPTER 37

I LOOKED AT PLACES in Cincinnati's Over the Rhine and Clifton areas, but ended up renting a house some thirty miles south in Kentucky, away from everything. I moved in with my one piece of luggage and stack of books. I was hoping for—what? Quiet? To be anonymous, hidden? Safe? I couldn't say.

Built in the 1940s boom years, when the steel factory brought jobs, the small house stood on a scrub of land. There were other houses around, but no neighbors. The jobs had bled off some years back. The people left. The houses stayed.

The kitchen in my place had a refrigerator that never got cold and a stove I didn't trust to light. Water stains colored the ceiling of every room. The entire house smelled like it'd been bombed for fleas. A poured-concrete deck out back was spidered with cracks. It was a house one rented when planning a suicide.

Early one morning, someone came by and raced a mower over the lawn, shearing the grass down to the dirt. I lay in bed listening to the engine whine and the blades of the machine kick stones and dirt against the house's siding.

I'd forgotten about the Midwest summer heat and the lightning storms that jagged the night sky. I'd forgotten how isolating rural areas can be.

I'd not forgotten about the cicadas. *Magicicada*. The North American genus. They blew in, buzzing and whirling thickly through the sweltering air. About an inch long, they had shiny, black shells and hard red eyes. Most people know the regular locust, the kind that come out in the summer. These were different; cicada nymphs spend most of their lives underground feeding on root juice, emerging once every seventeen years.

Their deafening *kkkerrrklick*-ing became the soundtrack for sweltering days.

At night, I'd sit on the patio in a rickety lawn chair, the cicadas careening their way past my head. The tepid breeze, like an aftereffect of their whipping wings, stirred little. I still wrestled with the thought of returning to Sarah. I kept telling myself I'd done the right thing by dumping her.

I'm not a bad person, I told myself, *it's just that my life is bad.*

Often, I fell asleep there, waking to dawn corrupting the sky and the entire deck covered with cicada carcasses, the insects having done what they'd been born to do.

Sweeping them up, I was amazed at how light their bodies were once life had left them.

CHAPTER 38

THE SUMMER BETWEEN MY fourth and fifth grade, my father set up a small aboveground pool in our backyard. Only three-feet deep and ten-feet wide, it still took the entire day to fill with the garden hose.

Nearly every afternoon, Clement would come over and we'd hit the pool with my dog, Mackerel. Panting excitedly, she'd circle around the tiny ring of water like a roulette ball, speeding in one direction then suddenly stopping to poke her snout over the edge and bark wildly.

We splashed her lots.

September rolled in. The weather cooled, and the swimming ended. Fifth grade began.

Draining the pool was a weekend to-do that my father never seemed to get around to doing. The draining would take hours and ruin the lawn, he said. So he bought a vinyl pool cover instead. Slipping the cover over the rim of the pool, he secured it tightly with bungee cords.

"To keep the leaves and muck out," he said to my mother.

"Emptying the pool would keep the leaves and muck out," she said.

"I'll empty it next weekend," he said and never did.

September crept into October. Halloween approached.

Coming home from school one afternoon in early October, I found Mackerel in the backyard. She'd somehow gotten on top of the pool cover without it collapsing and lay there with the head resting on her paws. "Mackerel," I said, "get off."

She barked once and tried to stand, but wobbled about on the slick surface of the cover like a foal first standing.

"Come here!" I worried the material wouldn't hold her, that the pool cover would break and drop her into the water like a teabag. I circled the pool, calling, yelling, demanding, but Mackerel couldn't move beyond the center, doing an odd dance of rising then sitting while barking joyfully. She found it all a game, fun.

Leaning over the pool, I reached for her. No luck. I leaned farther, my waist hard to the edge and my hand on the cover for support.

It was then that bungee cords snapped and the cover gave way, folding into the icy water.

Mackerel and I both yelped. We both went in, hitting the murky wet.

When my mother came home, she found me sitting on the kitchen floor, wet and crying. Mackerel, soaked but happy, wandered the house, leaving muddy paw prints on the carpet.

Instead of soothing words or a comforting hug, my mother tore into me for my stupidity. "Let the dog drown next time!" She grabbed my damp T-shirt at the waist, skinned it off me like a rabbit. "Now clean up this mess," she said, pointing to her soiled carpet.

My father caught hell for being too lazy to take the pool down. "The boy nearly died," my mother said, cursing. It was a rare moment that she showed her true anger. "Empty the fucking pool, now!"

My father knew better than to argue. He went to the garage, took out the garden hoe, and attacked the pool, hacking the frame and lining to bits. A torrent of water gushed over him and the lawn.

As for me, I was packed off to bed without dinner.

My father woke me later. He was drunk. "Don't let your mother know," he said, turning on the light. He handed me a ham and butter sandwich, then stepped back from my bed like he was afraid of me. "That trick nearly got you killed, huh?" He laughed, the sound hollow and joyless, then stared at me gravely. "There's a lesson in all this."

The pool cover, the dog, my head slipping under the water. "What is it?"

"I'll let you think on it," my father said, turning out the light and leaving me alone with my sandwich.

Aside from *Don't be stupid* or *Pool covers don't hold my weight,* I wasn't sure what lesson my father thought I'd learn. Lying in the dark eating my sandwich, the only other glimmer of new wisdom I gained was realizing I didn't like ham with butter.

It's only now that I realize the lesson of that day, one that would have saved me from the trouble I'm now in. *Walk away. When things look bad, walk away.*

CHAPTER 39

I'D BEEN LIVING IN Kentucky a couple months when, exiting the Piggly Wiggly one Thursday morning, a chubby boy in a Cub Scout uniform positioned himself in front of me and held out a small, padded envelope. "Take this."

Instinctually, I took it, then, panicked, tried to hand it back.

The boy retreated with a frightened look on his face. "He gave me twenty bucks to do it. Said to tell you"—he tried to remember the message—"it's clover." Turning, he ran.

A chill spiked me. Higgles had found me. Again.

I looked up and down the street thinking I might see him. Nothing.

I ripped the envelope open. A SIM card.

I popped it in my phone. A text. *Book 4. Tuesday.*

Book four was *The Memphis Sky Above*, a memoir by a twenty-nine-year-old woman who went by the initials ES. No name. She didn't like her name, didn't like her family. She didn't like much of anything according to her book, even though she seemed to do just about everything. Drugs, sex, stealing. It was the standard "hard life, hard lessons" memoir. I didn't believe a word she wrote.

ES was the worst kind of full-of-shit. Technically, she told the truth, but her truth was stripped of any truthfulness. Instead of saying a cup was white, she'd say it wasn't exactly red. She made unimportant events sound life-changing and poured gallons of emotion into a simple conversation. She didn't have friends but soul mates. From her book, she came off sounding like someone who'd accuse you of betrayal for not returning a call quickly enough. Sure, she'd done her addictions, battled her demons, endured her lumps, but then who hadn't? It didn't justify a whole book.

Why people under the age of sixty wrote memoirs, I couldn't figure.

I once had a chance to find out. After Sarah and New York, when I was back living in Seattle, ES did a reading and book signing in Portland, Oregon. I drove the three hours, curious to see if the real-life ES mirrored the one she'd crafted in her book. The woman at the podium didn't have the luxurious mane and ample cleavage of her author photo. Meek and dressed down in a Hüsker Dü T-shirt, she was unrecognizable.

An old woman and I were the only one's to show up. ES read a profanity-filled section about falling in love at AA, her voice rising querulously at the end of each sentence.

Afterward, the woman in the audience asked ES what it was like to have fondled a former vice president's genitalia. "I think you have the wrong author," ES said, in her tilting voice.

"No, I don't," the old woman replied.

ES asked if there were any other questions.

There weren't.

A twinge of sympathy hit me. I bought two books, had her sign both. I asked her if she had plans, if she'd like to go to dinner.

ES looked at the tall pile of her unsold books. "I've a bus to catch in an hour," she said, pulling out her phone.

"There are other buses," I said.

She looked up at me, her eyes tired yet questioning. "Have you read my book?"

"I've read it."

"Then you know I'm an alcoholic, so don't expect me to drink," she said, biting a hangnail. "And don't expect any fucking either."

I took her to Macaroni Grill. She drank. A lot. I offered to take her to the bus station. She took me to a motel room.

We fucked.

Afterward, she cried. I felt bad, not for what we had done, but for her, for myself. I could see why she did what she did. She was lonely, confused, and reached out any way she could just to make human contact, even if that meant destroying a bit of herself in the process. I knew the feeling firsthand.

She wiped the tears from her face with the bedsheets. "It's not you," she said. "It's just this whole thing—my life, my memoir. It's difficult opening yourself up to the world, displaying your life. I'm not proud of my life. That's why I don't use my full name, why I go by ES, to stay anonymous."

"Anonymous?" I sat on the bed next to her. "Your photo is on the back cover. You just did a public reading."

She ignored me. "People read my book and think they know me. I don't even know me."

What do you expect? I touched her leg gently, feeling her heat. "Listen, you put yourself out there. Of course people are going to think they know you."

She got out of bed and started dressing. "Fiction writers want the reader to believe their lies. But memoirists just want to believe their own lies." She paused, lost in the middle of a shabby hotel room in a strange city. "I don't know what's real about me anymore. And you know the worst part? My parents love me unconditionally," she said, stepping into her skirt. "No matter how hard I try, they won't hate me." She asked if I had any money, fifty or sixty bucks.

I gave her a hundred.

She wadded the money, put it in her purse. "You seem like a nice guy and all, but this isn't going to work out between us. You just don't seem"—she searched for the word—"generous."

"I just handed you a hundred dollars."

"Maybe generous is not the right word. Rich is probably better. You don't seem rich, and I need someone who's not only willing to give me money, but has money to give. I mean *money* money. You know, real money."

Now I was insulted. In an odd way, I liked ES and wanted her to like me.

She finished dressing in silence. I drove her to the bus station. "So, why don't you give me your phone number," I said, dropping her off.

She looked surprised. "Why would I do that?"

And now I was wandering into her homeland: Memphis. I wanted to see her; I didn't want to see her. She was the first real connection I'd made since Sarah. The prospect of stumbling across her rumbled strangely in my stomach, making me sick with excitement.

I drove the four hours straight and parked my car near Beale Street. I strolled around a bit, grabbed a pulled pork sandwich, then texted Higgles: *ELVIS HAS LANDED.*

Instructions came an hour later. The address was outside the city, in a suburb called Cordova.

Not knowing Memphis, I decided to grab a cab. The cabbie let out a short, hard laugh when I told him where I wanted to go. "Six Flags over Jesus," he said, heading toward the highway.

"What do you mean?"

"You'll see."

I saw. Our meeting spot was a church. Three towering crosses, each four stories high, marked the exit where it sat. They could be seen from three miles away.

The cab cruised through a crowded parking lot and dropped me off at the entrance where a poster advertised a Mozart's Requiem sing-a-long. Five dollars. The woman at the door handed me a score. "Soprano, alto, tenor, or bass?" she asked. She squeezed my bicep. "You look like a tenor, but I bet you're a bass in bed."

I thanked her, though I didn't know why.

Signs divided the space into four sections. Sopranos sat to the far right, bass to the far left. Altos and tenors made up the middle.

The place was near full, a sea of short-sleeved plaid shirts. Even the women wore them. It seemed a bad joke, all that plaid.

I scanned the room, each section, looking for Higgles.

Nothing.

Finally, I saw someone in the bass section waving at me. Higgles. Gaunt and sickly, he'd stripped at least thirty pounds since I'd seen him in Brighton. His face was filmed with a milky sweat. He always seemed to be sweating.

I took a seat beside him on the hard pew. He smelled of heated coins, metallic and foul. His once close-cropped black hair was now shaggy. Neither of us spoke for a minute. Finally, I said, "You look like shit."

"Tahiti does that to a man," he said, flipping through sheet music. "You know, I have no idea what I'm looking at."

The conductor's voice boomed through the speakers as he introduced the soloist for the evening. The organist hit a G flat and the crowd opened their throats to match the note. "Are we really planning to sing along?" I asked.

Higgles glanced about like he was just now noticing where he was. "I was told there'd be snacks," he said, standing. "I thought they'd serve snacks." He motioned me to follow. "Let's find some privacy."

Higgles directed me to the men's restroom, which was empty.

Higgles kicked open a stall, dropped his pants, and sat down on the toilet. The door stood wide.

I turned away.

"Did you know I was married once?" he asked. "Had myself a little lady, a house. We even talked of starting a family."

"You've told me." I wasn't in the mood to bond. Strains of Mozart filtered in, pitching and driving as the organ moaned along. "How did you know where I lived?" I caught glimpses of him in the mirror. "Close the stall door, would you? You're making me uncomfortable."

He didn't close it. Spinning the toilet paper roll, he mittened his hand. "So you want the good news about our next freelance project?"

"Good usually comes with bad," I said. "You know, I'm still waiting to be paid in full for all these other jobs."

"We'll even up, cousin—once this job is done."

"I get paid before I do another job." I asked again, "How did you find me?"

"You're like a comet."

"Why, because I burn bright?"

"Because you're constantly casting off bits and pieces of yourself," he said. "You leave a trail that anyone can follow." He flushed the toilet, buckled his pants, and exited the stall. "The others aren't too happy."

"What others?"

"The ones wanting retribution on the Africa job."

"Retribution for what? The Africa job fell through."

Higgles suddenly seemed exhausted, like he'd been playing at something for far too long. "Listen," he said, leaning against the sink basin. "Staying low-key and cautious is smart, but stop trying to be invisible. It's *good* that you can be found. People get suspicious if you're invisible. Only the guilty hide." He studied himself in the mirror. "The good news is you're going to Korea. The bad news is that the fallout over Africa has turned into something bigger than I expected. A lot of pissed-off people, the kind of people you don't want to piss off. But nothing we can't handle, right?" He laughed. "Do you know what my first real paying job was?"

I didn't.

"Robbing mailboxes."

This whole "pissed-off people" bit worried me. Who was pissed off, and why? I hadn't done anything. "Yeah, well, you seem like the kind of guy who'd steal fabric softener samples," I said. Our eyes met in the mirror.

"Not my style." He smiled. "I only hit the big boxes, the blue ones on the corners. And I'd only hit them once a year. Mid-April."

The cruelest month. I thought it through. "Tax returns."

"Yahtzee." Higgles turned on the faucet.

Address, social security, name, financial info. "Identity theft?"

"That's long-haul stuff. I was a sprinter. In and out," he said, washing his hands. "I'd cash the tax payment checks written to the IRS."

"How?"

"How indeed." There was a childlike glee in his face. "That was the brilliant part." He pulled a marker from his back pocket, wrote IRS on the mirror. "Simply changed the 'pay to' line." He deftly made the I a capital M, placed a period after the S and then added a name. IRS now read MRS. SAMANTHA SMITH. "Then I'd get my little lady to make a visit to the bank."

His eyes coldly met mine in the mirror. "But they caught on. Now all the tax checks are made out to the Treasury Department." He pocketed the marker. "God, I'm hungry. Let's get out of here."

Out in the parking lot, he hotwired a Honda Civic.

We drove back into Memphis, to Corky's, a barbecue joint. "The blooming onions are fantastic here," Higgles said, ordering double of everything, more food than he'd ever be able to eat.

I ordered a beer.

"Let me tell you a little something about this game," he said. "It's all about salvo chasing."

"Meaning?"

"The enemy fires at you," he said, making a pistol with his fingers, "then notes how far to the right or left of the target it landed, whether it was too long or too short. He makes adjustments. And while he's making the adjustment, you race to where the shot just landed."

"Because he's not firing there again."

Higgles tapped his nose. "You catch on fast." The food arrived and he set into a bowl of chili. "Tell me about your childhood, your aspirations."

Fuck you, I thought. Higgles already knew everything about me. He was just bating me about like a wounded mouse, letting me run a distance before pulling me back.

I told him details from Ray-Ray's life.

"Iranian?" He acted surprised. "You're pretty light skinned for an Arab."

"A Persian. And my father's side was famous for their light skin. The Ivory Wonder they called him."

"Huh." He sat back in his chair, folded his hands across his stomach. "So being Iranian, I guess you can speak whatever that language is that they speak there."

"Fluently," I said. "In fact, I use to be a translator."

"Really?"

I nodded. "For the UN."

"Wow, the UN." Higgles eyed my skeptically. "Did you ever get to meet anyone famous?"

"The Ayatollah."

"The Ayatollah?"

"We were drinking buddies."

He acted confused. "He doesn't seem like the kind of guy who'd drink."

"You'd be surprised."

He picked at a piece of blooming onion. "I already am."

Flagging the waiter, he asked for everything to be wrapped to go. "God, I'm stuffed. Couldn't eat another bite." He'd barely touched his food. "Enough of this chin-wagging," he said once the table was cleared. We got down to business. Seoul, Korea. He sketched out the particulars of the new gig on a napkin.

"What's the take?" I asked.

It was solid. Not a new Lexus solid, but solid all the same. "That doesn't include what you owe me, right?"

He sucked his teeth. "About what I owe you—"

"No 'about' bullshit," I said. "I get paid or I don't play."

He glared at me a moment, then pulled an envelope from his back pocket and tossed it on the table. "What's fair is fair, I guess."

I took the envelope and peeked inside. A stack of hundreds. "Do I need to count this?"

"Only if you want the practice."

I pocketed the money.

The bill came. He got up to leave. "So we're good to go on Seoul?"

I thought it through. I tapped the table with my knuckles. "We're clover."

"I'm confident you can find your own way home, yes?" he said, leaving his bagged food on the table. Leaving the bill.

On his way out, I saw him pick up the entire bowl of mints at the hostess station while the hostess was seating a couple and walked out with it.

I ordered another beer but didn't drink it. My thoughts flowed back to ES. This was her hometown, where she'd been weaned. I knew all the clubs she'd done her coke in, knew all the beer shacks where she'd had clumsy, drunken sex, where she'd found her eternal love at happy hour and then lost it at last call. I knew where ES had crashed into the sharp rocks of life. And I knew I had to find her. It's an odd feeling knowing all about a person you don't really know, feeling a closeness to someone you spent only a handful of hours with.

I left Corky's, left the food, and found a low-lit, foul bar with a great jukebox. I looked for ES, thinking, somehow, she might be sitting on the stool waiting for some guy to buy her a drink. Waiting for some human connection.

That was why ES lingered in my mind, I realized. While she wanted to be anonymous and unknown, she'd revealed a bit of herself the evening we'd spent together. Our time together was far from soul-shaking, but something had happened. Brief and raw, it was like live wires sparking across each other, making a small seared mark. There'd been a human connection, something I wanted to explore further.

I pulled out my phone, decided to give her call. "Hey, remember me? I'm here," I'd say. "Why don't we hang out a bit?"

But I realized I didn't have her number. I couldn't even look her up in a phone book.

I didn't know her name.

◉ ◉ ◉

INITIALLY, IT HAD BEEN about the money. I needed it. But once I had it, had squirreled away more than enough to survive on for some time, I realized I was doing this for something else altogether. Something I couldn't clearly define, but something money definitely couldn't buy.

CHAPTER 40

SEOUL WAS SIMPLE. I landed, had a traditional *hanjeongsik* meal that left me with a bellyache, made the pick-up, and then was viciously beaten down by my contact. I barely escaped with the package, let alone my life. Fourteen hours after touchdown in Korea, I had twelve new stitches in my head and I was winging my way back Stateside.

Back at my house in Kentucky, I sent the package to a PO Box Higgles had set up in Seattle. A week later, I got my cash.

Creeped out by the stains on the ceiling and absolute silence at night, I ditched my old place and got a Craigslist sublet in Cincinnati, one that that overlooked The Great American Ball Park, home of the Cincinnati Reds.

A week, then three passed. I had nowhere to go, nothing pressing to do. *Up for gig,* I texted Higgles. No reply.

So I waited.

Another two weeks. Nothing. I kept trying to convince myself that I was safe, that there was no way Higgles would find me. Still, it was like waiting in a dentist's lobby. I dreaded what was coming, but I wanted it to arrive quickly so I could have it over and done with.

I thought of heading elsewhere, maybe back to Seattle. But I stayed, figuring whatever was to happen, this was as good a place as any.

Fall, then winter took hold. The Ohio River froze over in rough jags. The icy air sliced through my clothes no matter how many layers I wore. The apartment never got warm.

Christmas came and went. I read, ate a lot of chili, drank too much beer. It's startling how quickly you can get fat. By late January, climbing a flight of stairs gave me heart palpitations, the sweats.

I needed a distraction. I needed a friend.

Rick served as both.

We met at an art opening. He'd come for the free cocktails, for the opportunity to meet women. I'd gone for the free cocktails, women, and to see the work.

As I studied a canvas of a naked man being attacked by geese, Rick sidled up next to me and held out a cocktail. "It's more lighter fluid than alcohol," he said by way of introduction, "but it's free." He stuck out his hand. Rick Flowers.

Sharply dressed, manicured, buffed, and plucked, he was as finely kept as an orchid. There was a story there, possibly something interesting. He told me he was a musician, had an album out on a major label that had been a critical charmer. Reviewed positively in all the magazines, it had hit the public consciousness like a birdbath launched into the river; it sank away instantly, selling fewer than three thousand copies.

"I'm more than just some guy on a guitar," he said. "What I do is art." He flicked his hand toward the works on the wall. "Unlike this stuff, which is average work at best. This artist is pure gimmick. She uses brushes made from her own pubic hair." He shrugged. "It sells, though. I'll give her that."

He asked if I liked sex.

"Depends," I said.

"On?"

"Who it's with."

He nodded. "Sagacious."

I expected a proposition. *A blowjob in the bathroom? A quick trip to his place where he'd strip out of his Armani motorcycle jacket and bespoke pants?*

Instead, he nodded at my glass and said, "Another drink?"

Standing by the makeshift bar, he pointed out a woman. "Yea or nay? She wants to have sex with you but…" He spun a story. With one woman, there was a fifty-fifty chance of catching a debilitating STD. "Blind for life," he said, "and a nasty rash on your face." Another, a violent boyfriend just out of jail. "He'll be home in less than an hour and the girl is a blabbermouth, will tell him everything that happened." A third, enduring the public humiliation of being arrested naked in a Port-o-Potty.

Sex couldn't just be sex. Each encounter had to have a threat to it, some danger had to be involved.

After he'd spun obscene tales of all the women in the gallery, he set his empty drink on floor and said, "Gotta cut. But let's meet tomorrow at Marco's Gym. It's down the block. We'll do a workout. A run, some weights."

He gave me the gym's address and a free pass, set up a time, then slowly made toward the exit, stopping to chat up a woman along the way. In less than two minutes, she was heading out the door with him.

The next morning, fatigued from a night of jerking awake at the slightest noise, I dragged myself down to Marco's Gym to meet Rick.

"That's right," he said, struggling to place me. "The guy from the art thing last night."

I spotted him on the benchpress. "That whole scene was gay. I probably seemed a bit gay, but it's all part of the game. Camouflage, you know?" he said, sliding on another twenty-pound plate.

"What do you mean?" I scanned the weight room, looking for— what? A glaring eye, a menacing smile, a man lifting weights in dress shoes. Something out of place, I guess. All I saw was a gym crowded with sweating, grunting guys.

"At all those things, art shows or cafés or poetry readings, you have to act emo and harmless to disarm the women. At clubs, it's different. The women are different. You have to be more direct, more aggressive. Basically, you've got to mirror the situation you're in."

As we ran on the treadmills, Rick overshared, telling me his process for picking up women, the situations and lines that were fail-safe. He was like his own reality TV show, irritating but intriguing, and always entertaining. He was honest, if somewhat vile, and made me feel we had a special bond, that he was sharing things about himself he shared with no one else. He probably made everyone he knew feel that way.

After the workout, we got a coffee. "Want to do me a solid?" he asked. "Want to be my Redshirt?"

I didn't understand.

He sat back in his chair, eyed me skeptically. "A Redshirt," he said. "You know, Star Trek. The one-episode extras who always got killed. Their uniform was always red. That's what I need. Someone to take the hit so I can survive the night."

"You need a wingman."

"Exactly. You distract the ugly girl while I score the pretty one."

Why not? I didn't feel like being alone.

That night, we made a tour of the clubs, moving swiftly from one place to another, never staying more than a half hour. "It has to torch," Rick said. "Seven seconds. If you aren't talking with her within seven seconds of making eye contact, forget it."

At the fourth club, he saw his mark—tall with a head of hair that made me think of a silk pillowcase. The girl's features were blank, forgettable, a screen on which you could project whatever you wanted. She was attractive enough, but not really my type. Rick, I had realized, had only one type: double X chromosomes.

Pretty Girl's friend was infinitely more interesting. Her face seemed to flash every emotion, every thought. She could tell you everything without ever saying a word.

The plan was for me to wedge myself into a conversation with the second girl while Rick made his play. "If I don't greenlight in two minutes, I'll give you the signal. We'll retreat, move on."

We made our approach.

Rick sidled smoothly up to the bar and dropped his line. "I feel I know you. Have we made out before?" Unbelievably, she actually laughed.

I held my hand out to the other girl, introducing myself as Clement Martin. Disgust filled her face, which threw me off guard. It was like she could see right through me, knew I was lying.

I held firm, smiling with my hand outstretched.

Rick had maneuvered the other girl away, splitting off from us.

I introduced myself again, said, "You probably didn't know, but Italy has only been a country since eighteen sixty-one. Prior to that it was just a bunch of city-states." I didn't move my hand.

Reluctantly, she shook it. "Actually"—there was the tiniest slip of a smile—"I did know."

Her name was Pansy, which she hated. "My mom wanted Nancy, my father Patricia. I got stuck with the resulting travesty."

Rick called over to us. "Hey, we're heading out," he said, his arm around his girl. His look made it clear that "we" didn't included Pansy and me.

Pansy glared at the two as they left, then her face fell blank, emotionless. After a moment, she turned to me. "You don't have to hang around," she said, her eyes cutting away. "I can make my way home."

The night was just starting. I couldn't leave her, not like that. Not so obviously.

I scouted the scene. The zooming lights, the thumping music. It was too much for me. "Is there a pub or lounge around here, someplace quieter we can get a drink?"

We went to a place a few blocks away, an old-man bar, the kind with a jukebox quietly playing and a floor canoed down the center from decades of people stumbling from the bar to the bathroom and back. We slid into a cracked, red pleather booth. Pansy ordered a vodka cranberry. I got a beer. She asked what I did for work.

"I'm in between unemployment right now," I said.

She laughed. "You temp, too?" she asked. "It's the same with me. I don't really have a career so much as a paycheck. I temp at a law firm. Make calls, file documents, send out invoices. My boss charges a hundred and fifty dollars an hour and what do I get paid? Nine. It's a farce." Born and raised in Cincinnati, she'd moved to Oregon after college, had only recently moved back. "Really loved Portland, but my family kept complaining that they never saw me, kept crying over the phone all the time. So I gave in, quit a job I really liked, gave up a nice apartment, left my friends, and moved back." She fiddled with the plastic stick in her drink. "There was something so nice about being able to slam the phone down on someone without the fear of them driving over and banging on the door, demanding to know why I hung up on them." She smiled. "At least my sister's here."

"That was your sister at the club?"

"God, no. That's just a friend. Or not so much a friend, but just someone I can't help but hang out with."

I liked Pansy. I ordered another round. She was funny. Dark, but funny.

She apologized for initially coming off cold at the club.

"I think you actually snarled at me."

She laughed. "Sorry. It's just, when I saw Rick—" She broke off, gazed across the lounge.

"How'd you know his name?" I hadn't told her.

"Rick and I use to date," she said, then amended her statement. "Dating is probably too strong a word. We used to fuck. Also," she said, "I know you're his Redshirt."

I sat back in the booth. Rick hadn't looked twice at Pansy, hadn't even acknowledged her. "Go on," I said, interested. "Tell me the story."

She looked down at her drink. "It's my sister's fault. She's much prettier than I am, but when I first got back to the city she was going through an awful period. She'd ballooned twenty pounds, had a terrible dye-job, and a swollen face from having her wisdom teeth removed. She wanted to go out on the town. I said sure, thinking it would cheer her up."

"So you got Rick and your sister got the Redshirt."

She nodded. "And the sad thing was that I really took to Rick."

"He's a good-looking guy."

"He's an asshole."

Then why'd you let your friend go with him? I wanted to ask.

She chewed on her swizzle stick. "But like you said, he's good-looking. And a musician," she said. "He's very upfront about the fact that he's an asshole. He told me he wasn't into a long-term thing.

I guess I hoped he was lying—to himself, you know?" She shook her head. "I actually thought I could make him change. The truth of it is I can't even make myself change." Her eyes found mine. "You want to hear something terrible?"

I nodded.

"He used the same line on me, the one he used tonight on my friend. And it worked."

A silence rose between us. I thought of asking why she didn't stop her friend from making the same mistake, why she didn't call Rick on his bullshit. I wondered if Rick even recognized her. Probably not. Pansy had been the number two girl, invisible. Fodder for me, the Redshirt.

She said, "I wish I'd never left Portland."

Then she invited me home.

In the cab ride back to her place, I asked about the last Redshirt, the one her sister got stuck with.

"Jerry," she said. "His name is Jerry. He's kinda like you."

"How's that?"

"Nice. A little bland."

"Thanks," I said. "You make me feel like a winner."

"You might be," she said, staring out the window. "Jerry was. My sister dated him for almost six months."

"Then what happened?"

"They got married."

As the cab slowed to a stop in front of her place, she said, "Moving back here, dating Rick, taking a shitty temp job. You know what? I'm done making bad choices." She took my hand. "Are you coming up?"

I wanted to. I had a terrifying erection. I felt a kindling of something for Pansy. I liked her. "I can't."

"Why?"

The reason eluded me. Then my phone chimed. A text. *Book 3. Be there Thursday.* Higgles.

"I've got work."

"Right now?"

I nodded.

She gave me a brief kiss, the kind you'd give a brother. "I'd give you my phone number," she said, opening the door and sliding from the cab, "but that would create expectations."

"I could give you mine."

"That'd be worse." The cab door *snicked* shut.

Snow banked against the apartment building. The icy wind raced the street. I watched Pansy unlock her building's front door and then disappear.

CHAPTER 41

BOOK THREE. *THE FROZEN GNOME: A Reykjavik Thriller* by Arnaldur Hegason.

Higgles texted me instructions when I landed in Iceland. I was to meet my contact at an espresso bar: a man carrying an orange trumpet case.

He was late. And when he finally arrived, he shot through the door in a rush, out of breath and his pale face flushed. An albino.

An ambulance raced by outside, then a police car. The sound of their sirens seemed to nail the man to the spot, his white hair standing in tufts like frayed nylon rope.

He scanned the place from the doorway. I made the agreed-upon gesture—scratching my chin—when his gaze struck me.

He strode over, said, "Rye bread makes the best toast."

"Not when you're diabetic."

I expected him to hand over the case, leave. Instead, he took a seat at the table next to mine, and set the case on the floor.

I reached for it.

He stepped on the handle.

Not good.

He grabbed my espresso and swallowed the dregs.

Another siren sounded far off.

"People think I'm an albino. I'm not." His pinkish eyes met mine. "Not technically, at least."

I looked away. The situation reeked. I wanted to walk away. "Well, at least they don't think you're an asshole," I said, staring out the café window.

"Oh, people think I'm an asshole. But I'm not that either. Not technically, at least." He handed me the case. "Go, flyaway. Be free."

I stood.

He grabbed at my jacket sleeve. "Listen, it's not the solitude," he said. "It's not the living with the awful thoughts of what I've done. Nor is it that this is a young man's game and I'm no longer a young man. All that I can handle. The number one worst thing about it all, the part I can't handle, is that there's no one I can talk to about what I do. That's the worst. I make handshake hand-offs to people who don't even acknowledge me, people who don't care to know my name." He held up my cup. "Foul espresso and clandestine meetings. It's not much of a life."

I stared at him. What should I say to that? I sat down again. "What's your name?"

He glared. "My name? That's the number one worst thing."

"You said the isolation was the worst thing."

"I misspoke. My name is even worse." He held out his hand. "Look at me," he said. "I'm a ghost. So guess what my parents named me?"

I thought. "Casper."

He sat back in the seat, folded his arms over his chest. "Casper." He smiled. "And what would be my last name, then?"

I thought. "White."

"Casper White," he said, the name rolling about his mouth. He got up from the table. "You'd best get a move on and take care of whatever you need to take care of." He nodded to the case. "I had to dirty my hands to get you that. Everything in there is souring as we speak. Come tomorrow, it's going to smell pretty bad."

After the door shut behind him, I took inventory of the case. It held a wallet, a passport, credit cards, three cell phones, a neatly clipped wad of cash, and an envelope with a certified check. *For the orphans*, the memo line read, with a number after it. But no trumpet. There was also a business card for the Blu 1919 Hotel with a handwritten note on the back that read, *We're fired from an unknown gun, shot at a target unseen. Life is making the best of a bad trajectory.*

All the identification held the name Wellem P. Steertal of Reykjavik, Iceland. Age twenty-eight. The photo gave me pause. Wellem looked eerily like me.

As Higgles had instructed me to do, I bought a business class ticket for a 10:00 a.m. flight to Boston the next day using Wellem's credit card and passport information. There, I'd leave the case in a gym locker.

I checked into the Blu 1919 Hotel—an old world, four-story white stone building—under the name Wellem Steertal.

At the bar, I settled in with a group of young Icelanders who were trying to make it through this moment of life, joyfully complaining about the collapse of the economy, the volcanic eruption, the relationships that had turned bad. I'd bought a round. The drinks kept coming.

One of the girls shifted her chair close to mine, blocking us off from the rest of the group. Her name was Layla. I told her mine was Wellem. "That's my ex-husband's name," she said, adding, "You even resemble him."

"Just the good parts, I hope."

I liked her, liked her laugh. Her hair was the color of a perfectly prepared crepe and her plump cheeks were covered in a light peach fuzz. She reminded me of a seal cub. And she liked me. "We are all depressed," she said, smiling. "An entire nation of depressed people. It's hereditary, in our genes. We've been bred to be depressed."

Layla had endured some tough breaks as of late. Freshly divorced, she'd lost her job and her apartment, and both her cat and mother had died. "Wellem, my husband—my ex-husband—used to handle everything," she said. "He kept me secure and comfortable. If it wasn't for the fact that he kissed me with his fist, I'd still be with him."

"He beat you?"

She rattled the ice in her glass. "Just around my face, neck, back, and legs. Still," she said, "I spoke to him this morning and he said he loved me. He wants me back."

"And I'm sure he promised he'd never beat you again."

Layla laughed and I lit up. It was a beautiful laugh. "No," she said. "He said he was certain there'd be times when he would." She lifted her shoulders. A shrug. "Telling the truth is one of his better traits."

"Are you going to go back to him?"

"He's coming to me. Or is supposed to." She looked around. "We were to meet here and talk about getting back together. But I'm going to tell him no." She paused. "Or yes. I really don't know." Her voice wavered. "You see, badness seems to pile up on me." Her eyes cupped with tears. "I'm not asking for all that much. Just want someone to appreciate me, someone who wants to be with me. Someone to spend the remaining minutes of the world's end with me. I could take my ex-husband back, or I could never see him again. I feel like a traveler trapped on an island." She laughed, trying to shake off her sadness. "Iceland. I guess I *am* trapped on an island. But I want to escape. Tell me, how do I escape?"

Leaving Iceland wouldn't solve her problems, I wanted to tell her. There was no escaping what plagued her. You have to face the bad things head-on, wrestle them down quickly, and make them your own. If you don't, if you try to keep them as something outside of you, something that unjustly came at you—which they may well be, though the truth won't change your luck—then they fester and spoil and serve as food for more bad to feast on.

I knew firsthand that, unstaunched, those bad breaks escalate. The world tastes blood. You become a continuous victim, and contrary to what all religions and governments and nonprofit organizations claim, mankind loves a victim, a loser, someone downtrodden—it loves someone to pick on.

Easy prey is just that—easy.

Instead I said, "Hold firm for a while. Things have a way of working themselves out."

While we talked, her friends had wandered off, heading out for a late dinner or to another bar or club. Layla and I drank more.

"Your friends seem nice," I said.

"I don't know any of those people." She opened her purse. "I just met them here tonight." She pulled out a set of keys, thirty-plus, packed tight on the ring, and laid them on the table. "That's my entire life here," she said, slurring slightly. "A key to everything I've entered or exited." She told me to pick one.

I set my fingers on a slim silver key.

She smiled. "Any one but that one."

"What's wrong with that one?"

"It's the one key I still use. It's to my storage locker."

I picked another one.

"Two twelve Kleinbaugur, apartment thirty-three, third floor," Layla said. "I lived there for five months with a girl I knew from school. We had big plans. We were going to open our own store, sell our own clothing line. Beautiful space but sad times," she says. "Pick another."

I picked another.

"My preparatory school locker. Locker three-oh-four. I loved the boy who had the locker next to mine more than anything else in the world. Or maybe it wasn't love, but it was whatever it is that tears you up inside when you like someone and they don't like you back." She looked away. "He runs a gas station now. He got really fat."

We continued the game, Layla telling me the story of each key, precisely and with detail. The joys and heartbreaks and expectations and accidents. We drank. We laughed. She pulled the key to her storage locker off the ring, and handed the rest to me.

"What am I supposed to do with these?"

She took my hand, and placed it to her cheek. The fuzz on her face was soft. "Keep them. Toss them. Do whatever, I don't care," she said. "Each one is some reminder of some part of my life I don't want to remember, some mistake." She kissed the palm of my hand. "No one should ever have so many keys. Especially useless keys. They don't unlock anything anymore."

"They unlocked your memories."

"I'm ready for new ones." She kissed my palm again. "Take me home?"

I took her upstairs.

She stripped, and standing in front of the lamp, a halo engulfed her entire body. Seal cub fuzz. It covered every inch of her. She crawled into bed, called for me to join.

I went to wash up first, and when I returned, she was thick in sleep, breathing the deep, desperate breath of the exhausted.

I unzipped her purse. A wallet, three different lipsticks, a couple of tampons, two cell phones, and a blue sock with no mate. I put her keys back, then threw in some cash.

As an afterthought, I put in the hotel business card with the note. *Life is making the best of a bad trajectory.*

I grabbed the trumpet case and closed the door quietly.

On my way through the lobby, a cold worry scratched at my neck. I was being watched, tracked.

At the front door, Casper White clamped my elbow. Paler than before, he now bordered on translucent. He had the look of a panicked horse, his eyes wide and rolling about. "I'm listening."

"For what?"

He looped his arm under mine, grabbed my thumb and wrenched it back. The pain was crippling. "Wrong answer." We moved straight into a cab. He spoke to the driver in Icelandic. Directions. An address.

The cab slipped into traffic, heading away from the airport, where I wanted to go. Morning harassed the sky. A new day. The trumpet case was wedged between my knees. Casper kept pressure my twisted thumb. "Let up," I said, swallowing a yawn. I was scared, but somehow—the lack of sleep, the alcohol lingering in my blood—my fear was fenced, held in check. My nerves were Teflon-coated. I'd get out of this, somehow.

"I called Higgles. He verified what I feared." He freed my thumb. The cab decreased speed as we merged onto a roundabout. "You're not him, my contact. You somehow—"

I popped the cab door. Fuck trying to figure out what he was talking about. The plan: escape. Hit the pavement running and don't look back.

Casper had other ideas. He grabbed at the case and bon voyaged me with a kick, launching me head-first onto the median. Shoulder, back, then ass. An oil drum halted my cartwheel.

I wobbled to my feet, the hot taste of blood carpeting my mouth. Traffic pylons, rusty rebar, and broken wooden shipping pallets. I'd landed in the dumping grounds for the nearby construction project.

The case sat a few feet off.

"You forgot to tip the driver." Casper. Like he teleported from the back of the cab. He rapped my ear, then took hold of my jacket collar. "Who are you?"

I coughed out a throat full of blood on his white shirt. "Wellem P. Steertal. Of Reykjavik, Iceland."

"Wellem of Iceland is dead."

I motioned toward the case. "Take it."

He pecked my forehead with his fist. "I will. But first I need a name. Who set this up? Who do you work for?"

My thoughts clattered like a drawerful of dropped silverware. Traffic sped behind us, oblivious to the scene. I'd often imagined how I might die, my last moments on earth. Killed by an albino on a roundabout in Iceland wasn't how I saw it happening.

I hacked out a name. "Higgles."

Worry darkened his face. "Bullshit." He leaned to me. "Tell me, then. What's he look like?"

I answered with a double-fisted chop to his larynx.

He hissed like a pissed-off goose and staggered back.

I had an opening. A chance to grab the case and bolt. I scanned the ground for a weapon of some kind. A pipe, a piece of broken board, anything to fight with. Running wouldn't get me far.

Casper ended my concern; he tripped on a piece of concrete, spun around in attempt to catch himself, and landed violently on a pile of loose rebar, stomach down.

He stayed down.

Cautiously, I tapped Casper with my toe.

He lolled his head upward, locking his hamster eyes on me. "Well played." His hand tethered tight to my leg.

I kicked free.

Whelping in pain, he forced himself onto his back. A two-foot length of metal bar harpooned his chest. How was that possible? He hadn't fallen that far or that hard. Open, shut, open. His mouth hinged like a landed fish as a sunset of red spread over his shirt. "I guess"—he chewed air—"it's time to retire." His blue-white fingers grasped the metal pole.

I bent down next to him, cupped his cold, sticky hands. "Leave it in," I said, envisioning a fountain of blood arcing out the moment the bar was yanked free. "I'll send for some help."

His head rolled from side to side. Dark froth bubbled from the corners of his mouth. "Help me now. Ram it in." His eyes shifted upward, looked beyond me. "If you don't, he will."

I turned, expecting to find someone there. There was no one. "Who?"

"He'll make me talk, then kill me." His voice wheezed like a damaged accordion. "Then he'll find you."

Walk away. Get free of the mess.

Casper reached out to touch my face. I slapped his hand away and was instantly disgusted with myself. The man was dying. He longed for human contact.

His breath smelled of rotting strawberries. "On three?" he pleaded.

I stood. A sourness squeezed up from my stomach. I couldn't do it. It tore against everything I was. Up until now, my Kam Manning had been a game. A dangerous one, but still a game. Now, though...

Casper huffed out red spittle. "One."

I stomped on the metal bar, driving it deep.

Cracking bones. A gurgling cry. Casper's hands shot up, quivered, then dropped to the ground. Dead.

I vomited, then grabbed the trumpet case and didn't look back.

Two hours later, airport security eyed my passport closely. Wellem P. Steertal it read. He studied my bandaged chin and blackened eye even closer. At least I'd washed my vomit off my jacket.

Security said something, pointed to my face. I forced a smile. *I just murdered a man.* "Bachelor party."

I was waved through.

Sitting in the business class cabin, my ribs throbbing and my nerves chaotically firing, I forced down a whiskey and orange juice and then a second.

The attendant served me a third drink. "Are you all right?"

I sandwiched my hands between my thighs to stop them trembling. *I've just murdered a man.* "I hate flying."

The engines revved. The plane taxied. Lift-off.

I'd gotten away, but from what or who, I didn't know.

Flipping through the Icelandic newspaper, I came across my face on page twelve. Or, not my face, but Wellem's.

I asked the attendant to translate the article. She skimmed the piece. "Crushed by a bus." She pointed to a word. "*Sjálfsvíg*. Suicide." Then she read further. "Or conspiracy."

"What do you mean?"

"Well, a woman swore she saw a man push him into the street." His finger settled on a line of text. "An albino."

How Casper White's death was described—accident or foul play— I didn't know. I killed him after the papers had gone to press.

◎ ◎ ◎

ONLY THE DEPRESSED HAVE a realistic view of themselves.

CHAPTER 42

A WALLET WITH NO ID, some cash, a cheap watch, and a cell phone. The Reykjavik police dumped the dead albino's things in plastic tray. The lead detective checked the phone's call log. One number. A Seattle area code.

On the fifth ring a man picked up. "Is it done?" he said. "Did you get the case back?"

"Yes, 'ello." The detective's English sucked. "I call the phone. The man who owned it. Who do I speak now?"

The line went dead. And while the detective tried calling repeatedly, no one every picked up again.

CHAPTER 43

I TEXTED HIGGLES WHEN I landed in Boston. *WTF? The albino tried to kill me.*

Did he succeed? came the reply.

I left the trumpet case in a locker at a gym near the airport, as instructed. My payment was to come later.

I went back to my place in Cincinnati, packed my books and my clothing, and relocated some forty miles west to Krotchersville, Indiana because—why? I knew nothing about the town and had only seen its name on a road sign. It could have been anywhere, really. I wasn't so much moving toward something as moving away from it. Cincinnati had started to become a home, a place I saw as my own. Part of me. And like Layla, I wanted the impossible, to escape the inescapable—myself.

Krotchersville, I tried convincing myself, would give me a fresh start.

What I got was raided. My second month there, I pissed off my asshole neighbor when I asked him to turn down his music. I've got nothing against techno, but not at 3:00 a.m. So the following night, he called the sheriff and said I was dealing drugs out of my place.

The sheriff pounded on my door at 10:00 p.m. then broke it down before I could even respond. I was tackled and cuffed, and had to lay face down my floor as his team tore my apartment apart. "Complaint from your neighbor," I was told.

Finally, they dragged me downstairs, tossed me in the back of a cruiser. Sitting cuffed and cramped, I remained quiet, holding my breath against the stench of bum-ass and ammonia.

Outside, the drug-sniffing dogs milled about, waiting for their orders.

"You're fucked, William," the sheriff said.

"Wellem," I corrected. "Wellem P. Steertal." I'd gotten an Indiana driver's license in Wellem's name, which was easy enough. I took his passport, the lease on my apartment—which I'd set up in his name— an electric bill, and a library card to the DMV. They issued me an ID, no questions asked.

The sheriff stared at the license he had in his hand, then glared hard at me. "What kind of name is Wellem?" I thought of asking him the same thing about his. His tag read *MZTET*. I'd seen the name on lawn signs around town. *Re-Elect Mztet for Sheriff*. It was like he'd been handed a name before it was finished. "Well, *Wellem*," he said, "there's enough evidence on you to put you away for a while."

He was right. Somewhere there *was* enough evidence to put me away. Fortunately, they didn't have any of it. They'd rifle through my closet of dirty clothes, my empty refrigerator, my stack of books. They'd find nothing incriminating. I slept there, little more. I was trying to live the simple life in Krotchersville. It wasn't hard. The three things the town was known for—growing corn, shooting hoops, and smoking crystal meth—didn't interest me. There wasn't much else going on, which was perfect. Exactly what I needed to clear my head, shake off the constant, low-level worry that had wrapped itself around me.

Since Reykjavik, since I'd murdered Casper, crippling panic attacks would shrivel my lungs to the size of sun-dried tomatoes. Fear would wire through my blood and my throat would twist shut. I felt garroted; I couldn't breath. So when I settled in Krotchersville, I launched into a Zen phase. I read the books, meditated, and tried my hardest to ingest shitty situations and spit out something clean, something pure.

That was why I took the apartment. I didn't like it. It felt off. The floor layout was forced, like it had once been a studio but had been built out into a two-bedroom. The corners appeared suddenly, the rooms were oddly small and claustrophobic. The ceiling hovered low. The space was cold. Daylight never found its way in.

It was exactly what I needed.

Discomfort isn't always a bad thing. It can be a teacher. Though what it teaches, I've yet to determine.

My landlord I liked. Xavier Yolando Zapitos, or XYZ as he insisted on being called. I liked him because there was no reason for me to like him. He wasn't so much a slumlord as a caricature of slumlord. It was a game for him; he wanted to see what he could get away with and for how long. Building's boiler broken? It doesn't really get cold until December. Mice? At least they aren't rats. Faucet leaking? At least you have running water.

When he showed me the apartment, XYZ promised a fresh paint job, and to fix the hole in the living room wall, the bedroom door that was half off the hinge, and the toilet that didn't flush.

I signed the lease and paid three months' rent in advance in cash. I wouldn't see him again. He wouldn't fix a thing. He wouldn't ever think of me again, his head filled with too many other worries. Which was what I wanted, to be left alone.

Not being noticed is an unappreciated luxury.

But now I was anything but, the star at the center of a scene.

The minutes clicked past. Ten, fifteen, forty. One of the cops came out of the building, held up his hands and shook his head. They had nothing.

A reporter showed up, asked for a statement from Mztet. His attitude shifted from cockiness to concern. "Not now," he said, nervously. Elections were this year. If today's bust was big enough, a few kilos of coke or the uncovering of a gun-running ring, then it would blaze a path to another four years for him. If it was a bust for one joint, that'd be fine too. But having seen his challenger's campaign flyers accusing Mztet of wasting taxpayers money and doing an all-around shitty job as Sheriff, I could understand why Mztet couldn't turn up empty-handed. He'd be mocked right out of his job. "Wellem," he said, "I'm a hardass with compassion. You help me and maybe I can help you."

I wanted to talk. He'd gotten the wrong guy, I was innocent—at least innocent of this crime. But it was the wrong time, wrong audience. I don't know why I craved credibility, but I did. I guess we all do. We want the small lies of our small lives to be real. "I love you." "Truth be told." "No, you don't look fat." When you get down to it, we're animals built on deception, on smoke and mirrors. But we still want to be seen as trustworthy.

XYZ appeared in the lights of the cruiser, his hands to his head as he paced back and forth, panicked. He didn't want attention any more than I did. Attention came with questions, and questions led to more questions. XYZ was not a man of answers.

Closing my eyes, I gathered my mind and tried forcing myself into the still, quiet space I'd been trying to reach with the stupid apartment, my deliberate self-denial. That place I knew nothing about.

I found myself laughing. Their systems would turn up nothing on Wellem P. Steertal. INS might find that the name belonged to a man now dead, though I doubted it. And I doubted Mztet would ever seek INS's assistance. He didn't seem the kind of guy to admit he needed help.

Mrztet shifted to face me. "You find this funny?"

I quieted, shook my head. "Okay, listen. If I offer information—" I broke off.

Mztet dropped his voice. "I'm going to be honest with you: talk straight with me and maybe—*maybe*—I can soften your situation." He had no intention of "softening my situation." He was like XYZ that way. All empty promises.

XYZ circled the scene, his face flush with fret.

I said to Mztet, "Have you checked under the floorboards in the bedroom and the kitchen?"

Mztet eyes sparked with excitement. "That's where you hid the stash?"

"There's no stash. I told you that."

He called a deputy over. "Get some crowbars, start pulling up the flooring."

"And in the walls behind the shower," I said, knowing they'd gut the place.

Before he hauled himself out of the cruiser to join the hunt, he flashed me a vicious grin. "Someone has just fucked themself proper."

By noon the next day, I had packed my few belongings and caught a flight south.

By evening, my lips were dusted with powdered sugar from the beignets I ate in the French Quarter. Four miles away was Tulane University, my number two college pick.

◎ ◎ ◎

WHEN PEOPLE SAY "TO be honest with you," I take it to mean that they typically aren't. That the act of being honest is something so uncommon for them that they feel compelled to acknowledge the oddity.

CHAPTER 44

I'D BEEN IN NEW Orleans less than a week when a package arrived at my hotel. A new SIM card and payment for the Iceland job. I'd stopped wondering or worrying how he found me.

Book 7. Thursday, Higgles' text read. *Macao Thunder* by Chet Tyson Miller. Published by Scepter Press, 1962, pure pulp trash. Fun trash, mind you, but trash all the same.

The gist of the book: an alcoholic advertising man heads to Macao, Brazil, to lock down a big account. Add a nubile girl, a dead body, a tropical storm, and a laundry bag full of money and, *voilà*, you have a thriller.

I prayed that the adventure Higgles had in mind would be less thrilling.

I bought a coach-class ticket on TAM Airlines and learned firsthand the difference been a nonstop and a direct flight. I had a direct flight to Rio, which meant we stopped in Miami and sat on the tarmac for nearly an hour.

In Rio I quickly cleared customs, then hopped on another flight to Macao.

I landed Wednesday night, wrinkled, constipated, and hungover from breathing airplane air for far too long. I cabbed it to a semi-cheap hotel, checked in under the name Clement Martin, then fell into a sleep that left me even more exhausted when I woke.

Thursday, I sat around the hotel room watching *Ugly Betty* dubbed in Portuguese and waited for Higgles to contact me.

My mind clouded with thoughts of Sarah. What if I had settled with her? What if I'd married her, built a life? She could have been my why. But I guess I was frightened I would end up like my folks, shackled to a relationship that I couldn't figure a way to free myself from. They'd shown me that marriages were contracts, agreements, business deals. One party promises to provide X while the other offers Y in return. Love, at least for them, was a negotiable point.

I couldn't settle and still keep Kam Manning. Each time I had to leave I'd have to lie. And lies have a way of taking on a life their own, tripping you up.

I stopped my stewing over "what if" when Higgles hit me with a text. *Hard Rock*, it read. *Second floor, northside slots.*

In the hotel lobby, I asked the front desk clerk to call me a cab to take me to the Hard Rock Café.

"In Rio?" he asked. "That is a many, many hours drive."

"Macao's Hard Rock."

He shook his head, thinking. He called his assistant over, who then called over two maids, one of them called her brother-in-law who was a delivery driver and would know such things. The forum agreed that there was a Breezy Café, Paulo's, Green Mountain, Morning Shine, 2202, Fresh Squeeze, Paradise, Emporio, Barraco, Paulista's, and BarBossa but no Hard Rock Café in Macao.

I texted Higgles the hotel lobby's phone number. *Call me now.*

Five minutes later, the phone rang.

"You made me break a winning streak. Where the fuck are you?" Higgles said. In the background, I heard pings and whoops, ringing bells.

"Macao," I said. "Where the fuck are you?"

"Macao."

"Brazil?"

The sound of the slots sang across the line. "There's a Macao in Brazil?" Higgles was in another former Portuguese colony: Macao, China. The gambling capital of the East.

"We must not have read the same book," he said, then complained about how expensive his call was going to be. "Can you get here in twenty-four hours?"

Forty-eight would be the best I could do, but why would I go to China? "You made the mistake," I said. "You come here."

"Can't," he said. "I'm in pretty deep with some things. You've got to get here, and fast. And bring lots of cash. The *Wheel of Fortune* slots are killing me."

"You just said you're on a winning streak."

"I'm fighting a multifront war," he said, then rang off.

CHAPTER 45

I LANDED AT MACAO International Airport at 7:00 p.m. Saturday night. Two Macaos in four days. I was sick with exhaustion and double jetlag. The city smelled like a wet wool sock stuffed with fried pork.

The old world clashed with the new; beautiful colonial buildings were bathed in blaring, ugly neon. Before the Portuguese colonized it, Macao was known as Haojing, the Oyster Mirror, or Jinghai, the Mirror Sea. Names change and change again. It made me think of Ray-Ray and his atlases.

Ray-Ray. While I owed my current life to him, he'd faded from my mind, disappearing into a fog of memories false and true.

I found Higgles camped at a video poker machine at the Hard Rock, hitting button after button. He was at home.

I sat down next to him. "Never understood the appeal of these things," he said, not looking over. "Kick me a few bucks, cousin."

"What's with the 'cousin' stuff?" I asked, pulling out some money. "I'm getting this back, right?"

"Just give me some money."

I peeled off five hundred-dollar bills, handed them to him.

"Maybe a bit more?" he said, holding the bills like they were a soiled condom.

I kept my hands in my lap. He shrugged, then pocketed the money. "Interested in some breakfast?" he said, standing.

"It's around nine p.m. Let's try for some dinner."

He led me out of the casino and into the chokingly humid night, sliding through the streets to a greasy place serving an all-you-can-eat buffet. "This place will change your life."

"I'm fine with my life as it is," I said.

He eyed me hard. "Really?"

Taking plates, we queued up. The room was crowded, the linen on the tables stained. "Try the shrimp rolls," he said, tonging six onto his plate. "Really good."

"I'm not real hungry." Digestive acid and airplane food battled for territory in my belly.

"Load up anyway." Higgles winked. "It'll save me from having to get up again."

I loaded my plate with shrimp rolls.

We settled at an empty table near the kitchen. My nerves were a jangled mess from lack of sleep. I kept flinching from the slam and clatter of dishware in the kitchen.

Higgles didn't speak as he worked through his plate. Finished, he attacked mine, then went back for more.

Finally through his third plate, he licked his fingers. "This is it, the big gig we've been waiting for. We hit this right and we can both take a nice vacation."

I asked what the take was on the job. He named a figure. "A straight-up fifty-fifty split."

The number was impressive, even more so because I knew Higgles was discounting the take by at least thirty percent, planning on pocketing the difference.

"How about seventy-thirty split," I said. "With me getting the seventy."

"How about," he eyed me, "we not get greedy." He said he'd burned a lot of bridges to get the information. "Believe it or not, you have the easy end of the job."

I didn't believe him. But I didn't push it either. "Okay, fifty-fifty."

"Good," he said, getting up once again for food.

Returning with a full plate, he thumped down in his seat. "Fair warning. We pull this off and the whole scene will be radioactive with suspicion. It's got to be pristine. Leave a trail like last time and the blowback will be pure misery."

"What trail?" I'd thought the Iceland job had gone smoothly, all things considered.

He laughed bitterly, bit into a shrimp roll. "If you only knew."

Pulling out a business card from his shirt pocket, he slid it across the table to me. There was writing on the back. Time, place, details. "All you have to do is meet this guy in Milan and get the documents." He started to say something more but bit the words off.

"That's it?"

"That's it," he said. "Get the documents, get back stateside with them, then you're off to Hawaii."

"Hawaii?"

"Or wherever you want to vacation."

It seemed straightforward, which meant it wasn't. "It feels like you're walking me toward a trap."

Higgles slurped his tea. "Of course it's a trap. There's risk. Lots of risk. If there weren't, the money wouldn't be so good. But I've cracked open a window of opportunity for us. We've got to grab it while we can."

"Why don't you do it yourself?"

"Because the contact knows me. I've worked with him before. And if he sees me he'll know something's wrong. Besides," he said, "the prick has a grudge against me. I nearly got him killed last time we worked together."

"How?"

Higgles shrugged. "I shot him in the back. Twice." He held up a finger. "Not without cause, mind you."

I looked at the business card. "Milan." I'd never been to Italy.

Higgles rose from the table. "Try the limoncello when you get there," he said. "It's to die for."

CHAPTER 46

Haven, Florida

THE WOMAN FINISHES HER gin, rises from the chair, and ambles to the bathroom. "Do you know what déjà vu is?" she calls to me through the closed door.

"Of course."

"I mean the scientific bit." Her voice sounds like it's trapped in a bottle, hollow and echoing.

I don't.

She comes out wearing nothing but her blouse, which falls to her thighs. "It's called—" She breaks off, trying to remember. "I've forgotten what it's called. But basically it has to do with your short-term memory getting messed up with your long-term. They somehow overlap and the short-term memory barely registers before the long-term grabs hold, making you think you've had that memory forever. So when you think you've experienced something before, you *have*—if just a fraction of a fraction of a second prior."

I wait for her to make some kind of sweeping statement, for her to say she's felt she's known me forever.

She doesn't.

She picks up her empty glass, holds it out to me. "Be kind," she says. "Refresh my drink."

When I hand her a full glass, her fingers linger on mine, sending a charge through me.

"You can't get me drunk, you know. Something about my genetic makeup. I get tipsy, but never drunk. No matter how much I drink."

"That's a handy trick."

"It's a horrible trick," she says, the morning light wrapping tightly around her. She seems to be miserable. Sweat plasters her hair to her face, turning it to yarn.

She rolls the icy glass across her forehead. "I have no way of knowing when to stop because I have no need to stop."

Seeing her sweat makes me uncomfortable, hot. Perspiration travels down my sides, down my back. "Take off your blouse."

Sighing, she sets her drink down and slips the shirt from her shoulders. She turns around, displaying herself. She has a fit body for such a heavy drinker, for someone her age. Small, teacup-sized breasts, an ample ass, a fairly flat stomach. She's shaved clean, no pubic hair. Turning around full circle, she bends over, allowing me a full screening. "Well?" she says, peering through her parted legs.

"Nice."

"I mean," she rights herself, "are you going to stay dressed?"

"Say 'Simon says,'" I say, kicking off my shoes.

"Simon says." She watches patiently as I strip.

Naked, I step toward her.

She lunges at me, grapples my torso in a bracing hold. We fumble to the mattress, kissing violently, awkwardly. There is something menacing, violent about her kisses. They're not about desire but something else. She kisses with an end goal in mind.

A foul burning taste kicks up from the back of my throat, choking me. I know this taste. I had it once before when I was swept from the beach by a riptide and pummeled along the ocean floor by an undertow. It's a taste of terror, of knowing too late that I'm in a situation I have no control over.

I stop her.

She starts again.

I stop her again and rise from the mattress.

She clasps my arm, holding me. "This isn't going to work unless you put some heart into it," she says, then takes my cock in her mouth.

I respond with more heart.

She pulls away just as I'm about to come.

I fall on her.

Elbows, knees, a few knocks of the chins. My sweat becomes hers. Sex is an endeavor one never truly masters. Even if you've had a hundred partners and done it a million times, there's something unnatural about it. It is not a pretty process. It's a sloppy, sweaty, primordial wrestle, all to satisfy a selfish yearning.

She cries out like a child getting her fingers slammed in a car door. "Jesus," she says, and wraps her legs tight around my torso.

Then she does something no one's ever done to me before. She sets her teeth deep into the side of my neck. Bites me hard.

A barbed wire of pain rams through me, snaking down my neck to my groin. Violent, dreadful, blissful. I come for what feels an hour while fighting to free myself from her.

I can't break free. Her legs are wrapped firmly around me, her jaws clamped solid to my neck. She's a crocodile, fast and unyielding.

I jab her twice in the ribs hard, which is enough to make her finally unlock her bite. Wrestling away, I get to my feet. "What the fuck is wrong with you?" I touch my neck. My fingers come away wet with brilliant red blood.

Lying on the mattress, she smiles up at me. Her teeth are rusted bright. "Sorry," she says. "It just something I can't help. Like dying." She rolls over, lies on her stomach. "You're not angry at me, are you?"

"I think it's time you go," I say, grabbing my underwear. I use it to bandage the bleeding.

She struggles off the mattress, picks up her glass, and strolls to the kitchen. "Where?"

"Charm's, your place. Anywhere," I say, heading to the bathroom. I examine the bite in the mirror. It's ugly, exaggerated, seeping blood. It looks like a Halloween wound made of a strawberry puree and maple syrup.

I splash water on it then dab it with a fistful of toilet paper.

After the bleeding slows, I return to the room to find the woman seated in ratty red recliner, the bottle of gin at her feet. She has a different glass, a large tumbler. It's packed full with ice.

"Weird," I say, holding a wad of toilet paper to my neck. "It looks like you're settling in when I know for a fact you're on the way out."

"Oh no," she says, catching me with a direct stare. "I'm here for the duration."

Anger frosts my lungs. "Get the fuck out."

"At least say please."

"Please get the fuck out," I say.

She politely asks me to hand her her purse.

I toss it to her, hoping she's going.

She smiles, though not with happiness. "I'm not leaving."

I surge toward her, grab her by the jaw, digging my fingers in.

She stares up at me, subdued.

"What's keeping me from throttling your ass and tossing you to the street naked?" I say, a flash of heat pounding at the back of my eyes.

She says something I can't understand. I release my grip on her jaw. "What?"

"I said, your upbringing," she says, touching her cold tumbler to her jaw. "That's what's stopping you. And one other thing." She opens her purse.

"And that would be?"

"This." She pulls out a pistol, small, silver, and beautiful.

Blood thrashes through my head, sharpening my vision, making me keenly aware of my surroundings. It's not fear I feel, even as I realize I've just handed her a gun—which she now points at me. I should be afraid. I'm not. If anything, I feel strangely relieved. The situation has been defined. I know where I stand.

But then she says something that does terrify me, something I haven't heard in at least four years.

My name. First, middle, and last.

◎ ◎ ◎

WHEN THERE IS NO way out, push on. Find a way further in.

CHAPTER 47

MILAN ENDED UGLY.

Gunfire, a taxi crash, both the cabbie and the contact dead.

Higgles' instructions had been simple. Fly in, pick up a packet of lithographed Chanukah greeting cards from a print shop, then meet my contact at Duomo Plaza. Hand him the cards and he'd hand me the documents.

From the start, things went bad. My flight out of Macao was delayed three hours. The trash collectors' strike in Milan created traffic jams. The address Higgles gave me for the print shop was wrong.

I finally found the place, got the cards, and made it to Duomo Plaza fifty minutes late.

I spotted the contact immediately. Higgles was always vague on the description, but this man stood out among the tourists. Italian, dapper, and impeccably coiffed, he looked refined and easily pissed off. He probably put on a tie just to make breakfast. I sat at the table next to his, and ordered a limoncello and an ice water. I said, "The Irish make wonderful pizza," to which he replied in a thick accent, "But the French make it even better."

It was the signal.

Without looking at me, he said, "You're late." His face was coated in sweat, glistening like it'd been dipped in butter. Still, he gave off an aura of comfort, coolness.

I said nothing, then laid the cards on his table.

He counted them out, his delicate fingers gauging the weight and texture of each. Done, he slid the cards back in the package, and pushed them toward me. "There's only ten," he said. "The deal was for twelve."

Bile spiked my throat. The three continents in five days, the exhaustion, the whole fucked-up situation enraged me. I wanted to stomp someone, maybe this pompous ass sitting next to me. But I swallowed my anger, kept quiet. It was something I had learned from my father.

For nearly a decade, my father leased and serviced photocopy machines to big businesses. High-end machines that could churn through reams of paper in a matter of minutes. One of the two things he said he learned from that job was to keep his mouth shut when someone had a complaint. "Often, they just want to vent. A lot of times it doesn't even have to do with the broken copier. It's just life chewing at them. The copier is the last straw," he said. "So you let them vent, you nod a lot, then you do what you have to do and move on."

The second thing he learned was that ninety percent of the time, the copier wasn't even broken. It was just a paper jam or that they forget to turn it on. "But I always go through all the motions, break the machine apart, service it, even if it's fine, just hadn't been turned on. The last thing you want to do is make your client feel like an idiot, even when they are."

The contact sipped his espresso, then said something in Italian. Then, as if speaking to a child, said, "That's what we call incompetence." His voice was even. He held up the cards. "How do you plan to rectify this?"

I took a breath, slowly released it. "I'll go back to the shop, check with the man I got the cards from."

The contact insisted on coming with.

The heat had set the whole town boiling with irritability. In our short walk to the cab station, we passed two women shouting and spitting at each other, a young couple arguing, and an old man being taunted by a teenage girl.

My contact puffed his cheeks, then let out a hissing breath of disgust. "I fucking hate Italians. Truth doesn't matter to them. All that matters is their honor."

"I thought you were Italian," I said.

"I am."

We found a cab. The seats were hot and the entire interior reeked of body odor and processed garlic.

I gave the cabbie the address. He made the sign of the cross, dropped the car in gear, and tore off.

When the cabbie made a left onto a narrow street, my contact berated him. It was the wrong way, the slow way, the out-of-the-way way that the cabbie was taking us. "The bastard thinks we're tourists, he's padding his fare," my contact said. He struck the cabbie on the shoulder, yelling.

Still driving, the cabbie wheeled his head around to glare at him. A shouting match erupted between the two, spit flying with each word.

His eyes off the road, the cabbie rear-ended a black Mercedes trying to park.

The Mercedes' driver got out of his car, his hand chopping the air like a maestro's while he screamed.

Perfect, I thought, sweating in the back seat. *More problems.*

Our cabbie stayed put, hurtling curses at him from the safety of the car, then let loose a wild scream that silenced his rival. The man stood stunned a moment, looking a bit lost, then turned back to his car. The incident was over, I thought, then I saw the man pull a pistol from under the driver's seat, calmly stroll back toward us. Seeing it too, my contact laughed. "Politics at its best," he said.

Our driver joined in, laughing as he revved the engine to take off.

His laugh was cut short by a sharp *boomthumt* from the gun. A bullet kissed the cabbie in the temple, opening his head in a spray of brains and bone that splattered the passenger side window. His body jolted, his foot jamming the gas pedal, and we rammed the Mercedes onto the sidewalk as the cab launched down the length of the street. We careened violently off one parked car then another, finally slamming to a stop when we hit the corner of a building at the intersection.

I found myself on the floor, wedged hard into some perverse contortion against the back of the driver's seat. "Holy fuck," I said, fighting to untangle myself. Extracting myself, I climbed from the cab and examined the situation. "Fuck, fuck, fuck."

The cabbie was dead, his shattered head poking through windshield. My contact sat upright in the backseat, no longer dapper. His face was a veil of blood. A flap of his forehead hung off of him like a cold cut.

I reached in to feel his pulse, but then jerked my hand back. I didn't want to touch him. I listened for a breath. No breath.

I turned to leave then stopped. The documents, the cards.

Fighting down a mouthful of vomit, I rifled his jacket pockets, retrieved the items, and then ran as fast as I could.

Twenty minutes later, I was on the A9 racing north toward Lake Como in a stolen Fiat, my nerves frayed and my leg, somehow cut, throbbing with pain.

Pulling the car to the side of the road, I dialed Higgles. It kicked directly into voice mail.

I texted him. *911. Call me now.*

He called. "This best be good."

"Actually," I said, "it's bad." I cranked the car's AC, fighting to stay cool. "We've hit a snag."

"You mean *you've* hit a snag," he said. "What happened?"

I explained.

"And you fled the scene?"

"Of course I fled the scene. What else was I to do?"

"Wait for the police. Give a statement. Get medical attention like any other normal, innocent person would," he said. "I don't appreciate the position you've put me in."

"You? What about me? What about the position I'm in?"

"You put yourself there." He sighed, then coughed. "Fuck, cousin. I'm going to have to do something I know I'll regret." He gave me a PO Box address in Haven, Florida. "FedEx the documents and the cards there."

"Then what?"

"Then forget the address, forget I ever mentioned Florida," he said, "and somehow find your way home."

CHAPTER 48

SHATTERED GLASS, CAR WRECK, dead bodies. Milan sparked a memory I'd fought to forget.

Driving back from my graduation dinner, my parents kept at each other until my father abruptly pulled to a hard stop at the intersection of Kelper Street and Jacoby Avenue and turned off the engine. "That is a real stop sign," he said, pointing to it. "And this is a real stop."

Off to the left, a single light drilled toward the intersection, heading our direction. A motorcycle.

Clement.

"You've made your point," my mother said. "You can go now."

Silent, my father glared straight ahead.

From behind, a truck's headlights beamed. The driver tapped his horn, waiting for my father to move.

Still staring ahead, his jaw tight, my father lowered his window and signaled the truck to go around.

The truck pulled past us, lumbering through the intersection.

I shifted in the back seat. "Can we please go?"

"Not until your mother apologizes."

"I'm sorry," she said. "Now can we go? I've got to use the toilet."

My father turned to her. "Never, ever tell me how to drive again." He started the car again and dropped the car in gear.

Clement was approaching the intersection full speed.

"Watch—" I never finished my sentence.

My father punched the accelerator, yanked the steering wheel left to make a turn.

A screech of tires, a strobe of light slicing through the windshield, then a spectacular explosion of motion and noise.

I remember my mother's scream, Clement launching through the windshield, a spray of glass hitting my face. I remember our car shuddering as it careened forward into a telephone pole, and then into the ditch.

◎ ◎ ◎

MEMORIES ARE SCARS CREATED by loss, not love.

CHAPTER 49

RIBES, FAVORS, AND JETTING across the country on a lead. Higgles finally tracked the man down. *Payback,* he thought, watching him stroll across the parking lot.

He thought about the situation, thought about all that had led to this moment. I'll hand it to him. Laughter welled in his throat, choking him. "Hand it to him," he said aloud. "I'll hand it to him."

CHAPTER 50

AFTER MILAN CAME ATHENS. My contact shouldn't have threatened me with blackmail. What exactly he had on me, I couldn't say. I could barely understand his English, though his threat was clear.

I gave him a firm answer in the form of a small marble statue to his head. But the fucker wouldn't go down. He lurched about the place like he was determined to get blood on every inch of every wall.

New body, new nightmares.

Higgles had me ship the package to the Florida PO Box. Again, he told me to forget the address. Forget he'd even mentioned Haven, Florida.

Back in New Orleans, a package arrived. Cash. The Athens job paid in full, with an extra thousand. Also, a new phone.

A text from Higgles. *Austin, Texas. A simple job.*

Unlike the other jobs.

I was to be there by Wednesday morning, wait for instructions. *Fuck that*, I thought. Being Higgles' surrogate, doing the dangerous work while he stayed safe and hidden, was bad for my health. Time I started doing a bit of Tom Sawyering myself, getting paid while someone else painted the fence.

"So how are you figuring this works?" the assistant manager of ReadiXpress, an Austin messenger service, asked skeptically.

My hopes bottomed out. The three other places I'd called required things I didn't want to provide, like my personal information and a credit card number. If I farmed this out, then I wanted to leave as small a footprint as possible. No records trailing back to me if something went wrong. "I'll overnight seventy-five dollars in cash to ReadiXpress," I explained, trying to sound everyday casual, two chums chatting. "Tomorrow, I'll call with the details. You guys make the pick-up, express the package to an address I'll give you. That's it." In the background, a phone rang. Someone laughed like a carnival clown, high and sharp. "A simple job," I said, Higgles' own words escaping my mouth.

"Yeah, well, here's the thing." His voice rattled with phlegm. "ReadiXpress is real prickly about no-record shit like this. They got in some trouble with some Mexican Viagra last year."

Austin, here I come. I already tasted the sweltering air, and felt the bites from vicious Texas mosquitoes.

"But I'm thinking..." He paused, grumbled his throat clear. "Tomorrow's my day off."

By the time we settled, he'd hemmed and hawed me up to two hundred dollars to do the job himself. "Personalized service," he said. I overnighted the cash.

Higgles texted me first thing the next morning with the details. The meet was to take place out front of the Sterling Hackfield bank in downtown Pflugerville. Ten a.m. sharp.

"Shit, Pflugerville?" my guy said, his voice sticky with sleep. The call had woken him. "That's like a forty-minute drive."

"Then you best get going."

"What I best do is nothing. Not until that money arrives."

"It'll be waiting for you when you get back."

"And if it ain't?"

"Then keep whatever's in the package you pick up."

The next three hours dragged on like a church fundraiser, each minute inching slowly into the next. Finally, my guy called. "Fucking traffic was crazy."

"You got the package?"

I pulled the phone from my ear as he hacked up a lung full of mucus. "What's with your boy?" he asked after spitting.

"Who?"

"The guy with the package. What's with his face? Looked like a bad asphalt job, all pitted and bumpy."

My kidneys throbbed. *Pockmark.* He was talking about Pockmark, from the shelter. What was his connection to Higgles, to all this? "But you got the package, right?" I forced the fear from my voice. Maybe it was just some other guy with a bad skin.

"Yeah, the money's here. Just like you said."

"I mean the package from Pockmark."

"Pockmark?"

"The guy in Pflugerville."

"Right." He grouches up more slime. "Got it. Thing is, that package I picked up doesn't weigh the same as the one you sent."

"Meaning?"

"Meaning I think we need to balance them out." He wanted another hundred for his efforts.

I gave him a PO Box number, said to overnight the package there.

"And the extra something-something?"

"I get the package," I said, "you get the money."

"What, I'm supposed to just trust you?"

I hung up.

The next morning, two packages were waiting for me, both with Austin return addresses. The first had a partially completed mortgage application, a stick of Juicy Fruit, and a flash drive clipped to a red lanyard, the kind conference attendees wear. Except this one had blue cartoon horses dancing the length, each with a letter or number on their belly. KTU9J7L it read. Or L7J9UTK, depending on which way it was read. A ship registration, a license plate number, or a fuck-up at the manufacturer, I didn't know.

The second package held a phone book with half the pages torn out. I flipped through it. Every few pages, a business name would be circled.

My Austin guy was fucking with me. He'd said he picked up
a package. Singular. What this second package was, I didn't know.
And which one was real?

Higgles had been blowing up my phone with texts, demanding an
update. *We're clover,* I finally wrote. *Austin packages in hand.*

Packages? More than 1?

Fat fingers, I replied. *Package. 1.*

Day late, Higgles replied, and instructed me to FedEx the package
to the Florida PO Box.

I studied the items, knowing I was overlooking something obvious,
a clue that pieced it all together and made everything make sense. I even
hit the Internet café to see what was on the flash drive. One document.
A thirty-two page PowerPoint of chicken recipes, clip art included.
I couldn't figure it out.

And what if I did? What then?

I deleted five of the recipes, swapped the Juicy Fruit with a pack
of Big Red, tore some more pages from the phonebook, filled out the
rest of the mortgage application with bullshit information, and added
a partially complete Sudoku puzzle. I packed it up in a single box then
texted Higgles that the package was off.

It wasn't. I stopped short of sending it and instead tucked the
package under my bathroom sink. Dependability is only appreciated
when it's missing. Higgles needed a reminder of how valuable I was to
him. He needed to realize that as long as I had what he wanted, I had
the upper hand.

There'd be blowback, for sure, but I'd handle it—somehow.

My Austin guy's game of sending a second package pissed me off.
I called him three times. He didn't pick up. I called ReadiXpress. MIA.
He hadn't shown for work that morning.

Let it go.

I mailed him a coupon for a McDonald's small coffee and a one-
dollar bill with *We're even* written on it instead of the hundred dollars
he was expecting.

I opened a beer, tried to do a crossword puzzle, but worry dug into my bowels like a porcelain shard. Pockmark in Austin? Higgles and him in cahoots? Who needs real conspiracies or enemies when your mind churns them out? I retrieved the package from the bathroom, deciding to send it to Higgles. No good could come from having it. Then I put it back. Hold firm, I told myself. Higgles would get the package once he showed me some respect. Gratitude.

By evening, my worries weakened. After my third beer, they collapsed all together.

I locked the doors and headed to bed feeling fairly secure about everything.

But then I woke Friday morning with what felt like a table leg jammed hard to my throat.

My eyes opened on a man dressed completely in green—ski mask, long sleeve shirt, and gloves. Had I seen him walk into a grocery store or church, I might have laughed. He looked like a frog. But standing over my bed pressing something knotty and hard into my neck, he wasn't so funny.

I smacked at whatever he was ramming me with, and rolled from bed onto the floor.

He wasn't holding a table leg. It was his hand. Or the stub where his hand used to be. He caught my head with it in three rapid whacks. I clambered to my feet and charged at the frogman, landing a punch to his face. He cried sharply and stumbled back, punching a hole through the cheap bedroom door.

I went at him, swinging wildly, blindly, and connecting more often than I expected. Frogman retreated down the hall. He whipped his stub back and forth, whapped me once on my left ear then followed it up with a homerun to my temple. I crashed hard to the floor.

Frogman bolted, making his escape out the open front door.

What the fuck? I struggled to my feet. If the guy was a burglar, he had picked the wrong place. I didn't have much to steal. The hidden Austin package, my Higgles books, some clothing. But no TV, no stereo, no computer. Locking the front door, I headed to the kitchen for water, my ear ringing and throat throbbing like my Adam's apple had been cracked.

I choked down some water, and tried to think. Blood trickled down my cheek. Who was frogman? What was he after?

A pounding on my front door kicked my heart into my mouth. I held to the wall, edged my way to the door. The banging sounded again, followed by a jiggling of doorknob. "Open up," a voice called. "It's me."

Fucking Higgles.

I let him in.

His hair was greasy and matted and he was covered in sweat. He wore a dingy white T-shirt and jeans. The right side of his face was red and swollen.

He took one look at me, said, "Shit, tell me I'm not too late."

"To save me? Yeah, too late." I felt like I'd swallowed gravel. I rubbed my throat, fighting off the urge to cry. "Looks like frogman paid you a visit, too."

"I meant the package," he said, heading straight to the bathroom. He retrieved the package from under the sink.

"How'd you know?"

"How'd I know what?" The package was securely under his arm. "Frogman? What are you talking about?"

I let it go, felt a sense of relief that he was actually there. I touched his face. He jerked back like I'd jabbed him with a branding iron. "Yeah, I got hit, too. Three guys. Hispanic and pissed off. But no frogman, whatever that is." He tapped the box he was holding. "So you shipped the package off safely, huh?"

"Yesterday, yeah," I said, in no mood for his bullshit games. "Safe and sound. You should have it by now."

He held the box up. "Well lookie here. I *do* have it." He grazed me with a look of contempt. "Get dressed. We're leaving."

"Who did this?" I said, needing to know what was happening, why we'd been attacked. He didn't answer. "Higgles?"

"Shit, no. That idiot? He didn't do this," he said, his voice spiking.

I was confused. "Who didn't?"

"Higgles," he said.

"I sure as fuck hope *you* didn't. And why are you calling yourself by your own name? What are you, royalty?"

Higgles forced a cough. "Right, right. You Ray-Ray, me Higgles." He rapped the top of his skull with is fist. "Higgles, Higgles, you idiot. Higgles' head is a bit messed up today. Higgles needs a vacation." He pointed to me. "Now get dressed."

Higgles had lost it and was freaking me out.

Once dressed, I cautiously followed him out to a dirty blue Prius.

He forced the keys into my hand. "Drive."

I took the driver's seat, buckled up. I always buckle.

He settled into the passenger's seat, calling out "Shotgun!" then tossed the package in the back. Laughing at his own bad joke, he pulled out a Gauloise and sparked the tobacco, inhaling like he'd surfaced from someplace deep.

I kicked over the ignition, turned to Higgles, waiting for instructions on where to go.

"Higgles says, 'Forward,'" he said, blowing a cloud of smoke at me. I'd never seen him smoke, but then I'd never seen him do a lot of things.

Questions pinged through my mind. What the fuck was Higgles doing at my place? How did he know I hadn't sent the package? And how did he know exactly where to find it? Instead, I asked, "Was it Pockmark who attacked me? What did this guy want?"

"Frogman. Pockmark. What is this, a video game? Cousin, whoever it was, they're pissed off," he said. "So. Austin. Good town, right?"

I struggled to swallow. "Beautiful. Hot. I can definitely see why it's the honeymoon capital of America," I said, not having a clue where that came from.

"Really, the honeymoon capital? Didn't know that." He dragged hard on his cigarette while motioning for me to turn left at the stop sign. "Thing is, cousin, that's the reason that guy was here, why you— why *we*—were attacked. Austin. You must have fucked something up."

He reached over, poked me in the temple with his index finger. "I mean, aside from the obvious. Anything you want to share, cousin?"

I shook my head.

"I'll let you in on a little secret: as with most everything, the problem rests with the translation. You know that when they translated the original text from ancient Greek, they went with the word 'betray' when the literal meaning of the word was 'handing over.' There is a different word for 'betrayed.' They have vastly different meanings."

"What are you talking about?" My throat ached dully and I was having a hard time swallowing. The smoke wasn't helping.

"Judas. The Bible. The crucifixion. The whole basis of Christianity. Christ wasn't betrayed. He was handed over." He pointed the glowing end of his cigarette at me. "Do you know what *akrasia* means? It's Greek, too."

"No."

"Unfortunately, I've forgotten what it means," he said.

Frogman, the attack, Higgles appearing minutes later with a battered face. The truth settled in my mind. Decked in green, Higgles had come after me, run off, stripped, then returned to finish the job. I glanced over at him. He still had both his hands. Meaning...I didn't know. Higgles wasn't Frogman.

The problem rests with the translation.

Just how fucked was I? Was I driving toward my own grave? So much for respect and gratitude. Sure, Higgles and I weren't equal partners, but I'd always thought he had my back, at least a little bit. Maybe I was no more than a means to an end for him, a disposable delivery boy—like my guy in Austin.

A briny goo dripped into my throat. *Kill Higgles*, the thought came, *before he kills you.*

Glancing over, I saw he didn't have his seat belt on. "Where are we going?" I asked again, my foot falling hard to the accelerator. I kept a sharp eye for a tree, a pole, or a parked car. Now was the time to sever our relationship. Get up a good speed and slam the car into something that'd launch my erstwhile partner through the windshield. Slam into something he wouldn't walk away from.

"You know," he said, "your paranoia isn't a bad thing."

"What makes you think I'm paranoid?" I said, paranoid. The car edged to forty, then forty-five miles per hour.

Higgles coughed up a laugh. "Cousin, you need a hobby, something to fill your spare time. Take up Facebook or knitting or something. Find an outlet for your pent-up energy." He turned on the radio, then turned it off. "Personally," he said, "I collect calling cards."

The car hit fifty. I blew through a stop sign without a flinch from Higgles.

"I said 'calling cards,' cousin," he repeated.

"Stop with the fucking 'cousin' bit," I said. "And who uses calling cards anymore?"

The lampposts ticked past alongside the road. I edged the car to sixty miles per hour. A straight-on impact, or an angled passenger's sideswipe? Which was best?

"Boy, this car's got speed for a hybrid," Higgles said as we powered through another intersection. "Poor people use them. Calling cards, I mean." He pulled out his wallet, showed me some cards. "Prepaid minutes. The ones for the Middle East and Africa are fantastic." He shuffled the cards. "Big Black Daddy. Allah Way Home. Pootie Ring. Who the fuck comes up with these names?" He pointed to the Sweet Dog Diner. "Turn in up there."

My foot slacked off the gas, hit the brake firmly, forcing the car to decelerate. Higgles hand pressed hard against the dashboard, keeping him from slamming into the windshield. "Jesus, cousin, this isn't NASCAR."

I rolled into the parking lot. "What are we doing?" I turn off the engine.

"Getting something to eat," he said, reaching over to pull the keys from the ignition.

Was this my last meal? Did he plan on letting me fill my belly before killing me, or was he really just taking me out for pancakes and sausage?

I followed Higgles from the car.

"No," he said. "You wait. Join me in seven minutes." He held up an open hand and two fingers on the other. "Seven minutes, got it? Not a second before."

I sat back down, massaged my tender throat. The dashboard clock read 7:04 a.m. I glanced into the backseat, expecting to find the green ski mask, gloves, and shirt. Nothing. Just the package. Maybe Higgles was right. Maybe I was paranoid. My worry broke like a fever, exiting my body with a shiver. Maybe I'd been wrong. Even though he was an asshole, maybe Higgles wasn't out to get me.

Through the diner's plate glass window, I saw my partner take a booth near the back. I saw him order. I saw his food delivered a few minutes later.

At 7:11 a.m., I headed in.

I slid into the booth. Toast, a coffee, scrambled eggs. It looked good.

"You have to remember," Higgles said, "we're magicians. We're in the art of making something appear one way when it really is another." He pulled a clipping from his back pocket and handed it to me. "Read it."

It was an article from the *Austin Chronicle,* dated two days prior, when I was to have been in Austin. The story showcased a magician and his tricks of making large objects—elephants, cars, a radio tower—disappear. The reporter himself had witnessed a house vanish from the middle of a barren field. There was nothing around for miles. The audience had been granted the opportunity to tour the house, touch the walls, see that it was real. Solid. A place a family once lived in.

Then, as complete night took hold, the visitors were directed to bleachers some thirty yards from the front of the house itself. Klieg lights drilled the brick house, illuminating it brightly for everyone to see. The magician said his words, made his motions. The white-blue beams on the house went dark and a long curtain was drawn before the bleachers, the field an impromptu stage. The moonless night stood black. Five minutes, ten. The crowd sat patiently in the dark silence, our intrepid reporter among them.

Finally, the magician boomed an incantation, and an explosion of light shocked the audience's eyes. The curtain dropped.

There was a collective gasp.

The spotlights cut the night, beaming without a break.

Nothing.

The house was gone. No sign of it. Just empty fields. A stunned audience. Then deafening applause.

Higgles tapped the table. "I have a hunch that you went off script on the Austin deal. And by going off script, you pulled the curtain too soon. You fucked up our magic trick." He slid from the booth, stood. "Someone rather nasty must have noticed. Now they're trying to pull a magic trick of their own and make you disappear."

Disappeared as in dead, buried in some scrubland outside of town, never to be found. "So what should I do?" I fought to steady my breathe.

Higgles picked up the butter knife, eyed his blurry reflection. "Relocate." He pointed the knife at me. "Breakfast is the most important meal of the day," he said, then tossed the knife on the table. It clattered to a standstill. "Eat hearty." He made his way to the door. "And don't forget to tip the waitress."

Through the glass, I watch him climb in the Prius and pull away.

I picked up the coffee Higgles had ordered for me and took a sip. It tasted like hot ocean, briny and foul. Chasing it with water made it worse. Higgles had spiked that with salt, too.

I studied the eggs, the toast, the hash browns, afraid of what he might have done to them.

I should have wrecked the car. I should have killed him when I had the chance.

◉ ◉ ◉

IT WAS SIMPLY SLIGHT of hand on a large scale. The house didn't disappear.

The bleachers were set on dolly tracks, slowly, imperceptibly, swiveling the audience so that the house, when "revealed" would be out of their sightline. While the breathless crowded stared at an empty field, the house stood off to the side, alone, empty and hidden by the dark.

CHAPTER 51

I WAS OUT. FOR good. No more Higgles, no more hiding or worrying about Pockmark, no more Kam Manning or strangers trying to kill me.

I booked a flight to New York. Sarah would be my salvation. I knew that if I got her back, everything would somehow be okay. We'd broken on a bad note, but I'd make it up. All I need was the chance.

It took me a day to find her. She'd moved from her old place on the Lower East Side up to Inwood. Upper State Manhattan. The top tip of the island. Quiet. Leafy. Residential. She'd made the first step on the journey toward the suburbs and her life of more, the life she felt she deserved.

I could get used to the normal life, I kept telling myself. Get a dull job at a movie theater or some magazine, have dinner parties with people I didn't particularly like, shop at Ikea, even endure holiday visits to Sarah's folks. I'd murdered men. There was no way domesticity was more difficult.

I staked out her place, waiting for the right moment. Tuesday she got home late, after eleven, looking exhausted. Not the best time. Wednesday she didn't come home at all. Thursday evening she popped out of the subway station just after six, smiling. She headed into her building. The light to her place flicked on. The fourth floor, front of the building.

Now was my chance.

I waited half an hour. Then I waited more. I was nervous, didn't know what I'd say to her, or how she'd react to me just showing up.

Play the long game, I told myself. I doubt she'd let me in. And even if she did, there was no way she'd fall lovingly into my arms the moment she saw me. Just be cool. It'd take time. Tonight was the reintroduction. Tomorrow, the rebuilding of the relationship.

I stood at her building's door for five minutes, working up the courage. When I finally rang, the door buzzed open instantly. Not a word over the intercom. It was like she was expecting me, knew I was coming.

I pushed in, pausing just inside the door to tamp down my jitters. It's only Sarah, I kept telling myself. A known element. Someone I had a bond with.

A voice stabbed me from behind. "Thanks, bro." Some guy slid in the building before the door closed. He bounded past.

Irritation lit through me. "Hey, you live here?"

"Seems like it." He took the stairs two at a time. "I'm here enough."

I followed, my eyes boring a hole through the back of his blond head. Second floor then third, he plowed ahead.

I should have gotten Sarah something, I thought, climbing. *Flowers or candy*. But no, no gifts. Not tonight. Too cheap, sentimental. A gift tonight would be a sure sign of guilt, a confession that I was in the wrong. Not a strong way to rekindle a relationship.

Nearly the fourth floor, my feet stalled. The blond guy was knocking on a door. Six apartments per floor, a one in thirty-six chance.

No fucking way, I thought, glancing around the banister.

He stood waiting.

When the door swung open, my soul curdled. There she stood. Sarah. Pretty, smiling, and welcoming. The guy kissed her twice, said something that made her laugh, and then stepped in.

The door clicked shut.

Sarah was gone, had moved on. *Of course she did*, I thought. *Of course.*

Outside, the spring breeze was raw. I walked the length of the island, down Broadway from 218th Street to Battery City Park. Not once did I see a telephone pole. In Manhattan, all the lines are buried, the voices traveling through the dark, cold earth.

CHAPTER 52

I settled in New York City, out in the Bronx just off the Major Deegan Expressway, and took to reading women's magazines—*Cosmo, Elle, Marie Claire*, and *Seventeen*. My dream of normalcy, of being with Sarah, had been ambushed, gravely wounded. I had nothing. I had to start fresh, anew.

Except I still had Higgles. He texted, *Book 8. George Orwell's* Homage to Catalonia.

One thing—one of the many things—I learned reading the women's magazines was that breaking free of an abusive relationship was tough. Nearly impossible. We can't do the hard work needed because we can't get past our own lies. We keep telling ourselves "this time will be different." It's not. It'll never be.

Every article advised the same thing: cut all ties with the abuser. No contact at all.

Love is a strong bond. Trauma is even stronger.

I bought a ticket to Spain.

Landing in Barcelona, I jumped on a train that clattered southeast along the coastline, per Higgles' instruction.

This time would be different, I told myself. *This time I'm in control.*

I met him in a wine bar in Alicante, Spain.

Nestled on a narrow street no car could manage, the tavern had the feel of a sea-warped schooner that'd been upended on the rocks. Timber beams, plank flooring, and oil lamps. The place smelled of baby powder and bacon grease, a smell that was oddly comforting.

Higgles sat waiting in the dim interior, holding camp at a corner table. My mind stormed with questions. I wanted to know what happened to the package I'd spiked and just how worried I should be. But Austin was over, forgotten. Higgles had turned the calendar's page. He was already into the next month.

Over a carafe of bad wine that grew better the more we drank, he said, "Montreal will be a curious one. It's not for a few months, so you have time to hone your fighting skills. You'll want to bring a knife along for the meet."

"Knife-fighting skills? Hell, Higgles, what are you sending me into?"

"A job."

"You're expecting I'll have trouble?"

"I know you will." He picked at a plate of sliced ham and olives. "Guaranteed."

"I'm not up for killing." *Except for you.* The strength of my anger surprised me.

"I'm not asking you to kill anyone"—he paused—"else. In fact, I hope you don't. Just cut the guy a bit. On the arm or something. You'd be amazed at how far a little blood can go."

I finished my glass of wine, leaned back in my chair. The smart thing to do would be to trail Higgles to his hotel room, strangle him in his sleep. Or lure him up to the Santa Barbara Castle that towered over the town and shove him off a parapet. Or invite him on a picnic at the beach then drown him as he swam.

I stood and pushed the chair to the table. "You still haven't covered me for Austin." It was pulling teeth to get him to pay for jobs these days. "Until then, I'm not doing anything for you."

The word "Austin" triggered him. Higgles face mottled grapefruit red. I'd never seen him enraged before and I felt a spark of fear. No matter the situation, his temperament seemed to rise to only annoyed. But now he was trembling with anger.

He forced out three hard breaths and the color in his face slowly drained. He held his hands up to the air. Peace. "I was just getting to that. Sit," he said, nodding at the chair.

Stay or go?

"I've got your money."

"Let's see it."

"Not until you sit."

I settled back down.

"Now, we've done supremely well together, yes?" Higgles fixed me with his gaze. "Aside from those times, that is."

"We've done okay."

He studied his fingernails, bit at one. "I've never really given you a thorough job review, have I?"

"It's not really that type of job." I poured the last of the carafe into my glass, downed it quickly. "We don't exactly have an HR department or play Secret Santa at the holiday party."

Higgles' face creased in confusion. "Well, I just want you to know, you're appreciated." He flagged the waiter for another carafe of wine, more tapas. "I want you to know that I'd be greatly indebted to you if you did the Montreal gig."

He *appreciated* me? The bastard was stringing me along. "You're already greatly indebted to me." I got up. "So unless you start flashing the money you owe me and get yourself un-indebted, we have nothing more to say."

Higgles stood up, too, came around the table and grabbed my arm. He threw a number at me. A big number. More than four times what he owed me for the Austin trip. "In euros," he said. "It's yours, free and clear."

I sat. "You mean a bonus on top of what you owe me."

He liked that term. "Yes. Exactly. A bonus. For all the good work you've done."

"And the catch?"

He made a face, wounded. "'Catch' has such an offensive connotation to it. I like to think of it as a prerequisite."

"Then what's the 'prerequisite' for the bonus?"

The new carafe came, another plate of ham and olives. "The Montreal gig." Higgles topped our glasses. "Think of it as one of those signing bonus, like in baseball."

It was a lot of money. I could travel the world for a year or buy a small house in Iowa kind of money. "I say yes to Montreal, you hand me the cash?"

He nodded.

"You've got the money on you?"

"Not physically," he said, "but it's here. In Alicante." He tilted his chair back, leaning against the wall. "So, are we in agreement?"

He's fucking with me. I'd end up agreeing and walking out with nothing. "Not until I have five thousand euros in my hand. A signing bonus to the signing bonus."

Higgles popped his eyes, trying to look stunned. "You think I roll with that kind of money?"

"Yes."

His lips tightened like he'd swigged sour milk. "A demanding lad," he said after a moment. Then pulled an envelope from his jacket, counted out five thousand euros. I pocketed the money.

Pulling a key off his key ring, he handed it to me.

"What's this unlock?"

"Your fortune," he said. "When you meet your contact, just hand him this key—"

"Whoa, hold up," I said. "My *contact?*"

"He has your money."

"You said *you* had the money."

"I do. In a sense. That key"—he pointed to the one I held—"gets you the money."

I dropped the key on the table. A bad situation, bullshit semantics. What little faith I had in Higgles had withered into a hard prune of distrust.

Higgles lightly touched the key. "Your behavior saddens, but..." He shrugged, then launched into a discourse about wines of the Spain, the weather, the region. "The Spanish Civil War was fought here," he said, pointing across the tavern like the entire ordeal had played out at one of the other tables.

I asked what he thought about Orwell.

A look of puzzlement peppered his face. "Orwell?"

"*Homage to Catalonia*," I said. "Book eight."

"Yes, right," he said, pouring out the last of the wine. He flagged the waiter for yet more.

"What'd you think about it?" I asked again.

"It was interesting," he said. "I liked the cover. The words in the book were very legible." He went on to say traveling to a foreign country always seemed to cause him dandruff.

We drank, talking about everything and nothing, mutually ignoring the topic of the key and the money. Talking like two friends who, after a nasty falling out years prior, had patched things up for the moment.

An hour later, my gut drowned in wine, I said, "All right, give me the fucking key."

Exuberant, Higgles held his arms wide for a celebratory embrace. He wasn't about to get one. "Wonderful," he exclaimed, then told me when and where to get the money.

I was drunk. "And you swear this is a quick snack," I said, emboldened. "No white-tie sit-down meal or a meet-the-parents-type thing."

Higgles licked his wine-stained lips. "What the hell are you talking about?"

"The money. The exchange," I said. "It's easy, yes?"

"Right, yes. Like you said, it's a snack. Just hand him the key and he'll give you the cash. Simple."

The following night, I found my way to a gutted house at the edge of town. Bags of concrete, boards, and stacks of bricks lay around the worksite like rotting carcasses. Abandoned for lack of funds. Like most of Spain.

The contact calmly smoked a cigarette on a half-finished stoop, waiting. A tiny man, barely over five foot. He couldn't have weighed more than a hundred and ten pounds. Eastern European, I'd guess.

We made the cursory gestures of greeting. I handed him the key. He handed me a knapsack. I inspected it quickly. It was solid with cash.

I nodded, turned to leave. Simple and quick. The gig was done.

Or so I thought. The contact had a different idea. He stabbed me in the back. Literally. The first jab hammered me at my waistline, hitting my hipbone and, fortunately, not driving deep. The second, though, found the meat of my ass and stuck.

I spun about, the pain pinwheeling through me, and caught my attacker in the temple with an elbow, staggering him back.

Small as he was, the fucker could scrap. Fists and chops and kicks and bites. We went at it for what felt like an hour, grunting, slapping, punching, and kicking. Finally, I got a hold of a brick and swung savagely at his head.

There was a crunch then the man folded like a broken lawn chair, dropping lifelessly to the dirty concrete.

Had the Austin mess followed me halfway around the world or was this guy just a greedy asshole? I searched his pockets but found only the key. No wallet, no ID. A nameless, nonexistent man.

I retrieved the knapsack, hobbled my way to the hotel, blood squishing in my shoe.

It was only after I'd had safely locked myself in my room that I realized the knife still protruded from my ass. A souvenir.

I labored through the papers the following day and the day after that, relying on my high school Spanish. No mention of a murder that I could find.

For three weeks, I holed up in a moldy flat with a stellar view of the Santa Barbara Castle and drank liter after liter of Rioja, recovering. The money never got beyond my arm's reach.

◎ ◎ ◎

IN *HOMAGE TO CATALONIA*, George Orwell tells of his time on the frontline fighting against the Communists during the Spanish Civil War. A muddle of confusion, propaganda, and a crippling need for supplies. Crouched down behind boulders on a hill, they'd fire random, wild shots across the valley, aiming at an unseen enemy defending the opposite hill. A lonely *pop* would sound, then a shot would be returned. The boredom of man.

Then he took a bullet in the neck.

No one thought he'd live. His companions thought he'd be dead before they could drag him off the battlefield, back to where an ambulance waited. When he got to the ambulance, the medics were positive he wouldn't live to the hospital.

But he lived.

In the hospital, the doctors didn't think he'd ever be able to speak again. He'd be forever a mute, his voice box scarred and mangled.

But they were wrong. Orwell spoke again.

CHAPTER 53

A BODY AT REST remains at rest. Unless acted upon. The knife wound laid me out for too long. My mind bubbled toxically, whipping up scenarios that weren't real. I'd been cramped up too long while my wound healed. I was imagining things. I could swear I saw Ray-Ray from my hotel window, strolling the cobblestone streets of Alicante. How could that be? Why would he be here?

I got back on my feet, packed the cash into a FedEx box, and shipped it to my PO Box in the Bronx. Then I switched out my passports, turned off my phone, and took a holiday.

As long as I was in motion, was moving toward a destination, I felt safe. Like no one could find me. It was only once I reached my goal and terminated my travel that the worry blistered up in me.

I flew down to Gibraltar and spent three days sitting on the hotel's balcony watching a parade of tourists ignore the signs saying not to feed the monkeys and trying to befriend them with Snickers or organic energy bars. When the animals attacked, stealing cameras, purses, or sunglasses—or just serving up a violent slap—the people were stunned, perplexed. *How could such a thing happen?*

I traveled on to North Africa.

In Tangier, the idea of Morocco soured. The whole scene was rotten with patchouli-dipped backpackers arguing the genius of Paul Bowles. A dream decaying from the inside out.

I moved on further, booked passage on a ferry to San Cristóbal de La Laguna on the island of Tenerife.

I should have flown.

The season was tapering off and there were few other travelers, maybe twenty, rattling around on a boat built to hold more than two hundred. The *Luxuri Freedom*. It was devoid of comfort. The foam cushions had been removed, leaving only hard plastic benches to sit on. The men's restroom was closed for repairs and the women's had no toilet paper. And the bar, the place I'd hoped to seek refuge, served only Diet Lemon Pepsi, Cheez Puffs, and warm Jägermeister.

Realizing I was American, a khaki-shorted woman from Alabama took to me like debt to a new credit card. The pale skin of her thighs glowed above her sunburnt cankles. She hated ferries, she said, leaning in toward me in confidence. "My husband thinks I'm afraid of those Somali pirates. But really, I'm just afraid of the boat flipping over and then the crocodiles eating me."

I gazed out over the calm Atlantic, a breeze cooling my face. "Somalia is in East Africa. And crocodiles aren't ocean animals."

She didn't believe me on either count.

I walked away, but she followed me as I strolled along the railing and peppered me with questions. Where was I from, was I married, did I have kids, what did I do for a living.

"I work for ARD," I said.

"ARD?" Her face, Christmas-ribbon red from too much sun, shined greasily. "What's ARD?"

"Audits and Retribution Department. It's a special division within the IRS."

"Retribution?"

I nodded. "We go after unique cases, people who've been cheating the government for years."

She made a noise that passed for a laugh. "Well thank goodness my husband and I are law-abiding Americans."

I said nothing, just studied her inquisitively.

"And anyway," she said, "you probably only go after the big fish, the off-shore-bank, hedgefundy, Wall Street kinda guys, right?"

"Everyone is equal in the eyes of the IRS. And you wouldn't believe how even a little cheating adds up over time. Hey," I said, turning on false warmth, "why don't you write down your name and address for me?"

She actually giggled, like I was asking her out on a date. "My name and address?"

"Or just your social security number," I said. "Then I can look up the rest."

I could see her mind churning, grasping for some foundation. "Why would you want to look me up?"

"It's a hobby I have, checking in on the people I meet on my travels."

She blanched under her sunburn. "You know, my husband is probably worried about me," she murmured, cautiously retreating.

At the bar, I ordered a shot of tepid Jägermeister and watched the blue waters of the Atlantic spread to the horizon. Africa was long forgotten. The island of Tenerife stood ahead. I ordered a bag of Cheez Puffs, a second shot, and a third for the bartender.

"How much longer?" I asked him.

My answer came in the reply from below decks. A *bbbkkkAAAANN-nngg* tore the air as the engine coughed up an explosive old-man noise, then a second. The ferry's engine died in a haze of oily smoke the color of egg yolk. The gritty cloud hovered tight to the water as our forward momentum slowed to a listing bob.

There was a crackle and screech as the PA system came to life. The captain's voice creaked over the speakers, his Spanish-African accent the stuff of B-movie villains. Help had been summoned, he said. Our rescue would arrive shortly.

A half hour passed. Then an hour. No additional announcements, no updates. We dipped and rose in the waters until finally, three hours later, an ancient tugboat chugged into view. There was talk among the passengers of being evacuated, put on the tug and taken ashore, but the boat slid up behind us, nosed us toward a dollop of foamy volcanic archipelago. The island of La Gomera was now the port of call.

Dusk spiced the sky as we finally docked. The PA hissed again and the captain made a one-word announcement. "Arrangements."

The others looked to one another for some understanding, for some answers.

I disembarked from our watery limbo and strode toward the town's cobblestone square, needing to distance myself from the group. They wanted to bond over the inconvenience and confusion. Hang together. Safety in groups. They wanted to share the experience. I wanted to be free of them and their forced community.

La Gomera. Christopher Columbus's last stop on his way back to Spain after discovering America. Rumor had it that a three-day resupplying had turned into a month when he saw the mayor's wife. Spanish influence marked the bright houses, the large central square, and the food and drink.

I found a room for rent, agreed on a price with the owner. The man spoke little English. I spoke broken Spanish. He showed me the room, then he showed me his daughter. She was fifteen, plump and pretty with acne scars high on her cheeks. "Yo!" she said, giving me a high-five.

"Yo to you," I said, returning the slap.

The man and his daughter showed me the backyard, the tree that had been growing there for decades, the flagstone path that the man had laid himself, and the small garden that he and his wife tended. After half an hour of being shown everything down to the grass, the man said, "Come, dinner."

I sat with them. The wife piled my plate with a mound of ham and roast potatoes, a bread hard and dark. She spoke no English. She spoke to her daughter, who then spoke to me. I told them how I'd been in Spain, had traveled down to Morocco, and how the ferry had broken down. The wife said something, which the daughter refused to translate.

"What did she ask?"

The girl, grudgingly, muttered, "She wants to know if you need a wife."

"Is she offering herself?"

The daughter laughed. "She had me in mind. She thinks you are rich and can take me with you to a big house in America."

"Ah, well, I have no house and I'm not rich. So stealing you away to America wouldn't be fair to you or your family."

The girl told her mother, who made the sign of the cross and then took my hand and kissed the back of it. She looked me in the eye and said something. "'Get rich,'" the daughter translated, "'then come back for me,' she says."

After dinner and coffee, we crowded into the living room and sat on plastic-wrapped furniture to watch satellite TV while the wife cleared the table. The man found a college football game, thinking I'd like it. Miami versus Nebraska. The Orange Bowl from some two decades prior, a rerun. "America," he said, pointing at the TV.

The daughter was talkative, intelligent. I liked her. She practiced her New Jersey accent while I practiced my basic Spanish.

"What do you call that thing?" she asked, pointing to the University of Nebraska-Lincoln mascot.

"It's a cornhusker," I said, trying to explain a cornhusker as best I could. "That's what the team is called, the Cornhuskers."

"And this bird?" she asked of the Miami mascot.

"It's a ibis, I think."

"The Miami Ibises?" she said.

"Hurricanes," I corrected. "They're called the Hurricanes."

She was confused.

I explained a hurricane.

That wasn't what she was confused about. "Why do they call themselves one thing when they are really another?"

I had no good answer.

The mother brought in a tray of Cognac and treats, served us all, then squeezed onto the small couch beside her husband.

Between bites of her cookie, the girl told me of La Gomera, about its history, about the rainforest I had to visit before I left, with its twisting trees and the lava fields of spiny, sharp pumice. She asked how long I planned to stay.

"A day," I said. "Maybe more. I don't know."

She took my hand in hers. It was clammy. "You were lying before. You are rich, no?"

I thought of the euros waiting for me at home, shook my head. "No, really, I'm not."

"That is okay. I like you even without money." She let go of my hand, laughed. "I like you even if you do not marry me." She suggested giving me a tour the next morning.

The next morning, it turned out, meant 5:00 a.m.

I woke to find her sitting on the edge of my bed. She touched her finger to my chin. "Ready?"

I was ready.

As we left the house, she grabbed two walking sticks by the door, handed one to me. The sticks were taller than I was, nearly eight foot. What was the point?

"I'm going to pass," I said, handing the stick back to her. "I like to have my hands free."

"No, you need it," she replied. "Without it, you can't come."

I awkwardly grasped it in the middle.

The cool morning air smelled of vegetation, of ocean, of gaining heat. The salty sharpness of the day filled my lungs. Darkness slowly crept away as dawn approached.

Strolling through town, she pointed out various houses as we passed. There, in the green house, was her high school teacher, who was jealous of her because of her nice hair. Over there was where the town council leader lived. He drank too much, but then what town council leader didn't? To the right, the home of the butcher, who had only seven fingers and whose four daughters, all in their thirties, were still unmarried. Up ahead, the market owner's house; he had a taste for exotic vinegars. The fisherman up the road never learned to swim. The hairstylist had rough hands. The seamstress tore more than she mended. The tavern owner who went through everyone's garbage in search of spare tinfoil. "And there," she said as we neared the town limits, "is my ex-boyfriend's house." They had been dating since they were five years old, she said, had only recently broken up.

"How is it possible for a five-year-old to date?"

She held up her free hand, open and empty. "All is possible if your parents say yes," she said. "Ten years we dated. It would never work, though, he and I."

"No?"

She paused, turned back to face the town. Tendrils of morning fog stretched over the land. "All these things I tell you, the people and stories, they make up the"—she pressed her lips together, finding the right word—"ribbon."

"The ribbon?"

She nodded. "Yes, the ribbon that is my life." She moved her hand in the air, smoothing its length. "I can see the whole thing. I see everything of my life. I know what is going to happen to me before it happens. I see my entire future."

I couldn't even see tomorrow. "You're fifteen," I said. "How can you know your future?"

"I know you will not marry me," she said, taking my hand in hers. "I know in a few years I will leave La Gomera. I know my parents will die. I know I will die." She shrugged. "It is very sad, life having no surprises."

We walked on, moving beyond the town's outer edges. The land tore open before us, the rocky crag of country a reminder of the earth's old tantrum. Pumice pikes swelled high then dropped sharp into jagged ravines. She vaulted over a black gully using her walking stick. Now I understood why they were so tall. "Come on," she waved. I poled awkwardly across, stumbling when I landed.

She laughed—"Careful"—then lifted her skirt to show me her knees. They were speckled black. "It is hard to get all the cinder out if you fall and cut yourself."

After a half hour more of walking this strange landscape, I finally asked where we were going.

"To talk to Stefan, my new boyfriend."

There was nothing before us but miles of rock and crag and scrub. "He lives out here?"

"In the next village," she said, pointing ahead.

There was no village in sight. "How far is it?"

"Two or three miles, maybe. I've only been there a few times."
She jabbed the lava plumes with her walking stick. "Stefan is not as tall
you," she told me, "but I bet he is stronger." Black hair, firm back, a good
set of teeth. She ran through his qualities as if he was a farm animal.

"You have a picture of him?"

She shook her head. "I have never seen him."

I stopped. "How do you date a guy you've never seen?"

"The same way you date any guy," she said, powering on. "Is that
hard to believe that love is not based on appearance alone?"

"It's a big factor."

"It is a wrong factor," she said. "Relationships based on a face are
like the faces themselves—they do not last. But if you know someone,
really know them, well, that part never changes."

We ascended a tall, bare ridge and the island spread out before
us, the Atlantic lofting into view. Finding a flat rock, I sat. I was out
of breath.

She clambered up to the edge of the stone to the peak, cupped a
hand to her face, and let loose a piercing whistle. The sound danced out
over the rocks, streaming outward the center of the island, the wind
holding it aloft.

A moment later, a reply was whistled. "That is Stefan," she said,
excited. "My boyfriend." She whistled again, the tone and infection
lifting and dropping as she fired back a reply.

The air quieted to the sounds of the breeze, then filled again to
with a whistle. "I told him about you. He says hello," she said. "Said he
will fuck you up if you try anything with me."

I laughed. "You're telling me you got all that from
whistling showtunes?"

"They are not showtunes," she said. "It is Silbo, our language."

"Yours and Stefan's?"

"My people's. Everyone on La Gomera speaks it. It is our culture,
our heritage. It is how we have communicated for hundreds of years."

I didn't believe her.

She pulled out a cell phone, handed it to me. "Text Stefan something. Just do not tell me what it is."

I thought a moment, then made something up. "My wife died last year," I typed, then nodded to her.

"Now I will ask him what you said." She whistled to him, long and plaintive.

A moment later, a reply sounded, pitched and long.

The girl turned to me, motioned for me to stand.

I stood.

She grabbed me by my ear, pulled my face to hers, and set a kiss to my lips. She tasted of bubble gum and basil, a taste of childhood aching to end. "I am so sorry," she said, her eyes soft. "I did not know you were a widower."

CHAPTER 54

THE DAY AFTER MY high school graduation, I woke in the hospital, a plastic tube snaked down my throat and my blood fighting to escape my battered body.

A smashed left arm, a shattered right wrist, a broken knee, eight cracked ribs, and a concussion that left my eyes panda black. My face, pebbled from shards of the windshield, was a topography of scabs.

People said I was lucky.

I didn't feel lucky. The pain was incredible.

My parents were dead. Clement was dead. At the hospital, no one wanted to take the responsibility of breaking the tragic news to me. I knew, though. Their absence shimmered and fizzled through my fractured bones like damp fireworks.

Officially, according to the sheriff's report I eventually read, it was Clement's fault. He was drunk. Vodka. He'd redlined his Nighthawk down Jacoby Avenue, and blown through the intersection. Either he didn't see the stop sign or he'd just ignored it. *A recommendation at best.*

My father, distracted, had wheeled our car directly into Clement's path.

All three had died instantly, which I guess is lucky. No suffering, no sadness of being left behind to deal with the grief.

Clement's parents, swollen in a rage of anguish, came to visit me in the hospital on the third day. Mr. Martin, unable to look me in the face, touched the frame of my bed like he was grounding himself for electricity then quickly left the room.

Mrs. Martin, jaundiced with heartache, pulled a chair alongside my bed. She breathed raggedly, uneven, like her lungs had been punctured. I'd always thought Mrs. Martin a pretty woman. Now her features seemed somehow displaced; her hair had climbed her forehead and her eyes no longer held horizontal. A choking odor of turned milk and rotting fish kicked off her.

She leaned to me, her lips close to my ear. "When I was a little girl," she said, "I wanted to be a movie star. Everything was geared toward that goal. School plays, summer festivals, acting camps. I learned everything I had to learn, then went to LA and did everything I had to do to be a success. I did things I now wish I'd never done, things I now try to blank from my mind. And just look," she said, her voice choked with tears. "I'm the wife of the small-town hardware store owner. I'm a mother without a child." She sat back, then reached out and touched my neck, running her finger along the skin as if I were an object she'd never seen before. A puff of a sigh escaped her and she leaned in again, her face close to mine. "What is the lesson in all this?" she asked, her body humming with sadness. "What's the takeaway?"

CHAPTER 55

AFTER LA GOMERA, I made my way back to Europe, working up through Portugal then jetting to Paris and on to Germany before heading back in New York. Home, the world seemed to have left me behind, though nothing really changed. Vacation was over, and instead of being calmed, relaxed, and refreshed, I was even more skittish. It was a battle not to constantly check over my shoulder when out. At night, I'd wake choking on dread. The rev of a car's engine, the slam of a door, or someone laughing sharply shot a fire poker of panic through my bowels.

Coming back from a movie one evening, my neighbor shouldered past me in my building's lobby. "Watch," she said, then stopped. Wearing a soiled white jacket and pink terrycloth sweatpants with the words *Deep Dish* written on the ass, she was firmly on the wrong side of voluptuous. She pointed a gloved finger at me. "Your dad is some totally angry cunt."

"I don't have a dad."

"Well, whoever that asshole is in your place." She grabbed her shoulders, hugged herself. "I can only sleep in the evenings, you know, because of my condition? So tell him to cool it with the crashing about. Next time," she said, heading off, "I'm calling the cops."

I shivered, but not from the cold. My blood pumped molten hot at the thought that someone was in my place.

Two flights, thirty-eight steps. It took me five minutes to make the climb, my legs burning with each step. I thought of taking my shoes off, going in stealth. I wanted the edge of surprise. But then I'd have my shoes in my hand when I confronted whoever it was. The shoes stayed on.

At my door, I put my ear to the wood and listened. *Wub thub, wub thub.* My pulse rang loudly through my skull.

I fumbled the key into the lock and then, standing to the side, swung the door open. No crack of a bullet, no slash of a knife, no fist to the face. The apartment was silent, dark. Empty.

I groped for the light, flicking it on. Everything stood exactly as I'd left it. If anyone had been there, all they did was dust lightly.

The stew of high-alert chemicals spiking my body drained away, seeping from my pores in a rank sweat. Exhaustion crippled me. I could barely think. A quick shower, then bed.

Trundling into the bathroom, I undressed and was about to take a piss when the icy fingers of fear gripped my balls.

The toilet lid was down. I never put it down.

Someone had been here.

Kicking open the lid, I expected to be greeted by a severed cat's head—or something equally gruesome. What I found was a yellowed newspaper clipping taped to the inside of the lid. An obituary. The kind the family pays to have published. The photo showed a chubby, youngish man wearing a Texas Rangers baseball cap. Smiling lazily, he looked high or mildly retarded. Not a great photo, I thought, but it was probably one of his best. Pulling the clipping free, I studied the picture. I didn't recognize the man. Then I read his obit. It was my Austin guy, the assistant manager of ReadiXpress. He'd been mowed down in a liquor store's parking lot by a hit-and-run less than twelve hours after he'd Kam Manned for me. Was the obit a warning, a threat, or just an FYI? And from who? Higgles, I hoped. At least he was the devil I knew.

I flushed the article, checked the lock on the front door, and then jammed a chair under the doorknob. The best weapon I could find was a foot-tall, wooden pepper mill, which I held through the night.

Higgles texted the next day, the first I'd heard from him since Alicante. I didn't know what to make of the message I received. Details weren't generally his highpoint. He broad-stroked everything, kept it simple. *Male, red shirt drinking wine, two p.m.* or *Woman, blonde, pearls, and black turtleneck, seven o'clock.* This time, though, his particulars were frightfully precise. It was like he'd been sitting directly across from the mark, crafting a profile for the police. Height, weight, eye and hair color, the brand of shirt, shoes, type of suit, and even the pattern of his tie. More details than usual. He was never that specific. He even noted exactly which chair at which table at the café the man would be sitting, what he'd be eating (poutine) and drinking (Diet Coke).

I had no idea what poutine was.

I was to steal a bag, the unnamed prize inside.

Enter front door, 3:00 p.m. sharp, he'd texted. *Not before, not after. Three on the nose. Walk twelve paces to table, grab brown calf's leather pouch hanging on back of contact's chair, exit through kitchen. Meet me in Baltimore Thursday. Bring flash drive from the bag.*

First the obit and now the sudden attention to minutiae. It bothered me. Was this Higgles' way of apologizing for nearly getting me killed in Alicante? Or was he sending me into more of the same?

I'd skip the Montreal job. I didn't need the cash. I was a free agent, could take or turn down a job, break out on my own. I could even set up my own shop.

I found myself laughing. What if I out-Higglesed Higgles, stole the bag before the real thief did? Then, somehow, sold it back to him. Or to someone else. Or maybe no one at all. Maybe I'd just destroy the bag and its contents and have the private pleasure of knowing I'd gotten one over on Higgles.

I texted him *Broke foot. Can't walk. Montreal off.*

Crawl then. Montreal is go.

It's all you, I texted. *Best of luck.*

I expected my phone to blow up with a barrage of texts. A minute, then ten, passed. Nothing. My phone remained silent. Higgles resigned?

Doubtful. I envisioned him collapsed on the floor, crippled with rage, maybe even foaming at the mouth. The image shot me with gooey glee. I'd pay for sure. I'd set myself up. But I'd also shifted the game, taken the upper hand. At least in my mind, at least for the moment.

The *why* for what I did wasn't clear to me.

Or rather, I was too afraid to face it. It disturbed me that I liked how my blood thumped and hammered through my veins each time I stepped outside the standard. It seemed unnatural, wrong to be excited by the possibility of danger. Like I had a death wish or something. But I couldn't help it. I liked the rush I got from uncertainty, the sharp flash of terror that shot through me when something went wrong. It made me appreciate being alive, which, ever since Clement's and my folks' death, I didn't often feel.

I booked a flight.

Montreal. My first time. It was a beautiful city of quaint cafés, friendly people who'd smile as they passed, lively nightlife, and really good food.

I bought a knife with a five-inch blade, not unlike the one I'd been stabbed with.

Unlike other Kam Mans, this would be no Sunday meet and greet, no quick, friendly exchange. Higgles had made it clear that the contact wasn't really a contact; he was a mark. It was a bash and grab. Flash the knife, punch the neck, snatch a brown leather pouch—a man-purse—and go. A poach and run. Right under Higgles' nose.

Mondo Et Fils, a corner café in Plateau Mont-Royal off Saint-Denis. That's where I'd find my man.

Approaching from the south, I scouted the scene from half a block away. The mark sat at a table near the front by the window, just as Higgles said he would. The pink page of the *Financial Times* he read blocked his face. Just as Higgles said it would.

I checked the time—2:39 p.m. Higgles instructions stated to enter the front door exactly at 3:00 p.m. It'd long be over by then. I wasn't going in on good terms. This was dangerous—or more dangerous. I was robbing this guy at knife point. The whole situation was dumb.

I reread the text. *Fuck Higgles*, I thought. *Fuck front door. Fuck three o'clock sharp.* I was doing it on my own terms and timeframe.

Making my way to the alley behind the café, I found the service entrance and banged on the door.

The dishwasher opened the door, a cigarette clamped in his mouth. "Yeah?"

"Sven thinks it's probably a cracked cogmount gasket," I said, pushing past him. "I'll take a quick look-see, get it back up and running in no time."

"What?" He was confused. "What's broken?"

I strode on without answering, moved past the silver stoves, past the waiter snacking on feta cheese, past the bin of food scraps and the stacked plates, and through the swinging doors onto the café floor. 2:43 p.m. The place was empty except for the mark, whose back was to me. Looped over the chair's back was the pouch I was after.

Approaching quietly, I slipped behind him. First the bash, then the grab.

I caught his jacket collar, clinched the fabric tight and yanked back as I kicked the legs of his chair out from under him.

A startled cry. An upended table. A clatter of dishware as he crashed to the floor.

I kicked the downed man in the ribs then seized his bag. I bolted.

Or tried to. The stranger wrangled my leg, tying me up midstep. I met the floor face first.

Lashing out, my heel connected with his head. I bound back to my feet, cut toward the front door.

Then he yelled, his voice freezing me. "Stop, cousin!"

It was Higgles.

Turning, I eyed him on the floor. "What the fuck is this?"

Higgles sat up and ran his hand down his food-stained front, frowning. "You ruined my shirt." Then he laughed. "Bravo on catching me off guard." He struggled to his feet.

I kicked him again, knocking him back down. "What the fuck *is* this?"

The café manager, now on the scene, shouted at me in mix of French and English, his voice rising in distress. "I call the police!"

"Yes!" Higgles said, crabbing his way across the floor, away from me to him. "The police! Call the police!"

The manager ducked into the kitchen for a phone.

"What the fuck?" I said to Higgles.

"Where's the knife?" he said, back on his feet. He kept his voice low. It rested heavily in my pocket. "No knife." I retreated cautiously, watching him.

"The police! Call the police quick!" Higgles said, his head turned toward the kitchen. Then he turned to me, hissed. "I told you to bring a knife, cousin."

Kill him now, my mind shouted. *Kill him with the knife.* "Got what I was supposed to get," I said, holding up the bag. "I didn't need the knife."

"You will," he said, charging me.

I caught him in the eye with an open slap. He stomped on my foot, then twisted me into a vicious headlock. "Bet you wish you had a knife now," he said, punching me twice in the forehead.

I dropped the bag, pulled the knife from my pocket. "I bet you wished I didn't." Flipping out the blade, I slashed savagely upward.

Higgles let out the howl of a crushed cat. The headlock fell away.

I sprang clear, grabbed the bag.

Turning, I saw that I'd caught Higgles in the face, parting his cheek down to his jaw.

Stunned, Higgles stared at me, his cut opening slowly. The blood spilled.

The manager burst from the kitchen, but on spotting Higgles, the blood, the knife in my hand, he quickly retreated back to safety.

Sirens sounded far off.

Higgles gathered his senses, a rage taking hold. "Cousin, that's twice you've surprised me today."

"Don't call me cousin." I provided him a third surprise by planting the knife tip deep in his left deltoid. The blade stuck like it was buried in a wedge of cheese.

Higgles paled, then sat heavily on the floor.

As I ran and ran, the pouch in hand and the crisp Canadian air burning my lungs, tears streamed down my face.

I'd never felt so alive.

◎ ◎ ◎

POUTINE IS CHEESE CURDS and gravy on French fries, a perfect cure for hangovers.

CHAPTER 56

A T FIRST, I DIDN'T understand why Higgles had done what he'd done. Why he'd demanded I stab him. Then it came to me.

Whatever was supposedly in the pouch, Higgles wanted the full profit from its sale to the highest bidder. But there'd be a storm of fury if his employers thought for a moment he had double-crossed them. So he needed a credible story to cover its disappearance. He needed the fight with me, needed the stabbing, the blood, the witnessed, the police, and hospital report stating he'd been violently attacked, all to cover the simple fact that he had essentially robbed himself.

Of course, whatever it was I was to steal, Higgles had kept. I'd come up empty. He got the goods and I was left literally holding the bag.

CHAPTER 57

THE MOMENT MY FLIGHT touched down at JFK airport, I knew I couldn't stay. I'd been there too long and Higgles had always found me, tracked me down no matter where I was. I was done waiting for him. Now it was my turn to hunt him down. Haven, Florida. Higgles' PO Box. My best lead.

I packed the books and a few items I cared to keep and I abandoned the apartment. I texted Higgles. *Shipped bag to Haven FL PO. Ready to talk.* It was a long shot. He already had what he wanted, had no need to go to Haven for the bag, but I had to try. Then I shipped my cell phone third-class ground to a Quizno's in New Mexico. It seemed farfetched, but if Higgles had been tracking me through the phone, then he'd be in for a road trip.

In Haven, I rented the apartment above a cigar store and bought a bike for seventeen dollars at a yard sale. I took to riding to the post office every morning at eight, hanging out in lobby for most of the day, and keeping an eye hard on Higgles' PO Box, hoping to see who, if anyone, came to open it.

Strangely, I felt safe there. Calm. A sanctuary. Nothing could harm me as long as I lingered in the hushed, marble-floored space.

Higgles would never come himself. He'd pay some kid twenty bucks to check the mail. It'd be that kid I'd follow.

It wasn't much of a ploy, I knew.

My third day staking out the box, the security guard, a wiry Cuban who wore both a belt and suspenders, strode up to me. "You got to go," he said, lowering his voice to a rough grumble.

I wasn't bothering anyone, I argued.

"You're bothering me with your crazy eyes," he said. "Plus, you haven't said hi to me once in the three days you've been standing there."

"Hi," I said, and left.

I thought about staking out the post office from the bus stop across the street, but why? I wouldn't be able to see who actually opened Higgles' box. Plus, with my paranoia spiking again, I felt positive I'd be an easy target. Anyone could roll up in a car and take me out with a shot. I needed to keep in motion. And I needed a new plan.

I took to riding my bike around town—ostensibly to locate Higgles, but really I just needed to clear my mind, plot a better attack.

Mornings were my favorite time for a ride. The day's light, flat and even, hadn't yet gained its full, brutal strength. People love Florida for that light. They love it for its bright, uninterrupted sunny weather, six hundred and sixty-three miles of beaches, its warmth. I found it all oppressive. Beautiful day after beautiful day, every minute spent indoors felt wasted; every minute outdoors I felt my brain baking.

I coasted my bike down ugly streets with calming names. Leechem, Mangrove, Coral, Kanahuatwa, Sea Pine. I pedaled lazily down Main Street, which wasn't much to look at: a Circle K, a nail salon, a tax and law office, a few paint-peeling houses.

The town of Haven proper was quiet, but Florida is a land of roads that connect one generation's dream-town to the next, and near the place I rented, the old highway ripped through. It was the favorite route of cement trucks and semis, offering a quick shortcut to their construction sites or drop-offs. They'd barrel through Haven like steel rhinos, claiming full right of way.

The intersection was unsafe. A handful of makeshift shrines and three or four crosses kept vigil alongside the highway, marking the places a life had been taken. Even with the stoplight, crossing the old highway on my bike was an act of calculation, bravery, and fast pedaling. I felt a charge of elation each time I crossed, defying death once again.

I stumbled onto Charm's Tavern my second week in Haven. There was no sign for the place aside from a half-dead Busch Light neon sign flickering weakly in the window, fighting the brightness of the day. I'd cruised past it before, never taking note of it.

One cool, sunny morning, they'd propped the door open and the sweet stench of stale beer and bleach hit me as I pedaled past.

Circling back, I chained my bike up and poked inside. Higgles might be holed up here, I told myself, knowing he wouldn't be.

It was about 10:00 a.m., close enough to lunchtime by my watch. Inside, three men sat silently on barstools, the hard shaft of day cutting across their cragged faces like a roller of whitewash. None were Higgles. None even acknowledged me when I entered.

Charm's was the type of place you went when you had some time to kill, a decade or two. I ordered a beer, then a second.

For nearly a week, I followed that pattern, a morning bike ride that ended at Charm's where I plotted and planned Higgles' demise over a fistful of beers. At about 3:00 p.m., I'd climb on my bike, take my life in my hands, and bravely clip across the old highway, and then sleep through the sweltering afternoon.

Higgles broke that pattern on Presidents' Day.

Returning from Charm's, I found him sitting on my mattress. He looked worse than he had in Memphis, unshaven and mangy like he'd been hiding in a forest all winter. The stitched scar hashmarked his cheek, shining the bright color of a baby's tongue, pink and raw-looking. Lazily, he flipped through *Macao Thunder*. The leather purse, which I had kept, sat on the floor next to him.

I tried to play calm, but my blood stopped. Once again, the fucker got the jump on me.

Higgles held up the book. "You know, I honestly thought you were yanking my chain when you said there was a Macao in Brazil."

Standing, he motioned at everything and nothing, like a priest consecrating a new building. "Your place needs a little something, some color or—I don't know—curtains. This decor is pure early poverty."

"You've got what you came for, I see," I said, nodding to the bag. "Let's say that evens us up and call it day."

He kicked the bag across the room. "You know," he said, glancing at *Macao Thunder*, "I've always wanted to be a writer. I come up with a lot of good stories." He tossed the book on the floor, paced the room, and proceeded to tell me one.

A soldier on leave in New York City buys some bootleg DVDs in Chinatown, three for ten dollars. He knows he shouldn't, knows he's only funding illicit activities. Still, the soldier wants the DVDs, so he buys them. The rest of the story, Higgles explains, is split. "Like they do in movies," he said. One thread of the tale follows the soldier as he is deployed to hotspots in the Middle East. The other part tracks the ten dollars as it moves from hand-to-hand through the underworld of counterfeit products to where it reaches the terrorists.

"And let me guess," I said, my voice breaking slightly from nerves. "The soldier's ten bucks ends up making its way to a terrorist who spends it on bullets used to kill the soldier himself."

Higgles beamed. "Actually, it's a bomb," he clarified, still pacing, "but yes. Exactly. What do you think?"

"It's a morbid *Gift of the Magi*. But how do you expect to write a novel when you can't even read?"

He stopped inches from me. "Just because I *don't* read," he said, his voice hard, "doesn't mean I *can't*, cousin. Or won't." He touched his stitched scar. "I believe you fucked me on the Montreal deal, something I don't appreciate."

"'Fucked' has such an offensive connotation to it," I said, fighting to hold my ground. Higgles' breath in my face crowded me, threatening. "Can't we just say 'disappointed'?"

He raised an eyebrow. "You *disappointed* me on the Montreal deal," he said. "But you can make it up now."

"Really? How's that?"

"By handing it over."

I pointed to the bag he'd kicked across the room. "That's all I got. But feel free to take it. It adds flair to your outfit."

"I'm talking about the—" He broke off, his voice sounding tired. "You didn't sell it already, did you?"

Was Higgles bullshitting me? It didn't seem so. But I definitely didn't have whatever it was. I'd rifled through the bag soon after I'd snatched it. Nothing. "I don't have it." The words came out of me before I'd fully thought them through.

Higgles fingers found his scar, gently touched it. "You don't?"

I'd just eliminated my usefulness. Without the drive he wanted, I was no use to Higgles. "On me," I said, clawing for leverage.

"Where is it?"

"Listen, I give it to you and I'm out of the game."

"I'm a fair sort of guy," he said.

I barked out a laugh.

He glared at me evilly, spit on the floor. "I'm a fair sort of guy," he said again, "so let's do this fairly. Let's go get it together, then—"

"Can't get it," I said, adding, "Right now."

"Because?"

I recalled it was Presidents Day. One of the barflies at Charm's had muttered over his drink, "How'd it get to be Presidents Day again?" It was the only thing I'd ever heard him say. "It's in a safe-deposit box. The bank's closed for Presidents Day."

Higgles made a face of disgust. He couldn't call my bluff, not yet at least. Still, my excuse didn't really buy me time, I realized. Now we'd just have a slumber party until 9:00 a.m. the next morning, when the banks opened.

But Higgles surprised me.

He left.

"Tomorrow, then," he said, opening the front door.

He paused at the apartment's threshold. "We'll meet here," he said. "Say noontime. That'll give you time to get to the bank, maybe do some laundry." He snapped his finger. "I'll tell you what. I'll bring some sandwiches, some sodas. You bring the chips and dessert. We'll head to the beach, picnic together. Then," he said, savoring the words that formed, "we'll talk about your severance package, because we're done working together." His scar seemed to glow as he smiled. "Sound fair?"

Before I could answer, the door *snick*ed shut behind him.

Almost instantly, the door swung open again. Higgles' head poked in. "I don't need to tell you what will happen if you try to run, do I?"

I shook my head.

"Good," he said, slowly closing the door again.

◎ ◎ ◎

THE FEDERAL HOLIDAY CELEBRATED on the third Monday in February is officially called Washington's Birthday, not Presidents Day.

Or Presidents' Day.

Or even President's Day.

CHAPTER 58

ASPIRIN, OR ACETYLSALICYLIC ACID, works on headaches by suppressing the production of prostaglandin enzyme, hormone-like messenger molecules that trigger processes in the body, including inflammation. It does that by crippling the cyclooxygenase—or COX—enzyme. Cyclooxygenase is needed for prostaglandin to synthesize.

For nearly a hundred years, doctors and scientists didn't know how aspirin worked. They just knew it did.

For the longest time, I didn't know how Higgles tracked me down. I just knew he always did.

It was only in Haven, Florida, after Higgles' visit, that I finally figured it out. I felt like an idiot for not realizing it long before. Picking up *Macao Thunder*, the book's binding broke loose and the pages fell out. There, glued to the inside of the spine, was a tiny GPS chip. All the books where the same.

Higgles was right. I am like a comet. I leave a trail.

CHAPTER 59

THE MORE I THOUGHT about Higgles' visit the more I started believing that there actually had been something in the bag, that I'd somehow lost it between the grab and checking the contents. Why else would Higgles give me a chance to produce it? Why else would he even show up here?

I locked the door behind him and crashed on the mattress. I couldn't think straight; my head, muzzy from the beers I'd had at Charm's, ached with worry.

A thick dream slowly carpeted me. I dreamt I was drowning in deep water, slipping under, choking.

I woke gasping for air, my lungs heavy with smoke. Bounding to my feet, I looked for the flames I was sure were licking the walls. Instead I found someone sitting in the red recliner, staring at me.

Ray-Ray. Or the ghost of Ray-Ray. Maybe I wasn't really awake yet, a dream within a dream.

But my intestines told me otherwise. They kicked violently, churning with a toxic mess that felt like vinegar and baking soda. It was Ray-Ray all right. He was real, sitting ten feet from me, tautly relaxed with a huge cigar clamped too casually between his lips.

"Jesus fuck, Ray-Ray," I said. "You're alive."

"Why wouldn't I be?" His voice was sharp, edged with anger. He wasn't here for a friendly visit. A pink duffel bag emblazoned with the words *Florida is for Retired Lovers* sat at his feet. "You don't seem thrilled to see me."

"How did you find—"

"You know, you've changed," he said, tapping ash on the floor. "Where's that innocent, beautiful idiot I once knew?"

I stood stock still, afraid to move. Higgles then Ray-Ray. I wasn't a lover of mysteries, especially one's I was tangled up in, clueless and confused. "What are you doing here? How'd you get in?"

He motioned to the door with his left hand, or what should have been his left hand. It was gone. All that remained was a rough, red, rounded stub.

My throat kicked off a phantom throb. New Orleans. Frogman. It'd been Ray-Ray who'd attacked me.

"I got in the way everyone gets in," he said, "through the front door. You really need to get better locks." He toked on the cigar, kicked out an impressive smoke ring. "The guy downstairs says you've only stopped by once, then insulted him by running out the door and puking in the street."

"I don't like cigars."

"They're an acquired taste," Ray-Ray conceded. He motioned at me with his stub. "Sit. You're making me nervous."

I sat on the edge of the mattress opposite him, a mix of emotions surging through me. I was thrilled. I was terrified. The buried memory of him had shot to the surface, ripping through the years. In a way, I was glad to see him. Yes, he'd tried to kill me in New Orleans—or at least cause heavy damage—but maybe he could help me out of my situation. I'd missed him, though he dredged up more worry than relief. I wanted to ask what he'd been up to, where he'd been, tell him everything that had happened since our shelter days. Instead, I blurted out, "What happened to your hand?"

He tapped more ash onto the floor, ignoring my question. "How long has it been, two years?"

"More. Three or so."

He nodded, thinking through the number, then took in the room, the apartment. "Ever think about sprucing the place up a bit? Maybe getting a plant or something? Doesn't seem much like home."

"I've only been here a few weeks," I said. "Probably won't be here much longer."

"You got that right," he said, his voice menacing.

I swallowed hard. "What's that mean?"

"Oh, before I forget." He reached into the pink duffel bag with his good hand and pulled out a bottle of liquor, held it out to me. Gin. "Call it a housewarming gift."

I took the bottle, looked at the label. Randerskin Diamond. I'd never heard of it. "Not a big gin fan," I said, "but thanks."

"Save it for guests."

"I don't have guests."

"You do today."

I wondered if he had seen Higgles stop by. Holding up the bottle, I said, "You want a drink?"

Ray-Ray shook his head. "That's a rare bottle," he said. "Only a few hundred bottles are made annually. It's the official liquor of the royal Nepalese family. It's what Crown Prince Dipendra was drinking when he massacred his family."

"Really?"

He nodded. "Really."

A silence fell between us. As I watched Ray-Ray slowly draw his cigar down, I fought the urge to pour out the past four years. I fought the urge to tell him how I'd traveled, how I'd killed.

He wasn't here for my stories, I could tell. But whatever he was here for wouldn't end well.

Finally, after some minutes, he held up his stump like he was seeing it for the first time. "I got bitten a year or so back. That's how I lost my hand."

"By what, a bear?"

"By a woman."

"A woman bit your hand off?"

The question seemed to tire him, like he'd explained it all once too often. "She set her teeth into my hand, tore a chunk of flesh out. I didn't take proper care of it. It got infected. Very infected. Doctors had to amputate." He seemed embarrassed by the whole thing. "I came to learn that human bites are worse than a dog's, more dangerous." He leaned forward in his chair, extended his rounded, rough stub toward me. It looked like a piece of driftwood dipped in iodine. "I owe you an apology."

"For what?"

"For all this," he said, looking about the place. "For you being here. For the situation you're in. I am, in a sense, responsible."

His stub was still extended. I realized he wanted me to shake it.

I gingerly took the end of his arm. The skin was knotted and dry beneath my fingers. Ray-Ray reached over with his good hand, clamped down tight on my wrist. "Sorry for this," he said, then swiftly twisted my arm upward and yanked me off balance.

I hit the floor face first. Ray-Ray cocked my arm back painfully, rammed a knee to the middle of my back, pinning me.

"It'd break my heart to have to hurt you," he said, hurting me.

"What do you want?" I said, my face rammed to the floor.

His voice was eerily calm. "What do I want?" he replied. "A young Latino lover, for starters. I want a better figure. I'd say I want world peace, but world peace would put me out of a job. Oh, and my hand. I want my hand back. But you know what I'll settle for?" He pressed his knee harder to my spine. Every pore on my body shot out sweat.

"Fuck, Ray-Ray," I said, in pain. "Go easy."

He didn't go easy. "I asked you a question."

"What would you settle for?"

He took his knee out of my back, leaned over me, and put his moist lips to my ear. "Whatever was in the bag," he said, his breath striking hotly. "I'll settle for that."

CHAPTER 60

THE BEST LIES ARE those kept simple. That way the story stays straight.

Ray-Ray got the same story I gave Higgles: I didn't have what he wanted on me. Safe-deposit box, bank, Presidents' Day.

Ray-Ray lifted his knee from my back, freeing me. "I believe you," he said, sitting back down.

I got up, feeling like I'd been snapped in half then jammed back together. I slowly sat down on the mattress.

Ray-Ray didn't believe me. The pinched sourness of his face told me he knew I was lying. "I like you," he said. "I want this to work out. I want to feel comfortable using the word 'amicable' here. That's how I want this whole thing to go down."

"I like the word 'amicable.'" I rubbed my shoulder.

"Unfortunately, another word that comes to mind, too. It's a Greek word. *Akrasia*," he said. "Know it?"

Higgles had thrown it out before, after the Austin trip and the attack of Frogman/Ray-Ray, but he didn't know what it meant.

Neither did I.

"It means weak-willed. Acting in a way that is in direct conflict with better judgment." He held up his nub like it was the Olympic torch. "Let me give you an example," he said. "There was this young man who seemed a bit lost, seemed to have nothing in his life. No home, no family, no friends. So this older, more experienced gentleman took him under his wing, started mentoring him. When the time came, he gave the boy some cash, set him up in the business. He gave him a purpose, a reason to wake every morning. And for about a year straight, our boy did a good job. So," Ray-Ray said, massaging his chin with his stump, "the boy's mentor decides the boy is ready for a promotion. He pulls some strings, sets him up with a new passport, and opens up a world of opportunity. He sends him to Cancún and other exotic places." Ray-Ray pauses. "Are you with me so far?"

My skin prickled hot. I was totally confused. Ray-Ray had directed me to the fanny pack, but Higgles controlled the Kam Man. Still, I said, "I'm with you."

"Good. Because this is where the boy fucks up. This is where *akrasia*, his weak will, comes in," he said. "You see, instead of appreciating all he'd been given, instead of being content working his way up the ranks, our boy is tempted to do something that he knows—he knows deep down to his core—goes against everything right. Does that stop him? No. He does it anyway. The gentleman tries to set him straight, beat a bit of sense in him, but no luck. The boy tries to disappear. But that's not the worst of it. He actually turns on his mentor, starts fucking him," Ray-Ray said.

"What exactly did this boy do?"

"For one, he teamed up with some asshole," he said. "An asshole who knows the ins-and-outs of the game, the value of certain materials and information." Ray-Ray stood, straightened his pants, then sat back down. "When I was young, all this cheap Shakespeare shit—the intrigue, the violence, the murder, the covert running around—used to be thrilling. Now, it's tedious." He hit me with a damp gaze. He looked like he was about to cry. "Please don't make me do what I don't want to do."

I tried to swallow but my throat wouldn't let me. "Listen, Ray-Ray, I made a mistake."

"You sure as fuck did."

"I mean, I didn't know I was working with you."

"*For* me, not *with* me."

"I just thought—"

"That's the problem. You *thought*. I didn't bring you into all this for your brilliant strategic insights. Now," he said, "the only thing I want to hear from you is that you have what I want."

"I have it," I said. "I'll *have* it. Tomorrow, noon. Here."

He ran his nub over his hair, smoothing it, then stood. He smiled, sincerely. "I like amicable arrangements."

Pausing at the door, he said, "I forgot to ask, what's the asshole's name, the one you've been working with? The one pulling everything together?"

I thought of lying, but why? If Higgles was in the same situation, he'd hang me out in a moment, instantly turn me over. "Higgles."

"Yes?" Ray-Ray said.

"Yes."

He stood a moment, his face brightening with contempt. His eyes drilled through me. Everything about him shouted *Don't fuck with me.* "Well, are you going to tell me his name or not?"

"Higgles," I said again, thinking he hadn't heard me.

"Yes?" His voice cut the air.

"His name." I didn't understand. Then something cracked in my brain. A blaze of clarity tore through me.

Ray-Ray *was* Higgles. He'd directed me to the locker, the phone. He ran the game. That was his last name, a name I'd never known, never thought to know. Ray-Ray Higgles.

Which meant that Higgles, the guy I've been calling Higgles, was—

I didn't know who he was.

CHAPTER 61

THE FIRST TIME WE met in Brighton, he laughed at my suggestion that I call him Higgles, that he call me Ray-Ray. The time in New Orleans when he referred to himself in the third person. *Higgles' head is a bit messed up today. Higgles needs a vacation.* I should have known.

Now it didn't matter. The faux-Higgles. Ray-Ray. They'd both found me.

They both wanted something I didn't have.

Both were determined to get it.

Yet, unbelievably, both had miraculously walked out of my sad apartment, leaving me alone. At least until tomorrow noon.

Evening entered the room, staining it with shadows. I felt flayed, my skin cut clean off of me and every nerve exposed. Even the slow breeze lazily pushing through the open window hit me with what felt like the tip of a whip.

The idea of making a run for it skittered across my brainpan, then died away. Any escape would be only temporary. And wasn't that my whole point in coming to Haven, to end all the running?

Tomorrow, I determined, I'd resolve the whole affair, one way or another. How exactly I'd do that I didn't yet know. And that scared the shit out of me.

Tangled in the immediate, I couldn't see the whole scene. I couldn't see my next move.

I couldn't make future plans because there was no future.

I needed a place to place my hope. Something to set my sights on. If I had that, I felt, then I'd have the strength to pull through whatever tomorrow brought.

If only I had someone to talk to, someone to snap me out of my panic—Clement or my parents or even the Ray-Ray I knew three years ago—then I felt certain I could see the course of action I had to take. Someone I could trust to talk me past my dread. There had to be a way free, if only I could see it.

Sarah. She could help. Or at least listen.

Since my attempt to reconnect with her, she'd been nibbling at my thoughts, forcing her way forward.

Maybe she'd broken up with that guy I'd seen at her place. Maybe he wasn't even her boyfriend but just some guy. Maybe, if they were together, I could somehow break them up.

Having no cell phone, I grabbed a fistful of change and headed down to the battered pay phone on the street corner. Sarah's old cellphone number kicked to the voicemail of a J. P. Ghahi. I poured more quarters in the phone, dialed up information, gave them her Inwood address, but couldn't find a new number for her.

I got the number for her parents, called them, and claimed I was a colleague of Sarah's from her old art gallery who wanted to get in touch with her. "I've just opened my business, thought she'd be an ideal fit," I said. Her father actually asked about salary. I threw out a high figure. "Plus three weeks' vacation."

Her father made a noise like a gas stove igniting. "That's near double what she's making now," he said excitedly, and handed over Sarah's information.

A 631 area code. So she'd made the transition to New Jersey. A bigger space, quiet, less chaos. She'd fully moved on to the life she thought she deserved. Hopefully, though, without the guy.

Mustering courage, I dropped in the last of my change and dialed.

She answered on the fourth ring, sounding tired.

My blood leapt just hearing her voice. "Hey," I said, my words rushing out. "I hope I'm not bothering you. And I hope it's not too late to call. It's just that—"

I broke off, unsure what to say.

"Listen, Sarah, I know it's been a long time, but I've been thinking about you. A lot. And I've been thinking that the way we ended, the way we left things, isn't the way I want it to be." It was true—at least at the moment. "I know it's a lot to ask," I said, my lungs aching for air, "especially coming now, after so long, but I'm going to be in the area soon, and I was thinking maybe, if you'd be up for it, we could have dinner or drinks, catch up a bit."

The phone connection clicked, sounding like a playing card in the spokes of a child's bike. I waited for her voice to travel the thousands of miles to my ear. I waited for what felt an hour.

Then she spoke, her voice coming like a flock of starlings, scattered then solid and swift. "I'm sorry," she said. "But who is this? Who's calling?"

CHAPTER 62

Haven, Florida

THE WOMAN HAS MY name, which means she has my life, or some part of it. Somehow, she has grabbed a thread and traced it back to my beginnings. She also has a pistol pointed at me.

The chat-up at Charm's, the hard come-on, the promise—and fulfillment—of sex, it was all a play. She had the upper hand from the start.

The room's air tastes of burnt plastic and arc welding. My mind runs hot, thrashing about. I recognize this moment. In Seoul, moments before catching a fist to my temple, I realized that just because my contact said he wasn't my enemy didn't mean he was my friend. It's a feeling of being fucked yet not clearly understanding how or to what degree.

Standing naked with a makeshift toilet-paper bandage on my neck wound, I feel ill from it all. I say, "I'd appreciate it if you'd leave. I'm expecting company."

"You've already got company," she replies.

"Other company."

The statement seems to confuse her, like I've dumped her moments after we'd been named king and queen of the prom. She rattles the ice in her tumbler, says, "Everything in life boils down to something very simple: two people meet. They either like each other or they don't. If they like each other, they may fall in love." She takes a swig of gin, then cocks her head to the side. "Am I making sense?"

"So far."

She nods. "I think he once truly loved me. But not now, not any more." She lifts her eyes to mine. "Why do you think he stopped?"

I shrug. There are too many reasons, too many possibilities. Plus, I have no clue as to who she's talking about.

"I can't figure it out either," she says.

The conversation halts, each of us studying the other. She says my name a few times, waves the pistol a bit like she's getting used to the weight of it, then, "Do you know who I am?"

"You're someone who doesn't think she's very pretty," I say, speaking in a controlled voice. A calm voice. A voice I hoped didn't betray my true feelings. "You're someone who's unhappy. You're someone who, for whatever reason, has done some research on me and is now sitting in my place drinking my gin."

She smiles her crooked-tooth smile. "It was never your gin," she says. "You know that, don't you? He brought it for me, knowing I'd be here."

How the fuck does she know? I think. The faux-Higgles and then Ray-Ray was too much, but now this woman? She's involved? It's impossible, insane. Or am I so stupid as to not see the set-up?

I'm not that stupid. I can't be.

So who is her ex? The man who once loved her? It can't be Ray-Ray, can it? There's no way they know each other. Plus, I can't see him saying he loved her, pulling it off. It would have been an Oscar-worthy performance.

The woman refreshes her drink, the gin gurgling from the bottle. "I'm surprised he didn't think to poison it."

"You're talking about the man who's stopped loving you?"

She makes a noise I take for a laugh. "Sweet Raymond? Ray-Ray's never loved anyone but himself."

I am that stupid. Ray-Ray. I can't believe she somehow knows Ray-Ray.

"No," she says. "I'm talking about Mason."

My mind struggles past the impossibility of her and Ray-Ray, tries to grasp what she's just said. Mason. Bearclaw boy.

I gingerly pull the toilet paper from my neck, bewildered. "So you're still in love with the king of pastries?" The toilet paper tears, comes off in damp, red pieces, the rest clinging to the sticky scab.

Confusion tints her face. "I'm talking about the other Mason. Mason One," she says.

It's my turn to look confused. *I think he once truly loved me,* she'd said. *But not now, not anymore.* She made it sound like Mason One was still alive. "The dead one?" I say.

"Who said he was dead?"

"You did."

She shakes her head. "I said I *lost* him. In the Gulf."

"So…what, he's MIA?"

She smiles. Then frowns. "Emotionally, yes. But technically…" Her voice fades, then comes back strong. "Actually, truth be told, he was dead. Literally dead. At least for a little while."

I wait for more.

There is no more.

I say, "You're talking like a drunk right now."

Taking a deep breath, she explains.

After the failure of her first marriage, she took to drinking. "Or drinking *more,*" she says. She met Mason One at Charm's Tavern. He was younger than her, in the army, and a bit wild. They took to each other instantly. "Like I said, he'd do crazy shit just because he was afraid to do it. I think that's why he married me."

"Because he was afraid of you?" I gesture to my clothing—can I get dressed? She waves the pistol at me, which I take to mean okay.

"Not of me," she says. "Of marriage. He was terrified of the concept. So we got hitched." She sips her gin. "We weren't together but six months when he got deployed to the Gulf."

"And that's when you lost him," I say, stepping into my underwear, then my pants.

She nods, her eyes filming with tears. "He was out patrolling the Kuwait-Iraq border in a Humvee with two others," she says. "The driver got hit, lost control, and ended up flipping the truck."

"Hit by sniper fire?"

She shakes her head. "Hit by Mason," she says. "Mason was riding shotgun. The guy driving said something he didn't like, so Mason cocked him." She powers down a swallow of gin, lets out a calm burp. "The Humvee ran off the road into—I don't know—an irrigation ditch or something. It turned over, trapping everyone. They all drowned, including Mason, which is a typical Mason move. Drowning in a desert." Tears salt her cheeks. "Anyway, Mason was the only one pulled from the wreck in time, the only one Lazarused back to life." She runs her hand over her face, wiping away weariness. "But death changed him. The Mason who came back wasn't my Mason. Wasn't the man I'd fallen in love with. The man who returned was some stranger in Mason's skin. It was like the face of the building had been saved while the insides had been gutted. He kept saying he loved me but then he'd do things to hurt me. I had to get away from him. And for a while," she says, "I did. I found my Mason Two. I made it out of Haven, made it to Indiana, built a new life." The woman forces a sad smile. "And now I'm back," she says, sounding exhausted, worn. "Back in Haven, back with Mason One, back doing the same shady shit I was doing before. They're right when they say you can never cure an addict, only manage the addiction."

Neither of us speak for some time. We remain still, a portrait waiting to be painted. Finally, she says, "The bank accounts, the fake names, the traveling about for flash drives, secret codes, and exchanges. Ray-Ray turned me on to the whole thing. He turned me on to it all, showed me the ropes, taught me the basics."

"Just like me," I say. "How did you two meet?"

She takes in a deep breath, like she hasn't tasted air for hours. "God, how did we meet?" She shakes her head. "I don't like to think about it." A smile sneaks to her lips. "You have to admit that it's exciting at first. Fun."

"But then it isn't so fun."

Her smiles wilts. "That's why I stopped. At least for a time." She brushes her bangs from her eyes. "What makes it all so sad is that I was the one to introduce Mason to all this. After he came back from the Gulf, I dragged him into the game. I taught him everything Ray-Ray had taught me." She pauses, thinks a moment. "Why did I do that?" She shakes her head. "I guess I just wanted my old Mason back. I guess I thought that if we shared that, had some special secret, we'd be brought together again." The hard morning light jets into the apartment, strikes her full and blanches her features. "It only made things worse. It only made him worse."

So it was a family affair. I wonder if I'd ever crossed paths with Mason One, if we'd made an exchange.

My lungs seize. I'd not only crossed paths with Mason, I'd worked with him. *For* him.

Mason is Higgles. My Higgles.

Like a bolt of cloth unrolling, the whole history of my Kam Manning flags out before me.

From the moment I got the fanny pack and cell phone to when I traveled to Brighton, I'd been aligned with Ray-Ray, working for the real Higgles.

Then, somehow, Mason One hacked the relationship. I went to Brighton, thinking I was meeting Higgles. Stupidly, I didn't question the set-up for a second. I just handed Mason that momentum, signed-on as his lackey, and began busting my ass across the world for him. Realizing you've been duped by someone sucks. Realizing you've duped yourself is crippling.

"Mason." The woman's throat knocks out a noise of sadness. "So many false starts," she says. "So many failed endings. How can you tell what's important? How do you tell what's worth fighting for?"

I say to the woman, "Mason got my name from Ray-Ray. You got it from Mason." It's the only thing that makes sense. But the why is more muddled than the how. "You're Mason's partner."

Sweat gathers in the hollow of her throat, runs down her sternum, following the valley of her cleavage. "No," she says. "Not any more. He needs to understand that there are repercussions."

"Repercussions for what?" I've dressed and now hold a clutch of ice cubes in a dishrag to my neck while I pace the room.

She lays the gun in her lap, rubs her temples. I could make a play, grab the gun. I'd have a good chance of turning the tables.

I don't move.

The menu is set; turning the tables won't change what's about to be served.

I sit in the chair across from her.

She frowns, closes her eyes. "For forgetting my birthday."

I want to laugh but bite it back. "You're doing all of this—whatever this is—because he forgot your birthday?"

"That sparked it," she says. "But there were a lot of other things, too." She wipes her forehead, looks at her damp hand.

"So what's your plan?"

The question catches her off guard. She lifts a shoulder, shrugging. "Resolution. Revenge. Redemption." She smiles, shakes her head. "Last night, it was all clear in my mind. But now—" She breaks off, rolls the sweating plastic tumbler of gin across her forehead. "Tell me about the confab."

"The confab?"

"This afternoon's meeting with Ray-Ray, Mason, and you."

"You seem to already know everything about it," I say.

"Not the details."

Strangely, I trust her. She's the closest thing to a friend I have right now, so I talk.

She listens attentively, then wipes her face again. "You're saying Ray-Ray hasn't figured out it was Mason you've been working with?"

I only just figured it out myself. "Seems not."

She laughs. "And they're both after it?"

I nod. What the hell *it* is, I still don't know.

She makes a face, either amused or irritated, I can't tell. "Ray-Ray will show up first. If he said he'll be here by noon, he'll show up by quarter to. He likes to arrive early, catch people off guard. Mason is the opposite. He'll get here late." She lifts her chin, motioning me over.

I move to her.

"Do me a favor," she says. "Bend down."

I bend, my head level with hers. The scent of lemons and warm cinnamon is soured with the smell of sweat and sex.

"Hold still." She pours a bit of her gin on my head then musses my hair. "Good. Now move the chair there," she says, pointing to the space at the edge of the day's shifting light.

I drag the chair over.

Placing the pistol back in her purse, she snaps it shut and holds it out for me. "Put it on the floor where the chair just was."

I take her purse; I have the gun. I can settle the immediate, but there is the rest.

She reads my mind. "That's not the way out," she says, her voice lazy.

There is no way out, I realize. *And when there is no way out, push on. Find a way further in.*

I push on, put the purse where she says.

Tipping the tumbler back, she downs the rest of her gin, then studies the apartment's stage. She smiles. "God," she says, "he's going to be pissed."

◉ ◉ ◉

SAVE IT FOR GUESTS. Ray-Ray had given me the gin knowing the woman would find me, would end up at my place. It was as though he'd been following the script of a play. He'd seen the third act long before I'd even taken my seat.

CHAPTER 63

WHEN I WAS YOUNGER, occasionally, after dinner, my father would call me out onto the back patio and offer me a seat beside him on one of the rickety lawn chairs. I was to play the audience for the life lessons he rambled out as he tucked in a couple more after-dinner cocktails. "Never eat fish at a restaurant on a Monday," was one. And, "Stay clear of women who giggle too much. They're a dangerous lot." Other pearls he offered: if there are two lines at, say, a cash register, always take the left; have your dress shirts washed and pressed, never dry cleaned; when out with others, never buy the first round; and always have an excuse ready for use, no matter the situation.

But the one I remember now was, "Know a man's full name before doing any business with him."

I should have known the moment I met Mason in Brighton that he wasn't Higgles.

Higgles are always Higgles.

Masons are Masons.

CHAPTER 64

WHEN I'D KAM MANNED in Côte d'Ivoire, I'd seen Clement again. I'd been ill for three days straight, every ounce of liquid exuded from my body via my pores, anus, or mouth. I couldn't stop shitting, sweating, and vomiting. Supernova flashes of light panned my vision with each visit to the toilet. I trembled, barely able to walk the ten-foot span from the bed to the bathroom.

Finally, an awkward reprieve arrived. Slowly, gradually, my stomach stopped lurching, my bowels stopped their spasms, and sweat no longer burned my skin. Lying on the bed, I finally fell into a rough sleep, a hard comfort.

But ten minutes in, the weight of something settling at the end of the mattress woke me.

Lifting my head, I saw him there, sitting naked by my feet, his back to me. I recognized him immediately. "Clement?" My friend, dead and naked in my hotel room in Africa, shaking and sobbing silently, his head in his hands. His skin, dappled with bruises the color of an oil-stained street, hung loose on his frame. His vertebrae made an uneven stack along the length of his back. Everything about him was misaligned, like the cartilage and ligaments that bolted his bones together had abandoned their task.

I worked myself into a sitting position. "Clement, what's wrong?" I reached for him.

He rose from the bed, trembling fiercely. I called to him again— "Tell me what's wrong"—but he wouldn't turn around, wouldn't even acknowledge me. It was as though he was too ashamed or angry to show his face. He lurched painfully forward, moving to the bathroom.

I forced myself to my feet. My stomach pitched, flooding my mouth with bile that I choked back down. Supporting my weight against the wall, I worked my way to the bathroom. "Come on, man," I groaned. Why was he making me chase after him? Couldn't he see how sick I was? "Talk to me," I said, but there was no one there.

The bathroom was empty. No Clement. Just a dank shower stall, a foul toilet, a dripping sink, and a fluorescent bulb overhead that stained everything a sickly blue-green.

"What the fuck?" I was incensed. I wanted Clement back more than anything else in the world. He'd finally come, and carried no message, no demands, no apology or closure, no dire warning, or even a shard of advice. Not even a ghostly moan.

All he'd done with his one chance was sit on my bed, cry a bit, flash his bruised ass at me, then leave.

What kind of haunting was that? He hadn't even tried to scare me.

CHAPTER 65

A T 11:44 A.M., RAY-RAY arrives. He enters the apartment like he's slipping into a theater midperformance, steady and quiet.

The place is stifling. The windows are closed. The woman sits in the far corner of the room, well over halfway through the bottle of gin. I stand by the windows, staring out into the street.

The gun is in her purse on the floor beside me.

Ray-Ray, the woman, me. I've thrown my lot in with the woman for the moment. Even so, none of the scenarios I've played out in my mind end well.

Ray-Ray pauses in between the two of us, turns a hundred and eighty degrees to study us each. He waves his stub at me, at the room, at nothing in particular, then his gaze settles on the woman. "Hello, Sweetheart."

"Hello, Mr. Raymond Higgles."

Naked, she seems comfortable, content, in control. She uncrosses her legs, scratches the inside of her thigh. "You look awful, Mr. Raymond Higgles," she says.

He does. Bloated face, dark-circled eyes, his pink button down is wrinkled, his white slacks stained. He looks like he's just untangled himself from a cramped airplane seat after a fourteen-hour flight. His knobbed stump, poking out of from the cuff of his shirtsleeve, looks like he's been trying to sharpen it on a whetstone. But his hair looks great. Parted evenly and coiffed to perfection.

He turns his attention to the sweaty plastic tumbler on the table. "If I didn't know better," he says, "I'd say you put that there just to piss me off." He sets the tumbler on the floor, wipes the ring of moisture off the table with his shirtsleeve. "The condensation will ruin the table's finish."

He paces the room, avoiding the swath of sunlight cutting the room. Ray-Ray hates direct sunlight. In the shelter, he told me he didn't tan but turned an odd, leathery orange. Like an Oompa-Loompa, he said.

He stops in front of the woman. "I honestly wanted to believe that it wasn't you, that someone else had corrupted my boy," he says.

She tilts her head, looks up at him. "Maybe someone else did, Mr. Raymond Higgles. Maybe I'm just visiting. Maybe you have more to worry about than you think."

"What worries me," he says, "is your nakedness. Throw on some clothing, please."

She doesn't move. "Have a seat, Mr. Raymond Higgles."

His voice spikes with irritation. "This isn't a goddamn coffee klatch." He turns to me. "Your hair looks like a dead opossum. Where'd you get it styled, at a homeless shelter? So," he says, "do you have it or not?"

I dig my hands into my pockets. Nervousness edges into terror. "Yes," I lie.

Ray-Ray crosses the room, still avoiding the sun. "Hand it up."

"First," I say, a brick of fear jamming in my throat, "I need something."

"You're not really in a position to make demands. Hand—"

"Sit for a spell, Mr. Raymond Higgles," the woman interrupts. She nods at the chair. "Let's do some catching up."

Distracted, Ray-Ray looks to the chair that is now held full in the harsh noon light. "Nice touch." He drags the chair back to where it originally had been, back to where her purse now sits. "You know how sensitive my skin is," he says, then adds, "And enough with the 'Mr. Raymond Higgles' shit."

"You know, I never liked your name," she says. "It makes you sound—what?—a bit gay."

"I *am* a bit gay," Ray-Ray says. "So I guess it's fitting." He hikes one leg of his pants, then the other, and sits. "I see you found the gin. You're a damn divining rod for alcohol."

She lifts her tumbler, a salute.

"I should have poisoned it," he says.

She runs her finger along the rim. "Once again, you missed your chance to assassinate me."

Ray-Ray laughs. "Assassinate? That only happens to important people. You? You'll just be put down." He turns to me. "Open a window, would you? It reeks of sex in here."

I open a window. A tepid breeze pushes in, mingling with the hot, rank air.

"Stay there," he says. "Where I can keep an eye on you."

"He's not the one you should be worried about." The woman smiles sadly. "How'd you lose the hand?"

Ray-Ray holds up his stub, glares at the woman. "Some alcoholic bitch got her teeth into me. Got a nasty infection from a bite," he says. "They had to cut it off." He points his stub at my neck. "She got her teeth into you, too, I see."

I say nothing, my hands still in my pockets.

Outside, a few birds sound, noting their positions, their territory. A truck lumbers past outside, grinding its way toward the Atlantic. A dog barks twice then sets into whimpering. The sounds of noon.

"He's coming, you know," the woman says.

"And who would this be?"

"Mason," she says. "He should be here soon."

Ray-Ray's face mottles. He struggles to play it off. "Yes, I know," he says, his voice betraying worry. He didn't know.

In the room, I've disappeared from the moment. Ray-Ray and the woman consume the immediate.

The woman tips her glass at him. "You're a terrible liar."

"Me?" Ray-Ray smiles. "I have no idea what you're talking about."

"I'm talking about how you operate," she says, anger flaring. "You want things just right but you're just too lazy to follow through. You're a half-assed perfectionist." She pauses to regain her composure. "But none of that matters now." Does he have a cigarette? she asks.

He says, "I thought you quit smoking."

"I have. I only smoke when I'm anxious."

He shakes his head. "There's a lot wrong with me, I admit, but self-control isn't one of them. You, though..." He looks at his stub like a woman would glance at her fingernails. "Whether it's a drink or a husband, you start with one and pretty quickly you've had three or more."

He's hit a nerve. The woman rises from the chair, her voice barbed. "I've only had two real husbands—"

"Three," Ray-Ray says calmly. "The Haven town hall will verify that."

The energy pours from her. She takes on the gray of a dying fish and settles back hard into the chair. She looks away, her eyes sparkling with tears. The fight is a fruitless one. A sob exits her lungs then turns into a full-on cry, a life's worth of tears spilling from her. "Mrs. Raymond Higgles," she gasps. "I never liked the name."

A tsunami of realization hits me.

To love and to cherish, to have and to hold.

Ray-Ray was her first. This was the woman Ray-Ray told me about, his *wife*. This was the woman he married for a green card.

Until death do you part.

Or at least until citizenship is official.

The woman's sobs stop. Her voice cracks the quiet. "You tricked me into marriage."

"I never tricked you," he says. "You knew what you were getting into. You knew the landscape."

"I *was* the landscape." Her voice is choked with grief. Tears gloss her cheeks, drip from her chin. "And you trod all over me."

My skin shrinks tight to my bones. Embarrassment, shame, disgust. Her pain chokes me. I fight not to cry myself.

The woman coughs out a string of snot from her nose. "Hand me my purse. I need a Kleenex," she says to Ray-Ray.

Ray-Ray grabs the purse off the floor and walks it to her.

He pulls up short of handing it to her. "What do you have in here, a knife?"

"A gun," she says, her face shiny with tears. "I plan on killing you."

He blanches a moment, then lights up with laughter. But his laughter stops cold.

Clamping the purse under his handless arm, he struggles to unlatch the butterfly clasp.

My stomach fills with concrete and glass. Was that the woman's entire plan? That Ray-Ray would hand her the purse, hand her the gun? Why didn't she just keep the gun when she had it?

Why didn't I?

Ray-Ray wrestles to unlatch the purse, unable to get a firm purchase.

I answer the question *Now what?* before I can even think it.

When there is no way out, push on. Find a way further in.

I charge Ray-Ray, let loose a wide swing.

He senses it coming, artfully steps to the left, stealing the force of the blow.

Instead of connecting with his head, my punch glances off his arm. But it's enough to knock him back, enough to make him drop the purse.

We both stand taut, a few feet apart. The purse is closer to him, but I'm now in the running. I can get it. I can get the gun.

A thought flashes through my mind, pushing out a bark of laughter: *the gun has no bullets.*

Ray-Ray glowers at me. "I have an expansive sense of humor, but there's nothing funny here."

"Let's not make a mess," I say, not quite sure what I mean.

"There's still time for you to redeem yourself. Still time to make your way back into my good graces."

It's a lie. Whatever redemption he has to offer is a redemption I can't afford. Still I say, "I'm listening."

He holds up his hands—or hand and stub—like he's surrendering. "Let's get one thing clear: I'm not the enemy here."

But you aren't my ally either, I think.

I lunge for the purse like Pete Rose hitting home plate.

Ray-Ray's foot is there to greet me. He stomps me to the floor and sets into some sort of *Riverdance* rendition. My face, my shoulder, my neck and back. He kicks and kicks, grunting the whole time.

Curled into a fallout position, I hold the purse tucked tight beneath me like a rugby ball in a scrum, taking blow after blow.

It's the woman who saves me. She lets loose a lung-freezing scream. "Stop!"

Startled, Ray-Ray pauses. It's all I need.

I clamber roughly to my feet, purse in hand.

Ray-Ray's on me instantly, ramming me in the chest with his stub.

I stamp on his foot, pin him in position, then hit him with a brutal headbutt to his face just as I grab his testicles and try to rip them off.

He howls then drops like a politician's campaign promises.

I stagger back, winded, bleeding, tired.

Ray-Ray lies on the floor. His nose is smashed, face bright with blood. He huffs noisily for air, moans.

I open the purse.

I pull out the pistol.

Dazed, Ray-Ray stares up at me a moment, then props himself up on his stub and struggles to his feet.

Standing hunched like an old woman, he makes a hissing noise and hacks out a mouthful of brown-red phlegm. He's hurt bad. "That's not the way I fantasized you would handle my balls."

He holds out his hand.

I stand some feet away, aiming the gun at his head.

"Make this clover, friend." He steps forward. "Give me the gun."

I give him the gun.

Or part of it.

I give him a bullet.

The air splits with a short, startling crack that surprises me.

It surprises Ray-Ray, too. His head snaps back and he wheels hard to the floor, landing in the swath of vibrant, punishing light.

At first I think he's playing opossum, but then I see a chunk of his lower face is gone. His eyes are filled with wonder, fright. And for the first time I've ever seen, his hair is mussed.

From some place deep and secret within him, a gurgle issues, fights its way out into the open through his now enlarged mouth. It's a language I don't know, a language only taught at death's door.

His stub rises like he's hailing a cab. He's hailing for help, mercy. He's begging for his life.

I pull the trigger again. A click. Nothing more. I pull it again. No shot.

One bullet. That was all the gun held.

His arm drops loudly to the floor. He exhales like he's blowing out candles on a birthday cake.

Ray-Ray's dead.

CHAPTER 66

O N March 13, 1964, about 3:15 a.m., on her way back from
work, Kitty Genovese was stabbed to death near her
home in Kew Gardens, New York.

Driving the empty streets, Winston Moseley spotted
a young woman walking alone on the street. He parked his car, stalked
her a half block, and attacked her from behind.

Kitty cried out for help.

Someone yelled from a window, "Let that girl alone."

Frightened, Moseley fled, leaving Kitty gravely injured.

But no one came to help her. No one called the police. No one
stepped out of their warm apartments to see what had happened.

Still calling for help, Kitty staggered into a back vestibule of the
building, and collapsed in front of the locked door.

Moseley returned in ten minutes, now wearing a wide-brimmed
hat to shadow his face, and systematically searched the parking lot,
train station, and small apartment complex, looking for his victim.

He found her half-conscious and bleeding profusely. He proceeded to
stab her several more times, then raped her, after which he left her to die.

The resulting investigation by *The New York Times* said that thirty-
eight people had either heard or witnessed the attack. But Genovese's
cries for help went unanswered. No one called the police until long
after she was dead. No one did a thing.

At first I worry that the shot I emptied into Ray-Ray's face will
prompt a call to the police. Then I think, *Maybe not.*

Maybe not.

CHAPTER 67

R AY-RAY'S BLOOD PERCOLATES THEN slows to a seep, blossoming on the hardwood floor.

Morning washes over all that can't be changed.

"The gun was empty," the woman says, stunned. "I checked. There were no bullets. I'm positive."

There was one, I want to say, but she knows that.

A taste of metal and grease, like a rusty bike chain, floods my mouth. "Shit," I say, and my voice sounds like cracking timber. My mind glitches on worries that make no sense. Will the blood ruin the floor? Will I get my rent deposit back? Will the woman cry more?

The room's air is sharp with a smell of burnt flesh and, strangely, wet wool. A fly punches in the open window. It buzzes past Ray-Ray's face, which is a bouquet of meat, and lands in his blood-matted hair.

The weight of the empty pistol is a boulder in my hand. I can't hold it any longer, and set it on the floor, then sit in the chair Ray-Ray had been sitting in. It's still warm, the ghost of his presence lingering.

The woman rises and steps to Ray-Ray, leaning over his body to make certain he's dead. She says nothing for nearly a minute. Then, "For the longest time, I believed that if I could figure out the moment I made my first mistake, figure out exactly what it was I did to drive myself here, to this juncture in my life, then I'd be able to atone for it. I'd be able to fix whatever it was that is wrong. But it doesn't work like that."

She rushes into the bathroom, closes the door. I hear her vomit in the toilet.

I find myself on my feet, rifling through his pockets, hoping for— what? A miracle, I guess. What I find is his gold-plated money clip straining with bills.

What comes next? I wonder. *What's my smartest move?*

I pocket the cash and sit back in the chair.

Returning, the woman slowly dresses, slips into her panties, slides on her skirt. She pulls on her blouse then pauses to study Ray-Ray. "Do you know how disheartening it is to realize that, even if you could relive your entire life, do everything different, it'd still turn out the same?"

A voice booms from the doorway in reply. "She loves asking questions like that. The kind of question you're not sure you're supposed to answer or not."

Mason.

He stands at the apartment's threshold, snacking on a foot-long sub sandwich. Lettuce, salami, cheese, I'd guess. Probably some mayo, too.

Mason/Higgles holds up the sandwich. "I don't think I brought enough for everyone." His scar seems to have grown since yesterday. "Guess we'll have to share," he says, striding in.

He swiftly grabs the gun off the floor. "I was wondering where this"—he holds up the gun—"went. Couldn't find it this morning. I couldn't find you, either."

Why I put the gun down, why I didn't just put it in my pocket, I can't say. True, it's empty, but Mason probably doesn't know that. I could have blustered, acted like I had a loaded chamber to back up my threats.

Mason sights the pistol on the woman. Taking a bite of his sandwich, he pulls the gun's trigger. It makes a hollow click. He lowers the gun. "There was a bullet in the chamber," he says, his mouth full. "Where'd it go?"

I hear myself say, "Ray-Ray has it."

Mason turns, plays like Ray-Ray's body just magically appeared. "Well, hello. What do we have here?" He gives Ray-Ray a hard kick to the head. Blood splays against the wall. "I guess I can take 'Kill Ray-Ray' off my to-do list." He toes Ray-Ray's stub with his boot, then tosses the remainder of the sandwich in the puddle of congealing blood. He turns to me. "So, you have it?" He pops the empty clip from the pistol, pulls a fresh clip from his back pocket, and rams it in the gun.

My mind whirls, trying to produce a strategy that will keep me alive. Mustering my energy, I prepare to mount a final fight. Find an opening and attack. It's a last-ditch effort. "It's still at the bank," I say, "in the safe-deposit box."

"We discussed this yesterday," he says, his face darkening. "We agreed on the plan."

"The plan changed when your boyfriend showed up," I say, nodding at Ray-Ray. "Your ex-wife didn't help matters either."

He studies Ray-Ray, then the woman. "Fair enough."

To my horror, the woman says, "He has it."

Mason sights the gun at my head.

"Not him," she says. "Ray-Ray."

He studies her a moment then says, "You're a terrible liar."

"I'm not lying."

"I know," he says, moving over to the body. "That's what I mean. I can always tell when you are and you aren't now." Keeping an eye on both the woman and me, Mason works through Ray-Ray's left pockets, rolls the body over and works through the right. He yanks Ray-Ray's shirt collar open, then pulls his shirt tail from his pants.

He finds nothing.

"I'm very confused," he says, standing. He tucks the gun into his waistband, steps to the woman. "You just told me the truth and yet it isn't true. Can you explain this to me?"

She doesn't get a chance. He coldcocks her squarely in the jaw.

Mason's ex-wife flips from her chair and is unconscious before her head bounces off the floor.

CHAPTER 68

Ray-Ray and the woman are sprawled on the floor. One's dead, the other is not.

The woman groans, her head lolling.

"God, she's gotten good at lying," Mason says. "I actually thought Ray-Ray had it." He stands over the woman, aims the gun at the back of her head, his finger firm to the trigger.

I could try to save her but there's no way to save her. I wait for the shot.

There is no shot.

Mason's arm drops. "Why are the simplest things the hardest to do?" Leaning over her, he shouts like she's hard of hearing. "I have to make a quick run to the bank, but I'll be back. You're not off the hook, young lady."

The pistol comes level to my forehead. "You have it on you, don't you?"

A voice fills the void. "Check," I hear myself say.

Mason holds still a moment then motions the pistol at me. "Best not be fucking with me, cousin." He nods toward the door. "Lead the way."

Out the apartment we go, my knees quivering as I lead the way down the long flight of stairs.

The sun stands hard in the sky. Mason slides on a pair of neon pink Wayfarer knockoffs with *Volcano Vodka* printed on the stems. He points to a powder-blue Smart car, hands me the keys. "Drive."

"I see you upgraded to luxury." I take the driver's seat.

"The car is a metaphor," he replies.

I buckle up. "For what?"

Mason slides into the passenger's side, leaves the seatbelt hanging slack. "Does it matter?"

I kick the engine over, drop the car in gear. "How'd you find me that first time? How'd you know I was working with Ray-Ray?"

"This isn't *Scooby Doo*, cousin. I'm not going to reveal everything just because you've asked. Plus," he says, "I have no idea what you're talking about." He rolls down the window. "Don't care, either."

Silence fills the moment. Then Mason laughs coldly. "Wow. You really have no clue what's going on here, do you?" He pokes my neck where the woman bit me with the muzzle of the gun. I flinch.

"She must really like you," he says.

"She seems to like anyone who buys her a drink."

"No." A slight shake of his head. "She only bites men who are special to her, men who have played an important role in her life." He scratches his stomach with the pistol's barrel. "You should see my chest."

A bit after noon, the traffic is light. I speed down the block, driving toward downtown. "I've only known her three hours."

"It doesn't take long to realize someone's worth." He keeps the gun leveled at me, runs his hand across his face. "I probably should have shot her. You think I should have shot her?"

I say nothing.

"God, I hate indecisive people, and here I am waffling," he says. "It's all your fault, cousin. You threw me off my game by killing Ray-Ray. I had everything perfectly laid out and you fucked up my plans."

"My apologies." I brake hard at the stop sign. Mason lurches forward.

"Apology accepted."

I accelerate through the intersection.

"It's just that, in my mind, I had Ray-Ray going out differently, by my own hand," he says.

The conversation dies.

I drive on, rolling through stop signs for a few blocks before pulling to a hard stop at the light.

My chance to break away is at the bank. Mason won't use the gun there. But then there's tomorrow and tomorrow's tomorrow. He'll keep coming after me, tracking me from state to state, country to country, until it's over. Until I'm dead.

The old highway stretches before us, running north-south. Trucks and cars and semis snap past in both directions, racing from one place only to be late for the next. The traffic light holds red for what feels an eternity. I look to Mason, look past him at the oncoming traffic. The bank isn't my way free. My way free is traveling toward us at sixty miles per hour.

I inch the car forward then hold. I say, "Is it true you died in the Gulf? That you were killed and brought back to life?"

Mason nods, studies the gun like he's never seen one before.

I pray the light stays red. Pray the traffic keeps coming.

Two cars zip past, heading south, followed by a light truck trudging north.

I hold.

"You know, things never turn out as you envision. Love, life, jobs, death. Nothing is ever really resolved. No happily ever after," he says. "We're bludgeoned into believing that there is a right way, an answer to everything. But there is no answer. There's only our daily lives."

I find myself laughing, even happy, as I ease my foot off the brake.

"Want to fill me in on the joke?" Mason says.

"Gladly, cousin," I say, and punch the gas, forcing the tiny car into the intersection. Forcing it directly into the path of a cement truck barreling south.

CHAPTER 69

THE IMPACT IS SPECTACULAR, stunning, pure.

A body at rest will remain at rest unless acted upon.

And it's a cement truck clipping at sixty-plus miles per hour that acts on us, slamming straight into Mason's side of the car.

Mason, unrestrained, blurs past me, launches through my side window, and hits the pavement face first. I see him skitter across the highway and under an approaching car.

Then I lose sight of him.

Fastened in tight, I am relaxed as I stay with the motion, trapped in the tumbling car.

My head concusses against the doorframe and a sharp light at the back of my eyes sears my vision, blinds me. My vision reemerges momentarily, flickering a whale belly blue-green that then floods to a pus yellow swallowed by grays then shadows then darkness.

Then I lose sight of everything.

Even darkness.

A ringing silence engulfs me. It lasts for days, months, lifetimes.

Then sirens.

My lungs are dusted with platinum and marshmallows, my heart pumping out liquid warmth.

I feel nothing.

I feel everything.

An immense pain shocks me conscious.

I'm in the hospital. Tubes and wires run off me like a failed science project. Every inch of my body, I swear, has been pummeled with a ball-peen hammer.

A thought, then another, breaks through the fog. The first: *I wish I were dead.*

The second: *I am alive.*

CHAPTER 70

THE ACCIDENT, I LEARN, resulted in a pile-up. Four cars in addition to ours, the cement truck, and a small U-Haul brimming with marijuana and counterfeit prescription pads. Nine injured. Two people dead.

One of the dead is the driver of the U-Haul, an ex-con with an outstanding warrant.

The other is Mason.

I know for certain because they ask me about him, ask if I knew him, if he was a friend or family member. *Knew* and *was*, not *know* and *is*. Mason has shifted to the past tense.

Also, I overheard a nurse talking about him. She said he looked like beef carpaccio. "I don't even know why they wasted their time bringing him to the ER," she said. "Should have taken him straight to the morgue."

Most of my injuries are not from the wreck, but from Ray-Ray's beating. I do have a mild concussion, though. The bite on my neck confuses everyone. How did I get those teeth marks?

Miraculously, the only bone I broke is my left wrist. Internally, though, I feel a mess. My urine is rust-colored.

As soon as I'm conscious and can speak cogently, the questions come. The nurses, the doctors, even the police. *What is my name? Who am I? Where do I live? Who was the man in the car with me?*

I shake my head, say only, "I don't know" or "I can't remember."

They hand me things they found on me in hopes of kindling a memory. Ray-Ray's money clip brimming with bills, the initials RH engraved in the gold. My keys, some change.

No ID. No wallet.

Do any of these things spark a memory? they ask.

I act like I'm studying them closely. I shake my head. "I don't know," I say again. "I can't remember."

Other questions, larger questions, remain unspoken, lingering in the air like fumes waiting to ignite.

But even with the police hovering about, I'm unconcerned.

I've seen my future and it isn't here, in Haven, in the hospital. In jail. I've seen my future and it isn't answering questions I can't afford to answer.

Night comes.

The nurse checks in on me every hour.

I wait until it's nearly 5:00 a.m., nearly time for the new shift of nurses to come on. Mustering my strength, I rise from bed, gather the cash and find my clothing.

One would think it's difficult for a bandaged patient with his left arm in a cast to just trundle out of his room, limp past the nurses' station and down the long hall to the elevators, nod a hello to a doctor, make his way through the hospital's lobby, pause a moment to ask a security guard where the taxi pick-up is, and then hobble his way out.

Fortunately, it's not.

CHAPTER 71

WHEN THE SMART CAR exploded in a shower of glass, screeching metal, and violent spins, I glimpsed the trajectory of my future.

I saw the rough arc of my life.

I'd like to say I saw myself taking the taxi from the hospital to Charm's.

I'd like to say I walk through the doors, amble to the bar, and position myself on a stool.

The bartender pours a gin on ice, then walks it down to me, the key ring looped on his belt jangling with each steps.

Charm's Tavern is empty save the two of us.

I place my fingers on the bar where the name MASON is carved. Both he and Ray-Ray wanted something I didn't have to give.

Whatever it was, it's brought me a fortune of grief.

The memory of Brighton, the first time I met Mason, flashes to mind. I think of the pipe-smoking old woman on the pier.

One line raced to infinity in both directions, while the other shot only in one direction.

The lines, I now realize, are the same length. Both are immeasurable.

The column of morning light, sharp and blanching, moves slowly across the bar, marking the gaining day. The rotation of the Earth. The progress of life.

I think of Ray-Ray. I think of the woman. I think of the trauma that binds strangers together.

She's not here. She's not coming.

I down my gin, then rise to leave. But I am struck by a smell. Lemons and warm cinnamon. It envelops me, cradles my battered body.

The woman.

Sliding onto the barstool next to me, she says, "Can I sit here?"

I sit back down, take her hands in mine. Hers are dripping wet. "They're still out of paper towels."

I catch the bartender's eye; the order is placed without a word. Whatever the woman wants.

She leans to me, her breath charged with loneliness. "Ask me a question," she says.

The bartender set two gins before us.

"What's your name?" I say.

"No, I mean a real question. Ask me something real." She grasps her glass with both hands.

I think. "Have you ever been in love?"

"Yes. What about you?"

I'd like to say I touch her hair, then her face, then her lips. I'd like to say I kiss her and kiss her and kiss her then say, "Yes, I know love."

I'd like to say this happens.

I can't.

None of this happens.

Free from the hospital, I climb gingerly into a taxi. I flash the cabbie my wad of cash in Ray-Ray's money clip, and tell him to drive me to Miami, some three hours away.

I tell him to drive me toward my future.

CHAPTER 72

A FTER CLEMENT SPIRITED OFF the bottle of vodka I stole, after my father had confronted me about it and I'd successfully bluffed, after the afternoon had waned toward evening, I went to my room to get ready for our dinner out.

My mother was there, sitting on my bed with my yearbook open. Her eyes were swollen, red. She'd been crying.

"What's wrong?" I asked.

She shook her head. "It all goes so fast." She took my hand in hers. Her voice broke as she spoke. "You're leaving me. My baby's leaving."

"I'm not leaving," I muttered, embarrassed.

"You're going to college in the fall," she sniffled.

"It's two hours away," I said. "You make it sound like you'll never see me again."

She let go of my hand, flipped through the yearbook. "It seems like just yesterday I took you to your first kindergarten class. And the day before that, I was graduating from high school myself."

She paused on the page with my graduating class's photos. "What happens to all the potential, all the dreams?" she asked. "What will happen to these people?" Her fingers lingered over Alan Adams, a goofy kid with a knack for playing the flute.

"I know what happens."

"Really?"

I nodded, pointed to Alan. "Well, Alan here ends up moving to Mexico and launching his own line of cat shampoos."

My mother smiled, wiped a stray tear. "Good for him." She pointed to the next picture. Beverly Anderson. "What about her?"

"Now Bev, she ends up being a toe model."

"A toe model?"

"For toenail polish," I said. "Unfortunately, her career is cut short by a terrible case of ringworm."

My mother laughed.

The game was on.

We worked our way through the class.

"Jasper Carpenter becomes a plumber," I said.

"In the desert," my mother added.

We determined that Kathy Eison, a tiny girl who weighed just over a hundred pounds, becomes the first woman to give birth to decatuplets—all ten of them in the back of the pick-up on the way to the hospital.

Randy Gersh grows the world's longest mustache, only to get it torn off when it gets caught in a rotating door.

Mandi Johnsen, who is dyslexic, becomes the president's chief financial adviser.

Luke Lickman, an ice cream taster for Breyer's, has to get a tongue graft after he burns off all his taste buds on a microwaved burrito.

And Janice Mabel is sentenced to seven years in jail for stealing corporate secrets from Victoria's Secret.

Then my mother's fingers touched Clement's photo.

"So what's Clement become?" I asked.

She studied the photo for some time, her eyes heavy. She said nothing, only shifted her fingers to the next photo.

The photo of me.

"Now this young man—" She broke off, looked away.

"Yes?" I said, trying to keep the game going. Trying to keep the smile on her face. "What's this handsome brute become?"

Evening came on. Soon it would be night and all that followed.

My mother turned back to me, her eyes brimming with tears. "This young man," she said, sorrow spilling out, "becomes a stranger."

END